THE CHAMBER

A DELPHI GROUP THRILLER

JOHN SNEEDEN

The Island
Copyright © 2020 by John Sneeden

All rights reserved. No part of this book may be used or reproduced by any means whatsoever without express written permission of the author, except in the case of brief quotations embodied in critical articles and reviews.

This is a work of fiction. Names, characters, businesses, places, events and incidents are either the products of the author's imagination or used in a fictitious manner. Any resemblance to actual persons, living or dead, or actual events is purely coincidental.

Cover design by Damonza
Formatting by Polgarus Studio

ISBN-13: 978-1-7329458-4-5 (Paperback Edition)
ISBN-13: 978-1-7329458-5-2 (ePub Edition)

Get a John Sneeden novella
FOR FREE

Sign up for John's newsletter and get the novella *Betrayal* for free. You'll also be the first to learn about John's future releases and special discounts. You can sign up here:

www.johnsneeden.com/newsletter/

The process is quick and simple, and your email address will not be sold to anyone else.

CHAPTER ONE

Alexandria, Virginia

ZANE WATSON OPENED his eyes to complete darkness. The room was silent save for the gentle whistle of air-conditioning blowing through a nearby vent. He moved his fingers a few times to confirm he was truly awake. His dream had been so vivid he thought he might still be in it.

Lifting his head, he looked at the digital clock next to his bed. It was three o'clock in the morning. *The witching hour.*

Why had he awakened at such a precise time? Why had he awakened at all?

He picked up his phone and read the lock screen. There were no calls, no texts, and no recent notifications. Nothing on the device would have awakened him.

Groaning in frustration, he moved to the edge of the bed and placed his feet on the floor. His throat was dry, so maybe thirst had wakened him. It wouldn't be the first time that had happened.

In fact, as he thought back on the last twenty-four hours,

dehydration seemed a likely culprit. His girlfriend, Katiya Mills, had been in town for one of her regular visits, and she had departed for New York on the previous afternoon. After dropping her off at the airport, Zane had decided to grab some Indian takeout on the way home. He ate the meal while watching a movie on Amazon Prime, washing it down with two glasses of sauvignon blanc. He was so engrossed in the film that he forgot to drink his customary two glasses of water after dinner. That omission, coupled with the spicy dinner, had turned his throat into a parched desert.

Zane stood and stretched. Before heading to the kitchen, he stepped over to the window and opened the blinds. Even though he was convinced thirst had pulled him out of his dream, it wouldn't hurt to see if anything was going on outside.

Leaning closer, he looked out through the slats. His condominium was on the top floor of a high-rise building in Alexandria, Virginia. It was one of three towers that formed a triangle around a small park. Looking down, Zane focused on the common area below. Even though the area was decidedly upscale, loud revelers occasionally found it necessary to shout well into the wee hours of the morning.

The park was deserted, so Zane lifted his gaze to the other two towers. A dozen or so lights glowed against the dark façade. Surprisingly, several people were still up and moving about. Either they were insomniacs, or they worked odd hours, he thought. Seeing nothing out of the ordinary, he let his eyes run past the towers to the twinkling lights of Old Town Alexandria. It looked peaceful, the calm before the storm. In just a few hours, the place would be buzzing with rush hour activity.

THE CHAMBER

Even though his primary residence was in Raleigh, North Carolina, Zane had purchased the condominium in order to be closer to his work at the Delphi Group. A private organization that contracted with US government agencies, Delphi typically operated in the dark and mysterious corners of intelligence. Their investigations encompassed such topics as futuristic technology, secret scientific discoveries, and the suspicious deaths of Americans overseas. Delphi had even investigated extraterrestrial incursions and artificial intelligence. Nothing was too bizarre for their portfolio.

But the world of intelligence was going through a metamorphosis, and that meant Delphi had to change along with it. The CIA and other intelligence agencies were facing greater and greater scrutiny, from both Congress and a skeptical press. Because of that scrutiny, those same agencies were asking Delphi to do more than simply investigate the bizarre—Delphi's operatives were being asked to take on routine espionage operations as well.

That increased workload meant Zane was spending most of his time at Delphi headquarters in Arlington, Virginia. In light of the challenging schedule, he had thought of selling his home in Raleigh and moving to northern Virginia. But in the end, he couldn't bring himself to break his Carolina connections completely. He had enough money to maintain homes in both locations, and the occasional trips back to Raleigh grounded him in the simpler life he craved. Nothing about living in DC was simple.

Before closing the blinds, Zane stared at his reflection in the glass. Despite the increased time in the office, his physique was as chiseled as it had ever been. His condominium came with a well-equipped gym as well as a running track on the roof. As it turned out, those amenities were all he needed to stay in shape. He had even managed to lose some weight, which was often difficult for someone north of forty.

Falling well past his shoulders, Zane's brown hair was even longer than usual. Katiya had encouraged him to get it cut short since she'd never seen him without the long locks. She'd even shown him a picture of the style she thought would complement his looks: shaved very short on the sides with a hard part and a small mop of hair on top. It was the modern style common among young male professionals. But Zane didn't see himself changing his look unless Katiya insisted. After all, he wasn't someone who followed trends.

Remembering his parched throat, Zane left the bedroom and made his way down the dark hallway. He would drink two glasses of water, visit the bathroom, then go back to sleep. Having woken up at an odd hour, he might need to turn on his white noise machine. The sound of crashing waves never failed to put him under.

After entering the living room, Zane reached for the light switch then stopped when a soft *thump* reached his ears. It sounded close and distant at the same time. He looked around the space, which included an open kitchen. As best he could tell, the sound hadn't come from inside. But if it hadn't come from inside, then where was the source? His condominium was on the top floor of the building, so he knew it hadn't come from above.

Another *thump* sounded, this one slightly louder than the

first. Zane's heart beat a little faster. His gaze moved to the floor-to-ceiling glass that ran along the far wall. The sound seemed to come from that direction. Thin curtains made it difficult to see the balcony beyond, so he took a couple more steps in that direction.

A shadow shifted on the balcony outside. Then another.

Was he dreaming?

His senses on alert, Zane took another step forward. As the blurry shapes came into focus, the hairs on the back of his neck stood on end.

Two men were crouched on the balcony.

CHAPTER TWO

IN A MATTER of seconds, Zane transitioned to fully alert operative. He had made that transition many times in his life, but this time was different. He wasn't walking down a dark alley in Europe with a pistol tucked into his waistband, nor was he hacking his way through a Caribbean jungle with a rifle slung over his shoulder. He was standing unarmed in the living room of his own home. Fortunately, seasoned operatives were always prepared to defend themselves, even in their own homes.

Zane watched the crouched figures move slowly along the balcony and toward the entryway. Their movements were careful and disciplined. They wore black military garb and carried semiautomatic rifles that looked like AR-15s, although it was difficult to tell through the thin curtains.

Professionals.

His heart hammering in his chest, he turned back toward the hall. After taking two steps, he stopped. On the far end, there was movement in the bar of light that spilled from underneath the front door.

Zane quickly processed the new information. The attackers

were pinching him from both sides.

He continued down the hall and turned right into the guest room. He then entered the L-shaped closet and followed it all the way to the back. He ran fingers across the painted surface on the right side until he found the hidden notch. He pulled the false wall back, exposing a hidden compartment beyond. A dim light came on automatically, revealing enough weaponry to outfit a platoon of soldiers: a 12-gauge Mossberg shotgun, three semiautomatic rifles, a half dozen pistols, several flashbangs, and a host of other weapons, including knives, a TASER, and a metal baton. There was even a set of dark clothes to change into.

As a plan crystalized in his thoughts, Zane grabbed the Mossberg, a .40-caliber Smith & Wesson M&P pistol, one flashbang, and several spare magazines. He didn't bother loading or checking any of the weapons. Every gun he owned was always filled with the maximum number of rounds.

Having everything he needed, he slipped on a black sweatshirt, black denim pants, and a pair of dark sneakers. He tucked the pistol and flashbang into his right pocket and the magazines into the other. After putting the false wall back in place, he picked up the shotgun and exited the closet.

Zane guessed he had about a minute to get ready for the pending attack. The floor-to-ceiling glass in the living room was bulletproof, which meant the attackers wouldn't be able to blast their way through it. In addition, the locks affixed to all of the condominium's doors were state-of-the-art products Zane had purchased through a top security firm in California. But even high-quality locks would only delay the inevitable. The attackers would get inside, and Zane needed to be ready to greet them when they did.

Zane's thoughts transitioned back to the odd way in which he had awakened. It all made sense now. Some sort of airborne craft had set down on the roof at precisely three o'clock. That meant it had been the bump, and not thirst, that had awakened him. Once on the roof, at least two of the men had rappelled down to the balcony with ropes, while the others had likely come down the stairs to breach the front door. They were attempting to crush him in a tactical vise.

The plan was sound, but the attackers hadn't counted on their target waking up. Zane was a light sleeper, and whatever noise they had made on the roof was enough to trigger his senses, even with the air-conditioning running.

As he came into the hall, a series of *clicks* came from the front door. He recognized the sound. It was a lock-picking gun, likely the version available only to law enforcement and the military. That meant he had no more than a minute to set up.

Zane opened the door to the closet that contained his washer and dryer. He reached up to the top shelf and grabbed a bottle of detergent. The slimy liquid would be perfect for his plan. After unscrewing the cap, he poured the cleaner onto the hardwood floor in the hall, starting with the area outside the two bedroom doors. Once he had finished there, he crept into the living room. The two attackers were at the glass door, using a laser to cut through the heavy glass. Ducking down, Zane poured the rest of the detergent onto the section of floor they would have to cross after entering. He then retrieved the Mossberg and crab-walked over to a large faux plant in the corner of the room, where he got down on one knee and waited for the uninvited guests to arrive.

THE CHAMBER

The breach at the front door and the balcony took longer than he expected. The attackers were probably taking their time in order to make less noise. That gave Zane the opportunity to think through what was about to play out. There were always unexpected developments, but he did have one advantage over his enemy: the element of surprise. They were expecting to find their target asleep in his bed. At worst, they thought they would encounter a groggy man with a pistol. Instead, they would find themselves confronted by a lion hiding in the darkness.

A *click* sounded at the front door, followed by the soft rattle of someone turning the knob. From his hiding place, Zane saw a brief flash coming out of the hallway, the result of the door being opened and light spilling in from the common area outside. Three or four seconds later, the hall went dark again. He guessed the door had been open long enough for no more than two or three men to enter, which meant there were at least four or five total attackers.

The numbers were against him.

Trust in the plan.

For the next minute, no sound came from the hallway. The ones who had come through the front door were likely waiting for the two men on the balcony to finish cutting through the glass. That would allow them to attack at the same time, a strategy that made sense. They wouldn't want one team to engage the target while the others were still trying to get in.

A half minute later, one of the men on the balcony removed a square of glass then reached in with a gloved hand to disengage the lock. There was a *click*, and the door slid open.

They were in.

From his place behind the plant, Zane raised the Mossberg slowly. He had chosen the shotgun for a reason—the intruders were likely wearing body armor, which meant that only a head shot would kill them. Zane was a skilled shooter, but even he would have difficulty hitting a small moving target in a dark room. And if he missed, that would draw a barrage of return fire that would quickly overwhelm him.

He listened for a few seconds, and the men finally crept inside. Green laser lights sliced through the darkness as they waved their rifles back and forth.

Zane watched and waited.

Just a little bit farther.

A panicked curse rang out as the first man's rubber-soled boots went out from under him. The second man went down a moment later.

The pool of detergent had done its work.

Zane stood and walked toward them, the butt of the shotgun pressed against his shoulder. As the two men scrambled to get up and raise their weapons, Zane squeezed the trigger twice, hitting each man's head with double-aught buckshot.

Both men went down, their arms and legs twitching.

Zane stepped closer and shot each one in the head one more time, pulverizing their skulls.

Two down.

The Mossberg carried eight shells in the magazine plus one in the chamber. He'd fired four times, which meant there were five shells left.

Shouts came out of the hallway as the other attackers rushed forward. The sounds that followed made it clear they had hit the slick as well. Zane went to the corner, pulled out a flashbang, and tossed it down the hall. A loud *pop* was followed by a bright flash of light as the device exploded. Zane leaned out and fired three times. He heard shouts of pain, then someone shouted instructions in a language Zane didn't recognize.

Foreigners.

He leaned out to fire again, but after getting off one shot, he was met with a ferocious volley of return fire. The glass on the other side of the room spiderwebbed as the rounds chewed it up. Zane maneuvered the shotgun around the corner without exposing his head and emptied the remaining shells.

Tossing the Mossberg on the couch, Zane drew the Smith & Wesson pistol. He heard sliding and bumping in the hallway, an indication the attackers were slowly making their way through the sea of detergent. The next few seconds were critical. Should all of the attackers come out firing, he'd have little chance of fending them off.

As Zane considered his next move, sirens sounded in the distance. Had someone called the police, or were they responding to another call? It seemed too soon for the former, although there was usually at least one black-and-white within a mile of his condominium at any given time. If someone had called 911 right after the first shot, then it was possible a unit was already responding.

Muffled speech came out of the hallway, followed by a flash of light a half minute later.

The front door.

They were retreating.

Sticking his head around the corner, Zane saw three black-clad figures sprinting down the hallway outside. Once they were out of sight, he sprinted after them. He ran past the elevator and around to the other side. Just ahead, a door on the left was propped open by a block the men must have brought with them.

His pistol raised, Zane entered the stairwell and took the steps up two at a time. As he burst through the door at the top, his eyes were drawn to movement in the distance. The gunmen were running toward a black craft that was perched on the other side of the running track. The craft had a body like that of a helicopter, with a cockpit, passenger seating, and landing skids on either side. But instead of one large rotor blade, it had four upward-pointing arms with propellers at each end.

A manned drone.

Zane watched as the three attackers moved toward the open door on the side. He ran in that direction, even though it would be impossible to prevent them from boarding. Two of the assassins ducked inside as the craft buzzed into the air like an irritated hornet. The third assassin was still standing on one of the landing skids, waiting his turn to get in.

Zane stopped and raised his gun, but the pilot—sensing what he was about to do—spun the drone around to protect the exposed man.

Zane squeezed off four shots. All four rounds hit the metal exterior without damaging the craft.

Once the drone cleared the building, the pilot maneuvered the craft down and out of sight.

Zane sprinted the remaining distance, but when he arrived at the roof's edge, the drone was already a hundred yards away and moving fast.

Seconds later, the men who had tried to kill him had disappeared into the night.

CHAPTER THREE

WITH THE SIRENS only a few blocks away, Zane returned to the stairwell. He needed to examine the dead bodies as quickly as possible, because once the police arrived, they would declare his home a crime scene. And once they did that, it would become virtually impossible to conduct his own investigation.

Because Zane was employed by Delphi, he knew the FBI would take over the case from the Alexandria police, perhaps within hours. And while the bureau would assign capable agents to the case, Zane believed he was best equipped to find the person or people who had tried to kill him. He was the target, and he knew his enemies better than anyone.

Zane couldn't even hazard a guess about who might have been behind the attack. There were too many candidates to count. Because he was an operative who had killed, injured, and brought down a large number of people, there were dozens, if not hundreds, of potential suspects. Once Zane's investigation was underway, he would examine his most recent operations first. That would narrow the list down substantially. The problem was that he couldn't think of any recent case that would have triggered such a reaction. Most of them either were mundane or had been carried out in the shadows. He had run across some bad characters in the last year, but he had either killed them or brought them to justice. He supposed there could be others out there he had missed, but they were likely minor players who wouldn't want to draw attention to themselves.

As Zane took the steps down, a troubling question entered his thoughts: How did the assassins know where he lived? He had purchased the condominium using a limited liability company, which was in turn owned by another entity. It wasn't the type of information someone could just look up online.

Because the ownership was a well-guarded secret, it shortened the list of those who could possibly have knowledge of it. Zane's real estate agent, a man named Brandon Greer, knew he lived there, but Zane trusted him completely. Greer was one of about a dozen real estate agents used by people who worked in the intelligence field. These particular agents specialized in sensitive transactions. But finding Zane in that way didn't make sense. How would someone have even known to contact Greer in the first place?

Another dark and troubling possibility surfaced. What if someone inside Delphi wanted him killed? Zane's colleagues were like family to him, but the organization had hired at least a dozen new employees in the last year. And while the application process was almost as rigorous as that of government intelligence agencies, there was still no guarantee that a bad apple couldn't slip through the cracks.

In the end, Zane didn't believe Delphi had a mole. More likely, someone had followed him home from Delphi headquarters. Although Zane's employment was a well-protected secret, discovering who he worked for was a more plausible way of finding him. Once they knew he worked for Delphi, then it would simply be a matter of tracking him from there.

Zane entered his condo and closed the door behind him. The sirens were close, which meant he had very little time to search the dead bodies for clues. He doubted the responding officers would know which floor the shots had come from, and that might buy him a few extra minutes. Still, he needed to move quickly.

After putting on a pair of latex gloves he kept in the kitchen, he turned on the overhead light and went to the bodies. Both men were sprawled on the hardwood floor, with pools of blood spreading out from underneath them. Zane knelt next to the first one, a blond-haired man of medium height. His face was a gruesome palette of bloody entry wounds and exposed flesh, making it difficult to note any distinguishing features. Zane was almost certain he'd never seen the man before. Not that he had expected to recognize him—whoever was behind the attack had undoubtedly hired a team of mercenaries to do the job since they were almost impossible to trace.

Zane shifted his gaze to the rest of the body. The man's black military garb bulged around his upper torso, a sign he had ceramic or Kevlar armor underneath. Zane rummaged through all visible pockets but found nothing. He was about to move on when he saw something on the man's neck. Zane used a gloved hand to turn the head slightly, exposing a dragon tattoo. It was probably nothing, but he removed his phone and snapped a photo just in case. Gangs and other criminal enterprises often identified themselves with inked symbols.

Seeing nothing else of interest, Zane moved to the next body. The man had close-cropped reddish-brown hair, a square, chiseled face, and large shoulders that hinted at a powerful physique. His face wasn't quite as damaged as the other attacker's, but Zane still didn't see anything familiar about him.

Zane found his first piece of valuable evidence when a search of the man's pockets yielded a burner phone. The fact that he was carrying a phone might mean he was the team lead. They were often the only ones allowed to carry such devices. Zane turned the phone on and was soon presented with a screen lock protected by a fingerprint reader. Thankfully, the owner's fingers were close by. Grabbing the nearest hand, Zane pressed the thumb against the sensor, and the screen opened.

As he had suspected, nothing was saved on the phone, at least not that he could tell. No calls had come in, and no calls had gone out. The man had obviously brought the device along in case their radios went out.

Keeping any piece of evidence from the FBI was an illegal and dangerous proposition, but Zane felt he had no choice but to keep it. Yes, the bureau had access to the best investigative tools in the world, but they wouldn't pursue any electronic leads as doggedly as he would. There was also the global nature of the investigation. One of the attackers had spoken in a foreign language, which meant the trail would likely continue overseas. And if it did, the FBI might decide to let the case die a slow death. After all, the intended victim had survived.

But Zane's desire to investigate the matter wasn't just

because he was best suited for the job. This was personal. Someone had tried to kill him, and they had attempted to do so in the one place he felt safe. Not only that, but if the attack had been sprung one night earlier, then Katiya would have been in harm's way. In that scenario, both of them might have been killed.

Before turning the phone off, Zane went to the device's settings and changed the screen lock from fingerprint access to password protection. He then chose a number that would be easy to remember. As he tucked the device away, he heard sirens arriving outside the building.

The police.

What should he do with the phone? They would certainly search both him and his condominium. He looked around the room then quickly realized there was no safe place to hide it. The FBI would go through the place with a fine-tooth comb, and there was zero chance they'd miss an electronic device, no matter how well it was hidden.

An idea pushed its way to the top of his thoughts. He was certain the lobby would soon be filled with people trying to get out of the building. Gunfire or word of gunfire had a way of making people flee. While the chaos played out, Zane would go down to the lobby and place the phone in his personal mailbox. As best he could remember, there were no cameras in the short corridor where the boxes were located. Once that was taken care of, he would approach the police and let them know what had happened.

Confident he had a sound plan, Zane pulled out his phone. It was time to send an important text before going down.

CHAPTER FOUR

Arlington, Virginia

ZANE ARRIVED AT Delphi headquarters a little after six that evening. He probably should have gone straight to a hotel once the FBI interviews were complete, but he was too wired to sleep, and he was also anxious to begin the hunt for the men who had tried to kill him. He would focus first on finding the team of assassins, but his ultimate goal was to find the person or organization behind the attack. And once they were found, he would make them pay a horrible price.

As he searched for a parking spot, Zane thought about all that had transpired since the attack. After examining the dead bodies, he had sent Delphi chief Alexander Ross a brief text explaining what had taken place. Calling him would have taken too much time. The Alexandria police were already outside the building, which gave him only a few minutes to hide the burner phone he had found on the assassin.

Before going down, Zane had entered the stairwell and pulled the fire alarm. The greater the chaos, the easier it would be to carry out his plan. After triggering the alarm, he waited five minutes then took the stairs to the lobby, which was already crowded. He then slipped down the back corridor and stashed the phone in his mailbox. Once the device was safely hidden, he returned to the lobby and approached one of the officers who was directing people out of the building. Initially skeptical, the officer finally believed Zane when the operative produced a picture he had taken of the bodies. Within minutes, a detachment of officers had sealed off the top floor of the building, now designated a crime scene.

A half hour later, Detective Margaret Lu arrived and took over the investigation. When Lu questioned Zane on what might have motivated the attack, he told her that due to the nature of his work, she would need to contact the FBI. Only then would he be able to provide any detail beyond simply a recounting of what had happened. He even provided her with the contact information for Special Agent in Charge Robert Powers, who was one of four special agents authorized to investigate matters related to government intelligence contractors.

Fortunately, Lu was able to reach Powers right away. The agent, who was in Houston on official business, asked Lu to surrender jurisdiction to the bureau. Lu initially resisted, citing a lack of information, but eventually relented when Powers offered to arrange a conference call with the vice president of the United States and the director of the CIA.

The first agents arrived on the scene a little after six o'clock. As they began to examine the scene, Zane realized he had been right to hide the burner phone. The bureau's Evidence Response

Team, or ERT, went over every square inch of his condominium, from the front door all the way out to the balcony and up to the roof. They even checked Zane for evidence, a process that involved him removing all of his clothing and submitting it for analysis. Obviously, the ERT would've found the phone had Zane tried to hide it.

Zane spent the next four hours being interviewed by Special Agent in Charge Grace Chappelle. Delphi CEO Alexander Ross was also present. Over several hours, Zane gave Chappelle a detailed account of all that had happened from the time he had gone to sleep until the moment he approached a police officer in the lobby. The only things he didn't mention were searching the bodies and hiding the phone. Zane had also decided not to tell Ross because he knew his boss would go ballistic. That and Zane didn't want his boss to be complicit in what was clearly an illegal act.

After parking his silver Lexus ES, Zane walked down the covered walkway and entered the building through a revolving glass door. The worldwide headquarters of Delphi occupied the top two floors of an office tower on Wilson Boulevard in Arlington. Ross had chosen the location due to its close proximity to several government agencies, including the CIA and the FBI. While Delphi personnel typically communicated through secure video and telephone lines, face-to-face meetings were sometimes necessary.

Zane was one of approximately two dozen operatives employed by Delphi. While working around the globe, the operatives utilized a sizable network of offices, safe houses, and support staff. As Delphi's senior operative and second-in-command behind Ross, Zane led the organization's most critical operations along with Carmen Petrosino, a senior operative born in Italy.

Before going up to the office, Zane grabbed a large coffee at the Starbucks in the lobby. Even though he was wired on adrenaline, he knew he would hit a wall unless he infused his system with a massive jolt of caffeine.

Coffee in hand, he entered a secluded hallway at the back of the building then took a private lift to the top floor. When the elevator doors slid open, he found the lobby unoccupied. Kristine Hirsch, Delphi's senior administrative assistant, was normally seated at the front desk, but she was currently on vacation. Zane was actually glad no one was around, because he needed to get to work right away.

Zane took the corridor to the left and stopped at the third door down, which was the office of Brett Foster. Brett's official job title was chief technology specialist, but to most, he was known as Delphi's resident computer geek. He had a distinguished background for someone in his mid-thirties. After graduating from MIT with honors, Foster worked for several research and development companies at the famed Research Triangle Park in North Carolina. The last private company he'd worked for was a consultant to the CIA, and there, his work had caught the eye of several government officials. Unfortunately, brilliant tech workers came at a price that was typically too high for federal budgets. That was why the CIA's head administrator at the Office of Information Technology had passed Foster's name along to Dr. Alexander Ross, who quickly brought the young phenom on board.

Zane knocked once then entered without waiting for an answer. Brett was turned in the opposite direction, typing something into a laptop. He was so engrossed in his work that he didn't even turn around to see who had entered.

"Just a moment," Brett said as he continued to type. "Almost done."

Zane closed the door behind him. "Take your time."

Brett swiveled around. "What the...? What are you doing here?"

"I work here, remember?"

"I'm sorry. I could've sworn you were attacked by a team of assassins last night."

Zane sank into a chair across from Brett. "What's the expression? All in a day's work."

"Seriously, what are you doing here?"

"The FBI ran me off, so where else am I supposed to go?"

"Last I checked, Alexandria has some pretty nice hotels." Brett seemed to study Zane's appearance. "I must say you look surprisingly good. No cast. No swollen eye. Not bad for an old man."

"I did break a nail, if that makes you feel any better."

"So you've already been interviewed?"

"I think *grilled* is the better term."

Brett's brow furrowed. "I heard Powers was a good guy."

"He's in Houston, so they sent over a female agent named Grace Chappelle. She's relatively new so insisted on asking me every question she could possibly think of, most of which were irrelevant."

Brett folded his arms across his chest. "Well, tell me what

happened. And not just the CliffsNotes version."

"Unfortunately, I don't have time. I need to jump on this thing."

"And I suppose you need my help."

Zane nodded. "My attackers took off in a manned drone, so I need to find out where they got it. Do you know where you can lease one?"

Brett paused for a moment then said, "First of all, I doubt they leased it. I don't know much about the industry, but I'm reasonably certain the manned models can only be flown by licensed pilots."

"So you think it was stolen?"

"That or they had their own."

"I don't think it was theirs. So are you familiar with the companies that rent these things out?"

"Well, there aren't many. Remember, manned drones are still new to the market."

Zane frowned, his thoughts turning back to an article he had read a month or two before. "I thought Dubai had air taxis flying all over the place."

"They do, but that's Dubai, one of the wealthiest cities on the planet. Manned drones are still a novelty here. A few big corporations use them to fly large clients around." He thought for a moment. "To the best of my knowledge, there are only two local companies that lease them."

"That's why I came straight to you. I knew you'd be up to date on the tech."

"Ross also had me look into leasing one for a small op we had a couple of years ago." Brett grabbed his laptop and set it on the desk in front of him. "You want me to get you the names of those companies?"

"No, I can do that. I actually need you to do something else." Zane reached into his pocket and removed the burner phone he had taken off the body. He had placed the device inside a plastic sandwich bag. "I need you to take a look at this thing." He tossed it onto Brett's desk.

Brett looked at the phone then back at Zane. "What's this?"

"It's a custom-made burner. One of the guys who attacked me had it on him. I need you to find out what's on there."

Brett lifted a brow. "Does the FBI know about—"

"No, they don't."

"*Zane*. What the…?"

"Look, this is personal for me. My guess is this whole operation originated overseas, and as much as I respect Powers and his crew, I don't think they're going to give it the attention it needs."

"Please tell me you're not going to conduct your own investigation."

Zane said nothing.

Brett shook his head then asked, "Does Ross know what you're doing?"

"No, it's just you and me."

Silence quickly fell over the room. Brett rubbed his face vigorously as though trying to wish the whole thing away.

"Are you going to help me or not?" Zane asked.

Brett stopped rubbing and exhaled. "Give me an hour or so, and I'll see what I can find."

"You're the best."

Brett pointed at the door. "Now get out of here before I change my mind."

CHAPTER FIVE

AFTER LEAVING BRETT with the burner, Zane managed to slip down the hall to his office without being seen by any of his colleagues. He wasn't being antisocial. He just couldn't afford to lose precious time. The men who tried to kill him were still out there, perhaps on a plane to any number of destinations.

After locking the door behind him, he sat down at his desk and took a sip of coffee. Assuming the attackers had stolen the drone, he needed to compare its appearance to those in the fleet of each company in the area. Unfortunately, it had been dark on the roof, and he'd been more focused on the men he was firing at. He did remember the exterior was black, and he also seemed to remember a silver corporate insignia on the side. Despite replaying the event in his head, he couldn't picture the insignia.

Zane turned on his computer. As he waited for it to power up, he pulled out his phone and noticed he had several notifications. It dawned on him that he hadn't checked his messages all day. He wondered if he should even bother to now. Most were probably texts from well-intentioned people wanting to know what had happened, and while he appreciated their concern, he didn't have time to go through them. Then again, what if it was a message from someone connected to the case? Special Agent Chappelle had his number, so it was possible she might have reached out.

Unable to resist a peek, Zane unlocked the screen and discovered nine texts waiting for him. He skimmed through each one. The most recent four were from colleagues who had heard about the attack and wanted to know how he was doing. Carmen Petrosino—who was currently on assignment overseas—had even sent him a message asking for an update. According to her text, Ross had sent a message to all employees letting them know what happened and warning them to watch their backs. It was good advice. Zane had been operating on the assumption that he was the only person targeted, but it was certainly possible this was a larger attack on the entire organization. Zane sent Carmen a quick reply, letting her know he was fine and that he would call her at his earliest opportunity.

Zane scanned the other five texts. There was one from his bank letting him know that two automatic payments had processed. The remaining messages were from people Zane had reached out to on other work-related matters. But there were no texts from Chappelle or anyone else connected to the case.

Seeing nothing that required immediate attention, Zane checked his voicemails. He had three messages, including one from his girlfriend, Katiya Mills. The time stamp indicated she had called at 6:37 that morning.

He played the message. Katiya spoke in a pleasant tone. "Hello, handsome. I'm on my way to campus to teach a seven thirty class. Fun, fun." There was a short pause before she continued. "You know, I still can't stop thinking about our time together. To be honest, I didn't want to leave."

Zane felt a rush of emotion. He hadn't wanted her to leave either, although in hindsight, he was happy she had.

"Anyway, I just wanted to hear your voice for a few seconds," she continued. "Knowing you, you're probably at work already, so don't feel like you have to call me back."

There was another pause, this one longer than the first. Zane could hear the soft sound of her breathing.

"I love you," she finally said before disconnecting the call.

Zane saved the message. He considered himself fortunate to have someone like Katiya Mills in his life. She was one of the most beautiful souls he had ever met. Despite her difficult schedule as an anthropology professor at NYU, she always made time for their relationship. She called him daily, even if it was only for a few minutes, and on several occasions, she had traveled to DC to take care of him when he was under the weather.

Zane had dated a lot of women over the years, but Katiya was by far the best match for him. The DC girls he had dated seemed preoccupied with themselves. He used to play a game in which he counted how many questions a woman would ask him on their first date. Some of the women had taken a genuine interest in his life, but most asked only a few questions. He had even been out with one or two who hadn't asked him any questions at all. Not one question about his background, his likes, or what made him tick. Despite being a relational red flag, not being asked about his work was probably good, as he liked to keep that part of his life hidden.

In fairness, Zane knew that type of behavior wasn't confined to one gender. Based on his conversations with colleagues Amanda Higgs and Carmen Petrosino, the men sounded even worse. According to Amanda and Carmen, even the guys who did ask questions did so only because they had an ulterior motive.

Despite their near-perfect relationship, Zane and Katiya had both ignored the very large elephant in the room, which was their future. A deep connection like theirs deserved a future, perhaps a permanent future, but neither seemed eager to bring it up. Zane guessed it was because a permanent relationship would require one of them to pull up their own deep roots. He was an intelligence operative, and there was really only one place he could work. A resident of Manhattan, Katiya was a tenured professor at one of the country's most prestigious universities. She truly loved her work, and Zane didn't feel it would be right to ask her to leave all of that behind. At least not now.

She had hinted that she wanted their relationship to be permanent, but she had never pushed the conversation as far as it needed to go. Not that it was her fault. Zane hadn't broached the subject either. But if things continued to go well, he would bring it up, even if it meant they had to make some extremely difficult career decisions. For the moment, he would enjoy and appreciate their time together.

Katiya's latest visit had been fabulous. They started each day with a late breakfast at one of Zane's favorite restaurants in Old Town Alexandria. They ate pancakes and sipped coffee as they watched boats sail down the Potomac. After brunch, they would usually take a leisurely stroll through the surrounding streets, stopping at trendy retail stores and cafés. At night, they made a few trips across the river to DC. One evening, they had dinner at a Russian restaurant Katiya had wanted to try. On another, they attended a musical at the Warner Theatre.

But it wasn't the places they visited that made Katiya's visits so special. It was the laughs they shared while people watching. It was drinking wine on Zane's balcony as they watched planes descend on Reagan National. It was also the time they spent watching movies on the couch together, their bodies entwined under a fleece blanket.

Zane found himself getting angrier with each passing moment. Rather than giving him a joyful reprieve from his work, the memories of Katiya's visit made him realize things could have taken a very dark turn. What if the assassins had attacked on Saturday night when she was still there? He shuddered. Although she was a tough cookie and could competently wield a firearm, Katiya wouldn't have been equipped to take on a team of professionals. Zane would have made her safety his first priority, and because of that, he might not have had time to prepare a counterattack. Even without Katiya to be concerned about, he'd had barely enough time to get ready.

A loud chime drew Zane back to the present. The computer had booted up. It was perfect timing, because Zane's anger was slowly morphing into rage, and too much rage would be counterproductive.

He began by typing "dc drone rentals" into the Google search box. There were way too many results, so he narrowed the search to include only those companies that leased manned drones. As Brett had indicated, only two firms fell into that category. In another five or ten years, there would probably be a dozen or more. That was how fast the industry was growing.

The first company listed was McKinney Drones, which had offices in Tysons Corner, Virginia, and Bethesda, Maryland. Zane clicked on the company's official website. After examining images of their fleet, he scratched them off the list. Almost all of their drones were white, and the company's logo wasn't silver.

Returning to the search results, he clicked on the website of a company known as Infiniti Air, which he soon discovered was no relation to the automobile manufacturer. As he tried to locate photographs of their fleet, his phone flared on the desk. He glanced at the screen. *Brett.*

He engaged the call. "Yes, sir."

"Hey, I found something I think you'll be interested in."

"That was quick. What is it?"

"I think you need to come down here and see it for yourself."

CHAPTER SIX

"SO WHAT DID you find?" Zane asked after entering Brett's office and shutting the door behind him.

Brett spoke as he typed on his laptop. "It looks like there were a few goodies hidden on the phone."

"And you already found them." Zane took a seat. "That's a massive amount of geekage."

"Hold on one sec."

Zane took a sip of coffee as he looked over Brett's shoulder. Brett scrolled through a list of names that appeared to be a manifest.

"Got you." Brett wrote something on a notepad then swiveled around and faced Zane. "I just found a very big piece of the puzzle."

"Tell me more."

"Let's start with the phone." Brett picked up the device, which he had connected to a smaller laptop using a USB cable. "I hooked it up to some new detection software we just got from the NSA. It scans electronic devices for hidden files. In this case, it was a hidden app."

"A hidden app?"

"As the name implies, it's an app that doesn't have a visible icon to click on, nor does it show up in the phone's application manager."

"Then how do you access it?"

"They're set up in various ways. This is probably the most interesting one I've come across. It's accessed by going to the phone's browser and typing *start* into the URL field." Brett turned the screen toward Zane and typed in the appropriate letters. As a blank page began to load, he toggled back to the phone's main screen. A small icon had already appeared. "The user now has five seconds to click on it before it disappears again."

Zane's eyes widened. "Wow."

"Whoever put this together knows what they're doing. If ninety-nine point nine percent of the population finds this phone, they'll likely never know of the app's existence."

"We need to be using those."

"According to my friend at the NSA, a few CIA agents already are."

"So we're dealing with some people who are tech savvy."

Brett nodded. "We're talking either a foreign government or an organization with deep pockets."

The mystery deepened with each new development. If the assassins had been sent by a foreign government, then why had they targeted him? Zane couldn't think of any operation that might have triggered a country to put a bounty on his head.

"Now let me show you what was in the app." Brett set the phone down then turned the smaller laptop's screen toward

Zane. "After scanning the file for malware, I transferred the contents over here for a better look."

Zane watched as Brett used the touch pad to open a folder marked START APP. Two files were inside.

Brett clicked on the first. "This is the information page of a passport. I'll enlarge it for you."

Zane leaned in and read the information displayed on the screen. The first thing he noticed was that the passport had been issued in Australia. It was not what he had expected based on hearing one of the attackers speak in a foreign language.

After giving Zane a chance to skim through the information, Brett adjusted the image until the passport holder's photograph came into view. "Recognize him?"

Zane leaned closer for a better look. The man had short reddish-brown hair and a neatly trimmed beard of the same color. His face was square and chiseled, and he was looking at the camera with a cold stare. Even though the hair was a bit longer than what he remembered, Zane could tell it was one of the men he had killed. Specifically, it was the one who'd possessed the phone.

"That's him," Zane finally said. "That's the guy I took the phone off of."

"According to the passport, his name is Andrew Parrish of Adelaide, Australia."

"Obviously a fake. I heard these guys communicating in a language I didn't recognize."

"Foreigners do live in Australia, but you're right. It's a fake, and I can show you the proof."

After exiting the first file, Brett clicked on the second, which was a PDF. The document was similar to ones Zane had seen many times over the years. It was a biographical sketch of an individual—in this case, Andrew Parrish. It listed his name, age, current address, place of birth, and a host of other pertinent information. There was even a short narrative at the bottom of the page, giving details of the man's life.

Brett looked at Zane. "When your attacker was given the fake document, he was also given a fictitious biography along with it. He probably kept this to refer to when necessary."

"Pretty much the same thing we do." Zane leaned back in his chair. "Good work. With a little luck, we may be able to find out where he and his friends were holed up and go from there."

Brett smiled. "I'm not done. There is more. I was able to find out who Parrish was traveling with, as well as their flight information."

"Are they still here?"

Brett shook his head. "They're currently on a commercial flight to Dublin, Ireland."

"That was quick."

"Once I had Parrish's name, it was pretty easy. Since he was using a foreign passport, I knew he must have flown in from somewhere. And if he flew in, that meant he was going to fly out. So I accessed the records of major airlines and discovered that Andrew Parrish was scheduled to fly from Dulles to Dublin at five p.m."

"So I guess that's also how you discovered who he was traveling with."

Brett nodded. "Once I had the information for his flight out, I looked back through the records and discovered he flew into DC last Monday."

"Which would give them about a week to watch me and set everything up."

"Correct."

Zane realized that if the attackers had been tailing him at various times over the last week, they had likely seen him with Katiya. And while they probably didn't know who she was, they might have been able to figure it out if they wanted to. He felt the anger he had previously suppressed rising again. It was one thing to come after him. It was another thing altogether to put someone he cared about in harm's way. This was a whole new level of personal.

But Zane was also angry at himself. He hadn't noticed them watching him. Yes, DC was one of the most compact, high-traffic areas in the country. And yes, that made it easier for someone to watch from a distance without being noticed. But Zane was supposed to be the best of the best, the senior operative at one of the most effective clandestine organizations in the world.

Brett continued, pulling Zane out of his thoughts. "Once I had both flights, I compared the two manifests and came up with a list of three names that were on both flights."

"I counted six at my building. Two are dead, which means four are on the run."

"Two got on the plane to Dublin, which means we can pick them up before they board their next flight. I'm still looking for the final two."

Zane frowned. "Let's get back to the ones flying to Dublin. So that isn't their final destination?"

"No, they're scheduled to fly from there to Sofia, Bulgaria."

"When?"

"They depart two hours after arriving in Ireland."

"Bulgaria," Zane said. "Maybe they were speaking Bulgarian. That would explain why I didn't recognize the language."

"It's possible they're Bulgarian, but it's also possible that's not their final destination. Who knows? They may get into a car, drive to another country, then board another plane. There's really no telling where they might end up after all is said and done. These hit teams will often travel for days in order to obscure their trail."

"Maybe, but my gut tells me that's where they're going."

"In the end, it won't matter, because we'll make sure they don't make it to Bulgaria."

Zane held Brett's gaze for several long seconds. "Maybe. Then again, maybe not."

Brett frowned. "What?"

"We need to let them run."

There was a long pause.

Brett's eyes widened as he seemed to realize what Zane was thinking. "Have you lost your mind?"

"You and I both know these aren't the men we're looking for. They're mercenaries. Someone else sent them to kill me, and if we're going to find out who that is, then we need to let these roaches crawl back behind the wall."

"We can question them once they're picked up. The Irish authorities will work with us to get them back here."

"You and I both know that's a dead end. If we have them arrested when they arrive in Dublin, they'll lawyer up, and we'll never get to the truth. And even if we were able to cut some sort of deal, that would take weeks, perhaps even months. That means that whoever is behind the whole thing would have plenty of time to disappear."

Brett shook his head. "You need to think this through."

"I have."

Brett appeared to think for a moment. "You really think you can do all this behind Ross's back?"

"We're not going to do it behind his back. We're going to get him on board with it right now."

CHAPTER SEVEN

"PLEASE EXPLAIN WHY you didn't take the time to call me first," Ross shouted, his face red.

Zane and Brett were sitting across the desk from their boss. Zane had spent the last half hour giving what amounted to a full confession. He hadn't held anything back. He admitted to taking the dead man's phone and hiding it in his mailbox in order to conduct a shadow investigation of his own. He assured Ross that only he was equipped to hunt the assassins down, and if he had allowed the police to declare his condominium a crime scene, he would never have had access to the best piece of evidence, the phone.

Ross had listened to the entire presentation in silence, his expression giving no indication of his state of mind. But once the operative finished, it was clear that Delphi's chief executive was furious. Zane had known things might get ugly, but he hadn't expected such a volcanic response. Even so, he couldn't quite determine whether Ross was truly that angry or was just making sure his operative had gotten the point. In all likelihood, it was the former. Zane not only had violated organizational policy but also had broken the law.

"I didn't call you because I knew you'd have a problem with it, and in the end, I couldn't take the risk that the police and the FBI would screw this thing up. This was personal."

"Did you ever think that this might be personal for me too?" Ross asked.

Zane thought about how to answer. "To be honest, I didn't have time to think about much of anything. As I said before, the police were pulling up outside, and I knew that once they declared the building a crime scene, we'd lose access to our best piece of evidence."

"They had no idea where the shots came from, which means you had enough time to call me so we could talk this thing through," Ross said sharply. "Besides, you know the FBI has shared information with us in the past, and there was no reason to think they wouldn't do that in this case, particularly since a Delphi employee was the victim." Ross sat back and crossed his arms. "So instead of calling me, you decide to play cowboy and put our entire organization in jeopardy."

"Look, the organization will be fine. I acted alone and—"

"But now you've brought me into it," Ross snapped.

Zane held his palms out in an attempt to calm Ross down. "I can get us out of this. Let me explain how. There's a park right next to my building. I'll tell them I found the phone in a bush down there while looking around on my own. Since there was no way to know who it belonged to, I'll say I brought it back here for analysis. They still won't like it, but that's not nearly as serious as me taking it off a body."

Zane didn't like to lie, but in this situation, they didn't have much choice. Hiding evidence was a serious offense, and even Delphi's ties to the intelligence community and the executive branch might not be enough to get him or the organization out of trouble.

"You're so deep into this mess that you're not even thinking straight!" Ross barked. "You've already told them that the hit team landed a drone on your roof. How is the phone supposed to end up in a bush next to your building?"

"That's easy. One of the attackers was hanging off the side of the drone when I fired shots at them. The phone could've easily fallen off when that happened."

"This is the FBI. You think they're going to believe a BS story like that?"

"Honestly? Probably not. But we won't turn it in until Robert Powers gets back and takes over the investigation. We both know Powers is a good guy. He'll probably realize what I did, but he'll also understand. There's no way in the world he's going to come after me for that."

Ross held Zane's gaze for a moment. "And what if you're wrong and he does come after you?"

"They can't prove anything," Zane said. "I'm sure they made a cursory search of the park, but I doubt they performed a grid search." Zane paused. "Look, if they do figure it all out, I'll take the fall."

"We're *all* in it now." After a brief pause, Ross looked at Brett. "So when did you learn about all of this?"

"A couple of hours ago," Brett said.

Ross let out a frustrated sigh.

Zane thought Ross was about to launch into a second tirade,

but instead, the chief rubbed his face then leaned back and stared at the ceiling. He appeared to be processing the information, which might be a good sign.

A half minute later, Ross looked at Brett again. "So you've figured out their flight plans?"

Zane saw a sliver of sunlight. The question might be an indication that Ross was willing to move on. Yes, he was still hot, but they didn't call him the Oracle for nothing. The man had an innate ability to focus on what was most important, and in this case, it was finding the assassins before they got away. They could worry about the FBI later.

"We know two are going to touch down in Dublin tomorrow morning, then two hours after that, they're scheduled to board another flight for Sofia, Bulgaria."

Ross's brow furrowed. "Bulgaria?"

Brett nodded. "That's assuming they board the flight. I guess it's possible they could be carrying more than one passport. They might walk out of the terminal and rent a car under a different name, something like that."

"I doubt it," Ross said. "First of all, we'd know if they didn't get on the next plane. And two, I'm sure they're going to try to put as much distance between themselves and the US as they can."

"Zane and I believe they could be Bulgarian nationals," Brett said, "but I just thought of something else. Maybe they're just trying to get to a country that doesn't have an extradition treaty with the US."

"That's possible, although I'm not sure it matters right now." Ross looked at Zane. "So you want to let them keep running?"

"I think it makes the most sense. As much as I'd like to take down the men who pulled the trigger, it's more important to find out who's behind it all. As you probably realize, they could be after all of us. Maybe I was just the first target."

"So what difference does that make?"

"Let's assume we pick up the two who are set to arrive in Dublin. Let's also assume we find the other two. Who's to say there aren't more teams in place out there? Our operatives could be under surveillance at this very moment. That means we need to get to the source and get to it fast."

"Let's say I agree to your plan," Ross said. "Even if I put you on a charter flight late tonight, I'm not sure you'll be able to beat them to Bulgaria. The planes we use would have to stop somewhere to refuel."

"That's one of the things we wanted to discuss," Brett said. "Do you have any contacts with Bulgarian intelligence?"

Ross shook his head. "No, I don't. I knew the last director of the SIA, but he's retired now. The Bulgarians tend to keep a low profile on the world stage, so we're not in touch very often. But I'm sure if we asked for help, they'd be happy to give it. They have a close security partnership with the US and the European Union."

"Can you make the call?" Zane asked. "They can have people at the airport long before the targets arrive. Just tell them to keep an eye on them until I get there."

"I think I can do better than that. Mort, Skinner, and Pratt are on assignment in Southeastern Europe right now." Ross was referring to Delphi field operatives Doug Mortensen, Cleavon Skinner, and James Pratt. "They can probably get there in time to follow the targets. That way, we won't even need to bring in the Bulgarians."

"Where are they specifically?" Zane asked.

"Split, Croatia." Ross picked up his phone and tapped the screen a few times. "They could drive to Sofia and be there before the flight's scheduled to arrive."

Zane looked at Brett. "Were you able to pull the fake passports of the other two travelers?"

"I did and can send them to Mort right away."

Ross asked Brett, "What about the two who aren't on the flight to Dublin? Where are they?"

"I checked all of the flights out of DC and came up empty," Brett said. "Next I'm going to check rental car companies and Amtrak. Don't worry. I'll find them."

Zane said, "It may not matter. I think they'll all end up in Bulgaria."

Ross nodded but said nothing.

"So when can you put me on a flight out?" Zane asked.

Delphi operatives often flew commercial, but they also had an arrangement with the CIA to use their chartered flights if speed was of the essence.

"I'll have to check. If it was a national emergency, I could get something tonight. Since I don't want to answer any uncomfortable questions, let's just send you out in the morning."

Zane stood. "Perfect. I need some sleep, anyway. I'm running on fumes."

Ross stood as well. "I assume that means the ERT won't be finished with your condo tonight."

"No, but Brett has graciously offered to let me stay with him."

Ross looked at Brett. "Don't you live in one of those cheap apartment complexes out in Reston?"

Brett was known for his frugality. The man would go to any length to save a buck. Zane had once quipped that Brett was so cheap that he probably rinsed off and reused coffee filters.

"I do," Brett replied with an air of indignation. "And I know what you're thinking. But trust me, it ain't cheap. They're some of the nicest apartments out there."

"Still, doesn't sound like the safest place in the world." Ross nodded at Zane. "He's already been attacked once. What happens when the bad guys show up at your place?"

"Then they'll have to deal with Caesar," Brett said.

Ross frowned. "Caesar?"

"His Boston Terrier," Zane said.

Ross shook his head. "I'll get someone working on your obituary right away."

CHAPTER EIGHT

Sofia - Varshets, Bulgaria

THE BEST-LAID plans of spies and spooks often go awry, Dr. Alexander Ross sometimes told his operatives, putting a new twist on the famous proverb. They seemed like the perfect words to describe Zane's multi-leg trip to Sofia, Bulgaria, which seemed to go off the rails from the very start.

Ross had hoped to secure an aircraft that could transport Zane to Sofia as quickly as possible. Unfortunately, world events got in the way. Due to various fires across the globe, the CIA was under heavy pressure to consolidate flights. That forced Zane to share a plane with five NSA analysts and two CIA case officers. The analysts would be dropped off at Ramstein Air Base in Germany, after which the case officers would be taken to Sarajevo.

The long trip got even longer when the group arrived at Ramstein. While making a routine check of the craft, mechanics noted an issue with one of the plane's engines. They wouldn't be able to procure the right part until the following day, which forced Zane and the CIA officers to stay at the base overnight.

To make matters worse, Zane had a difficult conversation with Katiya later that night. When he called to tell her what had happened at his condominium, he discovered she already knew about it from news reports. She had recognized his building during live coverage then figured out the rest when the reporter indicated "two robbers" had been killed by a heavily armed resident after they tried to break into his penthouse suite. And while she was happy that Zane was safe, she was upset that she had to learn about it from the media.

Zane had tried to call Katiya while staying at Brett's apartment but had been unable to reach her. She'd been hosting a webinar for anthropology professors that evening. Zane had meant to try her again before going to bed but had crashed in sheer exhaustion. He had then gotten up early the next morning to catch the plane.

Despite the tension between them, Zane eventually smoothed things over. He apologized for not staying up long enough to reach her, and she apologized for not understanding the pressure he must have been under.

Fortunately, the second and third legs of the journey went much better than the first. Other than ten minutes of extreme turbulence over the Adriatic Sea, the flights to Sarajevo and Sofia had been smooth and uneventful. In addition, the dinner served by the crew was better than that at most restaurants Zane frequented. He chose the corn-fed New York strip steak over cauliflower risotto, roasted corn, steamed asparagus, and a basket of warm pumpernickel bread. Despite a surprisingly good selection of both reds and whites, Zane had refused the wine.

The sleek white Gulfstream G550 finally touched down in

Sofia at 1:37 in the afternoon, more than twenty-four hours after the journey began. Following a smooth landing, the pilot directed the craft onto a secondary runway that took them away from the main terminal.

Once on the ground, Zane took a quick look out the window. A steady rain thumped rhythmically against the glass. The pilot had announced that local temperatures were hovering in the high thirties, which meant misery would greet Zane and the others when the crew disembarked.

The jet slowed as it neared a small gray hangar. Three men stood outside the hangar's office, umbrellas in hand. One of the three was Delphi operative Doug "Mort" Mortensen. An American of Danish descent, the blond-haired operative stood just over six feet tall, with a body that looked like it had been chiseled out of rock. Although he could certainly do damage with his hands, Mortensen's skill with firearms was what set him apart. He was a former US Army sniper, and few could fire long guns and pistols as well as he could.

During the flight, Mortensen had sent a text that Zane had just received as the plane made its final approach. The message was short and simple. Mortensen would drive to the airport to pick up Zane while operatives Pratt and Skinner kept the mercenaries under observation.

The plane made a wide arc then approached the hangar nose-first. Two men in bright-yellow vests used paddles to wave them inside. Once the craft came to a stop, everyone on board got up and gathered their belongings. The crew and the two CIA officers would stay overnight in Sofia before continuing on to Istanbul the next day.

"Welcome to Bulgaria," Mortensen said as Zane arrived at the bottom of the airstairs.

"I see you failed to follow my instructions to order up some good weather," Zane said.

"I don't get paid enough to arrange good weather. Besides, it's good for divas like you to get dirty and wet once in a while."

"Diva? I guess I'd better not tell you about the meal they served on board."

"Please don't."

"I did refuse the wine."

"You've always been a man of sacrifice."

After thanking the crew, Zane followed Mortensen through a door at the back of the hangar. Mortensen used a fob to pop the trunk of a silver Dacia Sandero hatchback. Not only was the car dented in several places, but also parts of the exterior were covered with mud that was so hard-packed even the rain hadn't washed it off.

"Nice limo," Zane said.

Mortensen tossed the luggage into the rear compartment then closed the hatch. "He gets off his fancy little spy plane, and he's already complaining."

"At least you could have given her a wash."

Zane wasn't surprised that his colleagues had chosen modest transportation. When possible, Delphi operatives rented smaller or older vehicles. Top-of-the-line sedans—particularly those that were white or black—were usually avoided since they resembled unmarked law enforcement vehicles.

"Actually, we're responsible for most of what you see... the mud, grime, and maybe even one of those dents," Mortensen said after they got inside. "It seems our targets chose quite the place to hole up."

"So where exactly are they?" Zane asked.

Mortensen smiled as he started the car. "It ain't Waikiki, I'll tell you that."

Before leaving, Mortensen snapped his phone into the dash mount then typed an address into the device's GPS.

Zane noticed the destination. "Varshets?"

"That's our first stop. It's actually a quaint little spa town about a hundred kilometers north of here. Quiet. Clean."

Zane liked what he was hearing. "So the bad guys are holed up in a spa town?"

"Not hardly. That's where our hotel is. They're about an hour from Varshets."

The drive to Varshets took just under two hours. The rain had ended by the time they reached the hotel. After dropping off Zane's luggage and picking up a six-pack of Coke, they took the 162 northeast out of the city. The emerald peaks of the Balkans rose in every direction, beautiful sentinels that seemed to watch over the rolling countryside.

"It may not be Waikiki, but this is one hell of a view," Zane said, taking a sip of Coke.

"Oh, the view is fine. The conditions at the farm are another thing altogether. I'll let you see for yourself."

Forty-five minutes later, they turned onto another highway that ran east from the 162. Two miles later, Mortensen took another left.

"The hostiles are staying at a farm about a mile and a half down." Instead of driving past the farm, Mortensen turned right onto a dirt road that cut through a thick stand of deciduous trees. Despite the growing darkness, he killed the headlights and slowed the car to a crawl.

"We think this is a private logging area," Mortensen said. "As best we can tell, it hasn't been used in months."

Five minutes later, a distant light blinked once. Mortensen flashed the Dacia's headlights once in response then drove another hundred yards and came to a stop.

After the two got out of the car, a tall figure came toward them out of the trees. Zane recognized the tall, athletic silhouette of James "Bull" Pratt right away.

"Patrick Zane Watson," Pratt said as he approached. "The man with nine lives."

"I think I used eight of them the other night," Zane said.

"I'm proud of you, my man." Pratt grabbed Zane's shoulder and shook it. "Always good to hear about some slime getting their due. Only wish I could have been there to see you do your thing!"

"You may get to see it again," Zane said. "Wouldn't mind getting my hands on the two you've been watching."

"Oh, there's more than two," Pratt said. "We found a whole nest of the little bastards."

"As they say, the more, the merrier."

Mortensen gave Zane a pistol, then the two followed Pratt to an animal trail at the edge of the woods. Keeping their flashlights off, they followed the narrow path through the tall trees, stopping every few minutes to listen. They were a quarter mile away from the farm, but Pratt still recommended they exercise caution. Patrols walked the perimeter several times a day, an indication the mercenaries were wary of a possible attack.

Fifteen minutes later, the trail turned left up a steep slope to a ridge that ran behind the farm. With high ground and plenty of cover, it was the perfect place from which to launch an offensive.

The group moved slowly through the trees, trying to stay behind large trunks as much as possible. After traveling a hundred yards, Pratt held up a hand, bringing them to a stop. Pursing his lips, he gave a series of whistles that sounded like the hooting of an owl. Seconds later, a whistled reply came back.

Given the green light, Pratt led them to a stand of firs, where Cleavon Skinner greeted them. A six-foot-tall African American, Skinner had a light complexion and an athletic build. Like Pratt, he carried an AR-15.

"Well, if it ain't the man himself," Skinner said in a soft voice.

He and Zane clasped hands and pulled together, patting each other's back.

"You really didn't need to come," Skinner said. "We could've taken these boys out for you."

"You think I'd miss all the fun? I still have a score to settle." Zane looked around the area. "How are you guys holding up out here?"

"Let me show you." Pratt stepped over to a pine tree and retrieved a backpack propped against the trunk. He pulled out two protein bars and waved them in the air. "This is dinner. And we won't even mention the facilities."

Skinner grabbed the branch of a nearby fir tree. "Not exactly soft."

Zane looked at Mortensen. "We should have stopped for a case of Cottonelle."

"You need to go get some Pepto for Bull." Skinner nodded at Pratt. "His persistent flatulence is going to give away our position."

Pratt held up his middle finger.

"Okay, give me a sitrep," Zane said.

"I'm not sure how much Mort told you, but it seems like our little friends are gearing up for a celebration down at the farm," Skinner explained.

"How do you know?"

"We've been here almost twenty-four hours," Skinner replied. "Up until this afternoon, it was all business... scowls, very little talking, and lots of patrols of the perimeter. Then this afternoon, something changed. There were more smiles and horsing around, that kind of thing."

Zane stroked his chin. "Interesting."

"That's also when they started stacking logs behind the house," Pratt said.

"I don't follow," Zane said.

"A bonfire," Pratt explained. "After getting the logs stacked up, they started setting coolers outside."

Zane nodded.

"Something happened that changed their mood," Skinner added.

"There were a couple of men who were involved in the attack that we weren't able to trace," Zane said. "My guess is they made it out safely."

Mortensen nodded. "And they probably figure if they were

going to get caught, it would've already happened by now."

"That's exactly what we want them to think." Zane looked at Skinner. "Has the party started?"

He nodded. "Last I checked, it was just getting cranked up. Want to have a look?"

"Please."

After reminding everyone to keep their voices down, Skinner led the group through a thick stand of trees that soon opened onto a granite ledge. Crouching, Zane moved to the edge and looked down. A meadow ran from the base of the ridge to the farm. At one time, it had probably been an agricultural field, but now it was overgrown with weeds and small saplings.

Zane cast his gaze farther out. At the center of the farm was a large ranch-style house that was at least three thousand square feet. In addition to the house, there was a barn, a couple of smaller sheds, and what appeared to be a series of animal pens.

As he continued to study the layout, Zane's eyes were drawn to a flickering glow behind the house. Even though it was partially obscured by the barn, he could tell it was the bonfire that Skinner had referred to earlier.

Mortensen handed him a pair of binoculars. "Here, take a closer look."

Zane aimed them at the distant splash of yellow then turned the focus wheel until the image sharpened and the large fire came into view. Two men in flannel shirts were seated in lawn chairs to the left. Both clutched beer bottles and waved their hands as they talked. A moment later, another man walked behind the two who were seated, a phone pressed to the side of his head.

Zane swept his binoculars to the right. Along the edge of the yard, two men walked along a hedgerow. One smoked while the other talked. Although it was dark on that part of the property, Zane could see that both men had rifles slung over their shoulders. The general shape of the weapons suggested Kalashnikovs, probably AK-47s or AK-74s.

They might be celebrating, but they're not letting their guard down completely.

A cool breeze swept across the ridge, and with it came the distinct scent of animal dung. It was the same odor that was common at state fairs and poorly run zoos. The presence of animals might be a problem, Zane thought. Livestock were often skittish, particularly in areas like the Balkans with high numbers of wolves and coyotes.

Zane turned to Skinner. "Any farm animals down there?"

"We've smelled them but haven't been able to figure out where they're at." Skinner pointed off to the right. "There's another farm about a mile down the road. If I had to guess, I'd say that's where they are."

It was possible, but Zane still tucked the information away for future reference. The scent was too strong to have been carried in from a mile away. They would need to be careful when they moved in. One horse neigh or pig squeal could ruin the operation.

"How many hostiles are down there?" Zane asked Pratt.

"We think seven, although I wouldn't bet my life on it. Just to be safe, I'd say ten or twelve."

"Is one of them in charge?" Zane asked.

Skinner nodded. "We think so. He's a big white dude that

looks like Grizzly Adams. Wavy black hair and a bushy beard."

"Big as in tall or big as in heavy?"

"Both."

"What makes you think he's the one in charge?"

"He's the only one who doesn't come out of the house much, and when he does, he's always looking around."

"That and all the others seem to get serious when he does come out," Pratt said.

Zane nodded. "He's the one we need, then." He looked at Mortensen. "We go down tonight."

Mortensen frowned. "Ross said you wanted to watch for another twenty-four hours. Look for weaknesses in their defense."

"I did say that," Zane said. "But that was before I knew about this little party we need to crash."

CHAPTER NINE

SEEING NO SIGN of guards, Zane came out from behind the tree and ran to a thick row of bushes. He was a mere fifty yards from the house, and that was as close as he was going to get. That was fine. His goal was to set up in a place with a clear view of the house, and he had accomplished that.

He and the rest of the team had spent the last hour moving into position. After coming off the ridge, they had split up before making their way across the overgrown field. Zane took the south side of the meadow, moving from bush to bush. Now that it was dark, the guards had confined their patrols to the area around the home. It seemed they were growing more and more confident that the Americans weren't coming, a development Zane hoped would play to his team's advantage.

Hearing nothing, Zane pushed his way through the bushes. The rear of the farmhouse opened in front of him. A lone apple tree partially blocked his view, but he could see enough to tell that little had changed since they were on the ridge. Three grizzled men were seated at a table near the bonfire, playing cards and drinking bottled beer. The conversation was loud and boisterous, an indication the alcohol had heightened their spirits.

As Zane watched the men, he realized one was the leader Skinner had described earlier. He had dark hair that was shaved on the sides and longer on top. His face was mostly obscured by one of the bushiest beards Zane had ever seen. Despite the night chill, he wore a tight black T-shirt that accentuated broad shoulders and biceps the size of cantaloupes. Even from a distance, the man looked intimidating.

While the card game continued, the man's dark eyes constantly scanned the area behind the house. The others might believe they were safe, but this man was still on alert. They couldn't take him lightly.

The loud *pop* of a cinder drew Zane's attention to the fire. A plume of cinders and ash rose into the air. *Perfect.* The noticeable movement of combustible material was vital to the success of the plan that they were about to initiate.

Pratt's voice crackled through Zane's earpiece. "I'm in place, and the targets are in view."

"Copy that," Mortensen said. "My targets are in sight as well."

"I'm looking at Papa Bear right now," Zane whispered, using the name they had given the group's leader, "and he's a big old boy."

"Nothing you can't handle," Pratt said. "The bigger they are, the harder they fall."

Skinner was the last to check in. "I'm behind the barn. All clear. I'll initiate in five minutes."

"Copy that," Mortensen said.

In the silence that followed, Zane's thoughts turned to the questions that had been running through his mind all night: who were these men, and why had they tried to kill him? He had assumed they were hired mercenaries, and seeing the leader's appearance only cemented that belief. Zane was certain he'd never seen the man before. Who could forget a man who looked like that?

Their ultimate goal was to take Papa Bear alive. Zane wondered if they could get any information out of him. He looked like the kind of man who could hold up under extreme interrogation techniques, but Zane wasn't about to give up hope. Experience had taught him that some of the toughest-looking men were often the first to break down under interrogation. These types of people usually ruled through intimidation, but when their position of authority was snatched away, they turned into sniveling cowards. He didn't know how this man would react, but they would find out soon enough.

Zane's thoughts were interrupted by the sound of approaching footsteps. He pulled back into the bushes. Soft voices came from the left, punctuated by the occasional laugh. At least two hostiles were about to pass by, so Zane remained perfectly still. But instead of going past, the men stopped a few yards away. Zane held his breath. Had they stopped because they could see him? It didn't seem possible. The bushes were too thick to see through, especially at night.

The distinctive *click* of a lighter broke the silence. A few seconds later, the scent of cigarette smoke reached Zane's nostrils. He cursed under his breath. If the two didn't move on, that smoke would be a problem.

As he waited for the men to finish, Zane reviewed their plans. Once all four were in place, Skinner would sneak up behind the barn and set it on fire. While scanning the yard from the ridge, Pratt had spotted several gas cans propped against an unused tractor. While they didn't need gas to start the fire, it would certainly quicken the spread of flames.

Zane hoped the mercenaries would assume the fire had been started by a stray cinder. If they did, they would likely focus on putting it out. That would allow Pratt and Mortensen to target them for quick kills.

But if the two guards remained near Zane, that would create a very large problem. It was Mortensen's job to take out any guards on the south side of the property, which in turn meant he'd be firing into the area where Zane was hidden. Mortensen was an expert marksman, but any number of factors could cause a round to move off its intended path.

Adding to their problems, the bushes were filled with smoke, and Zane felt a sudden urge to cough. He covered his mouth and tried to suppress it, but he still made a soft grunt. Immediately, one of the guards said something Zane couldn't understand. He had heard the noise, although it was likely he didn't know what it was. As Zane remained perfectly still, a light clicked on, and a beam pierced the bushes just a few feet away. Moving carefully so as not to make any noise, Zane removed his Glock. Firing his weapon would sabotage their plan, but he would do what he needed to survive.

The guard barked a loud command. Even though Zane didn't understand what was said, he assumed it was an order for him to come out. Hearing no response from the bushes, the guard shifted the beam in Zane's direction. It was three feet out and closing fast.

His heart pounding, Zane aimed his pistol at the silhouette behind the flashlight. He wouldn't be able to make a head shot, but he could certainly hit center mass.

Just as the cone of light came close, someone shouted in the distance. Zane turned his head slightly. *The fire.* Skinner had initiated the plan.

More shouts came as flames licked up the side of the barn. The two guards who had been standing near Zane ran off to help. Zane waited for several seconds then crawled out into the open. Two of the men had found a hose behind the house and were pulling it toward the barn. More men rushed toward the fire. None had their weapons up.

The plan is working.

Remembering his assignment, Zane looked at the group's leader, Papa Bear, who was now standing. Staying outside the light, Zane ran to the house and crouched behind an HVAC unit. The mountain of a man was only about twenty yards away. Interestingly, he wasn't focused on the fire. Instead, his dark eyes scanned the perimeter of the yard. He seemed to sense something was wrong, that the fire hadn't started by accident.

Zane considered his next move. As soon as the shooting began, he would rush the brute and try to get close enough to shoot him in the knee. It was a difficult shot to make, but if he could get close enough, it might work.

A shot rang out, and one of the guards holding the hose dropped to the ground. A second shot sounded, and another man fell.

It was time to move in. But as Zane stood, he realized their plan had just taken an unexpected turn.

Papa Bear had disappeared.

CHAPTER TEN

CEZAR RUSSINOV HEARD the loud *pop* of a gunshot as he slipped into the house. Seconds later, the first shot was followed by several more. He wasn't in the least surprised. Soon after seeing flames shooting up the back of the barn, he had sensed they were under attack. He had been around hundreds of bonfires over the years and had never seen one of them spark a second fire, even when plenty of dry brush was around. Most cinders that launched into the air cooled off long before they hit the ground.

But even if a cinder had somehow started a second blaze, it wouldn't have erupted so quickly. No, one of their enemies had ignited the barn's siding, and they had likely done so with the help of gasoline or some other accelerant.

Russinov's gut told him the Americans were behind the attack. He believed it was the group that the longhaired target worked for and not an official military strike. The US military wouldn't have conducted such a brazen act on foreign soil. He supposed the US could have asked the Bulgarians to help, but if that had been the case, they would have simply surrounded the property and demanded the men give themselves up.

This was something entirely different. This was an attempt to wipe them out. This was revenge.

Russinov guessed the Americans had somehow tracked the first two men who flew out of the United States, the same ones who were traveling through Dublin. But how had the men been traced? They had flown back to Europe under false identities and had never once been questioned by authorities. The Americans had probably found something on the two assassins who had been killed. Russinov's lead man carried a phone with hidden files. The technology was supposed to be impregnable, but the Americans could probably find anything. While their human intelligence capability was poor, their electronic surveillance capability was second to none. If they could knock out entire computer networks in North Korea and Iran, they could certainly find hidden software on a burner phone.

Inside the house, Russinov flicked a nearby switch and extinguished the overhead light. That allowed him to move around in the darkness without fear of being shot through a window. They would probably try to take him alive, but it was also possible they would seek cold-blooded revenge.

As Russinov turned left down a hallway, he heard the continued rattle of gunfire outside, punctuated by the occasional shout. That gave him hope. At least some of his men had found cover and were fighting back. That would give him enough time to do what he needed to do.

A half minute later, he arrived at a utility room just off the garage. It was the place where they kept their large stash of weapons. At least a dozen pistols were arranged on a laundry table, but Russinov needed more firepower. He needed something that could deliver the maximum number of rounds in a short time. With that in mind, he chose one of the AK-74s that were propped against a nearby wall. He would find a window and return fire from the relative safety of the house.

Russinov was about to look for additional cartridges to take with him when a thought stopped him in his tracks. Did they really have a chance to win this fight? Probably not. He figured at least two or three of his men had been killed when the fight first began, which meant that at best, only three or four were left to fight back. The Americans were hiding in the darkness, firing at men in a lighted area. It was simply a matter of time before the enemy gained the upper hand.

Russinov put the rifle down and grabbed two pistols instead. He would live to fight another day. It was really the only smart choice. Yes, he could try to be a hero and go down with his men, but what would that accomplish? Nothing. His men had shown themselves to be fools, rushing to put out a fire that had clearly been set. It was probably better that he start over, and this time, he would find men of higher quality.

After making sure the magazines were full, Russinov slid one pistol into his jacket pocket and kept the other in his right hand. He made his way to the front of the house. They always kept one vehicle ready to go in case they needed to evacuate quickly.

Russinov peered out through the tiny rectangular window set into the front door. There were four vehicles parked outside. All of them faced the house except for the Renault SUV. Russinov's gang always had one car positioned that way in case they needed to leave quickly. You simply got in and drove off.

Russinov scanned the front yard and the surrounding trees. As best he could tell, there were no attackers positioned to prevent an escape. *Perfect.* It was the one flaw in their plan. He felt a small measure of guilt about deserting his men but quickly set that thought aside. This was about surviving to fight another day.

Satisfied he wasn't walking into an ambush, Russinov opened the door and hurried to the SUV. He climbed in and tossed his phone and the pistol onto the passenger seat. He then reached his hand into the cup holder on his right and felt around.

Nothing.

He frowned. They always left the key in this particular vehicle. Had one of his men used the vehicle and taken the key with him by mistake?

Russinov briefly sensed something was wrong but pushed the feeling aside. It wouldn't be the first time his men had failed to follow his instructions. All the more reason to leave the idiots behind. *Survival of the fittest.* He was fit, they were not.

Russinov turned his attention back to the problem at hand. The keys weren't in the cup holder, but maybe they were somewhere else. On more than one occasion, he had found them on the seat or in the ignition. It wouldn't hurt to take a quick look around.

He reached for the overhead light, but before he could flick the switch, he felt the muzzle of a gun press against the back of his head.

Someone spoke from behind him. "Don't do anything stupid."

CHAPTER ELEVEN

IT TOOK ZANE several minutes to maneuver the mammoth man out of the vehicle and pat him down. Not only was he physically imposing, but he also seemed cagey, the kind of person who could turn the tables if his captor averted his eyes for even a second.

The ambush in the SUV had been prompted by a hunch. When Zane realized the man had retreated into the house, he had considered going in after him. But the more he thought about it, the more he became convinced that wouldn't be a good idea. For one, the man knew the house better than he did, which meant he might be waiting to ambush whoever came in. More importantly, Zane believed the man was going to flee. As leader of the gang, he had to know his men would be wiped out. Exposed in the glow of the fire, they didn't stand a chance against snipers targeting them from several different directions. It would be like shooting fish in a barrel.

Once Zane became convinced the man would try to escape, he had circled around to the front of the house, where he found four vehicles. As he waited for the man to come out, Zane remembered that criminal gangs often left keys in one or more vehicles in case they needed to make a quick exit. Delphi operatives did the same thing when the situation warranted.

Zane conducted a quick search and discovered that one of the vehicles, a gray SUV, was unlocked. Not surprisingly, he also found a set of keys in the cup holder of the center console. Knowing that was the escape car, he grabbed the keys and hid in the back seat.

From there, it had simply been a matter of waiting for Papa Bear to enter the car and sit down.

After searching the man thoroughly, Zane marched him toward the front door. The gunfire seemed to have ended. Zane hoped that meant his team had finished the job. Nevertheless, he approached the house with caution. The absence of gunfire could simply mean a break in the fighting.

As Zane followed the man up the steps, the door swung open. Zane pointed his pistol at the dark silhouette standing in the entryway.

"Whoa, whoa," the figure said.

Pratt. The Southern drawl gave him away every time.

"Next time, let me know you're coming," Zane said.

"I didn't know you were out here. You disappeared on us."

"All clear out back?" Zane asked.

"Ten-four," Pratt replied. "Unfortunately, they're all dead." He looked at Zane's prisoner. "But I guess you got the one that mattered."

"I think our friend is in a foul mood. Probably thought he'd be flying down the highway by now."

Zane jabbed the man's spine with the pistol, letting him know it was time to go in.

"Sorry to rain on your plans, big guy," Pratt said as he passed by the captive.

They took the leader to the living room at the back of the house. The other operatives were already there, and all of them appeared to be unscathed. So far, their plan had worked to perfection. Then again, phase one might have been the easy part. Getting the captive to talk would be a monumental task. He was the leader for a reason.

After telling Skinner to bring over a chair, Zane looked at Pratt. "See if you can find something to tie him up with." He turned to Pratt. "How about checking the gray SUV that's parked outside? When I patted him down, I didn't find anything, which was strange. If he was making a run for it, he should've had a phone, a pistol, and who knows what else. They're probably somewhere in the front of that truck."

"Roger that."

As Pratt set off, Zane pushed the captive down a hallway to the left. "Walk, and keep those hands up."

While keeping one eye on his prisoner, Zane reached into the first door on the right and flicked on the light. It was a bedroom, which was perfect for what he had in mind.

"Turn around." When the man turned and faced him, Zane waved the pistol toward the door. "Get in there."

The man entered with Zane right behind him. Two unmade beds were positioned on either side of the filthy room. The smell of smoke and cheap liquor hung in the air, and the floor was littered with crumpled packs of cigarettes, empty potato chip bags, and porn magazines.

When Skinner arrived with the chair, Zane nodded toward

the area between the beds. "Set it right there then close the blinds." Once he was done, Zane nodded at a small bedside table with a lamp on top. "Now set that in front of the chair."

Zane had questioned bad guys many times before and knew how to get them to talk. The first step was to establish the right environment. When he'd first started working in the intelligence field, Zane had always assumed the use of a bright light in a dark room was just Hollywood drama. But he soon learned that it really did help to bind a subject up in a dark room then blind them with light. He didn't know the science behind the results, but he guessed it had something to do with establishing control.

"Sit," Zane barked at the man.

He took his seat and looked at Zane. He had the cold, empty eyes of a psychopath. It wouldn't be easy to break this man, but Zane was going to find a way to do it, even if it meant straying across the line. Someone had ordered the man to kill Zane, and Zane was going to find out who that was.

Mortensen stepped into the room and held up a roll of duct tape and several USB cables. "How about this?"

"Perfect," Zane said. "How about doing the honors."

"My pleasure."

When Zane turned his attention to the captive, he realized something was wrong. The man had a hand inside his jacket. Zane had patted him down thoroughly, but it was always possible he had missed a thin blade or other small weapon.

"Hey!" Mortensen shouted.

The man removed his hand, revealing a large white pill pinched between two fingers.

Mortensen rushed forward and grabbed the man's arms, but it was too late. The man's Adam's apple was already moving. The pill was on its way down.

Zane pressed the muzzle of his pistol against the man's temple. Maybe there was still time to get some information out of the man. "Who sent you?"

He laughed. "What you going to do, kill me?"

"No, we're going to keep you alive." Zane looked at Skinner. "See if you can find something under the kitchen sink. A harsh cleaner, bleach, anything. We need to get him to throw up."

Zane had no idea if it would work. The idea had simply popped into his head. If they could somehow get the man to vomit the pill, that could buy them some time.

The man laughed again. "Won't work. I take another pill before. End will come soon."

Zane thought back over the last ten minutes. He supposed the man could have slipped another pill into his mouth at some point. But why even carry them to begin with? If these were paid mercenaries, why go to such extreme measures to avoid being questioned?

"Who sent you?" Zane asked.

The man leaned closer, his lips quivering. "They'll find you. They always do." He managed a grin. "They have tentacles everywhere, even in government."

"Who are *they*?"

The man's body shook uncontrollably as a thin line of drool oozed out of the corner of his mouth. He was fading fast.

Skinner came into the room and held up a bottle of toilet bowl cleaner. "This is all I could find."

THE CHAMBER

Zane waved him off. It was too late. They'd never bring him back now. The toxin had already made its way into his bloodstream, and while it might take hours for him to die, his mind had already descended into a foggy haze.

Zane looked at Skinner. "Are you sure all the other men are dead?"

"All the ones we *found* were dead. I can't guarantee one of them didn't run off."

Zane nodded.

Pratt entered the room and held up a phone. "I found this on the front seat."

"Let's have a look." Zane turned to Mortensen and Skinner. "How about watching him for a minute."

"Roger that," Skinner said.

Zane followed Pratt down the hallway.

"He didn't have a screen lock, so I took the liberty of looking around," Pratt said as they entered the living room. "Take a look at this text he got a few hours ago."

Zane took the phone and read the short message that had been typed in English: *Remain in place. Should be able to fly into Tel Aviv soon. Waiting to schedule with our person on the inside.*

"They were supposed to fly to Tel Aviv," Zane said as he read the text a second time.

Pratt nodded. "It looks like they may have someone working for Israeli customs."

Zane went back to the text app's main screen and noticed there weren't any other texts. "Looks like he's been erasing his messages as he goes along. I guess we were lucky to find one."

"He didn't erase everything. Check the photos."

Zane opened the photo gallery and found two thumbnails. The first was a distant shot of two people walking down a street. He tapped the image. A wave of rage swept through him. It was a photo of him and Katiya walking down a street in Alexandria. They had just left the breakfast place they frequented. He couldn't figure out who he was angrier at, himself for not spotting the tails or whoever was trying to kill him.

Pushing his anger aside, Zane tapped the second image. It showed an older heavyset man with gray hair and a bushy gray beard. He was working on a laptop while seated at a table outside a restaurant or café. Zane stared at the photo. Whoever took the image was seated just a few yards away, which meant they were probably using a phone camera.

"I wonder if that's their next target," Zane whispered.

Pratt nodded then pointed at something behind the man. "Notice the language on the sign."

"Hebrew," Zane said.

The target lives in Israel.

"And based on the text, it's probably Tel Aviv."

"Not necessarily," Zane said. "Almost everyone who travels to Israel flies in through Tel Aviv." Zane zoomed in on the man's face. "This is a high-quality shot. I need to get it over to Brett to—"

A distant wailing cut him off. *Sirens.* Someone on a nearby farm had likely seen the flames, heard the gunfire, or both. He had hoped to ransack the place, but that was no longer an option.

They needed to get out, and they needed to get out fast.

CHAPTER TWELVE

THE KNOCK ON Zane's door came just as he stepped out of the shower. After drying off, he threw on a terry cloth robe. It would have to do. Another knock sounded as he came out of the bathroom, this one harder than the first.

"I'm coming, I'm coming."

Even though he had a pretty good idea of who it was, he followed protocol. After retrieving his Glock from the nightstand, he eased up to the door and looked through the peephole. *Pratt.*

"Any day now," the Southerner barked from the other side.

Zane opened the door and waved him in. "So much for keeping a low profile."

"I come bearing caffeine." The Southerner entered clutching two large mugs of coffee. "You'd think that would have put a little jump in your step."

Zane shut the door behind him. "Would you have preferred I come out naked?"

"Not on your life."

"I trust you got my order right."

Pratt set one of the mugs on the table. "You're a creature of habit. I can probably predict what color boxers you have on right now."

"Now you're starting to scare me."

"I should probably warn you, it ain't Starbucks."

Zane picked up his mug and took a sip. "Actually, that's not too bad. In fact, I'd say it's pretty good."

"I thought the same thing, although it might be because I'm going on three hours' sleep. Gas station coffee would probably taste good right now."

They were running on fumes, although if Zane had his way, they would have stayed at the farmhouse all night looking for evidence. Instead, the approaching fire trucks had ended any hope of that.

Zane did stay long enough to complete one task that was meant to throw off local law enforcement. Using a knife found on one of the guards, he carved an odd-looking symbol on the foreheads of the deceased. He wanted the disfigurement to suggest the killings came by the hand of a rival gang within Bulgaria. If authorities ruled out an international hit, they wouldn't be as likely to watch all points of entry, including airports. They would eventually figure out the symbols were bogus, but it might at least buy Zane and the team a day to get out.

"Where are Mort and Skinner?" Zane asked after taking another sip.

Pratt took a seat at the table and looked out the window. "Down in the restaurant getting breakfast. Now that you're up, you should do the same thing. We need to hightail it out of here, and who knows when we'll be able to eat again."

"I wish I had that luxury. Brett is supposed to be calling at any—"

As if on cue, Zane's phone buzzed on the table.

"Speak of the devil," Pratt said.

Zane looked at the screen. It *was* Brett. He engaged the call. "Good morning."

"Well, I guess two a.m. is technically morning," Brett said.

"I have Bull here with me, so I'm going to put you on Speaker."

After tapping the speaker button, Zane placed the phone on the table and sat down across from Pratt.

"I have you on Speaker as well. Our fearless leader is on the line."

"Greetings, gentlemen," Ross said.

"So both of you are burning the midnight oil," Zane said. "Please tell me you found something. That photograph is all we got."

On the way to the hotel, Zane had texted Brett the photograph of the heavyset man with gray hair and beard. Making positive identification was a long shot, but Zane knew Delphi had some of the best facial recognition software out there. Not only did it analyze images extremely well, but it also connected to the world's largest database.

"Actually, we did," Ross said. "Or I guess I should say Brett did."

"The man in the photograph is Solomon Glaser," Brett said.

Zane didn't recognize the name. "Who is he?"

"He's an Israeli archaeologist."

Archaeologist. Although Zane didn't have a preconceived notion of who the man might be, he certainly hadn't expected him to be an archaeologist. Were these mercenaries working for two separate clients, or was Zane somehow connected to this man?

"You said he's an Israeli," Pratt said. "Does he actually *live* in Israel?"

"Yes. Based on what we've been able to find out, we believe he lives in Jerusalem."

"We believe this Glaser may be a target," Zane said. "Do we have any way to contact him?"

"Not yet," Ross said. "We found a landline number for him, but it's been disconnected."

Zane wondered if that was significant. Did the archaeologist know he was a target? Had he gone underground?

"What about an address?" Pratt asked. "We probably need to get the Israelis to pay him a visit."

"We do have an address, but for now, we're not going to get them involved," Ross said. "No other agency knows we're looking into all of this, so any warning needs to come from us."

"They can get to him quicker," Pratt said.

"I'm fully aware of that," Ross retorted. "You took out the hit team last night. Even if another team is sent, it will probably take some time. That means our archaeologist should be safe for the next day or two."

Zane nodded. "I think you're right. Remember the text we found? The one that said the team was being sent in once their inside guy was working at the airport? That means whoever is behind it all will have to make other arrangements, and that will take time."

"Which brings me to the next point," Ross said. "Watson, we have another plane on its way to Sofia to pick you up this afternoon. I want you to go to Israel to warn Glaser and find out what's going on."

"What about the rest of us?" Pratt asked.

"You can return to Croatia. I don't expect Watson will need any muscle."

"I would like to ask for something, or I should say someone," Zane said. "If Amanda's available, I'd like her to join me. She's our resident archaeologist, so I think she needs to be there."

"I'm already one step ahead of you, Watson. She's packing as we speak."

CHAPTER THIRTEEN

Jerusalem

AMANDA HIGGS PULLED to the side of the street, put the car in Park, then pointed at the row of houses ahead. "Glaser's should be the fourth one down on the right."

Zane lifted his binoculars and trained them on the home's front gate. Even though it was dark, there was enough light from a nearby streetlamp to read the numbers. "Yes, that's it."

They were in Rehavia, one of the three garden neighborhoods of central Jerusalem. While Rehavia's residential streets were known for their solitude, its upscale retail district was known for its vibrant and hip wine bars, coffee shops, and restaurants. It wasn't the sort of place where Zane had expected to find an archaeologist's residence.

Like most properties on the block, Glaser's home was encompassed by a stone wall. The wall wasn't particularly high, but the interior courtyard was filled with numerous large trees, making it difficult for Zane to see the house clearly. Apparently, the archaeologist liked his privacy.

"Can you tell if anyone is home?" Amanda asked.

"No, too many trees." Zane put the binoculars in the glove compartment. "I guess we'll find out when we get there."

"The whole thing seems odd," Amanda said.

Zane turned toward her. "How so?"

"I know dozens of archaeologists, and this isn't how most of them live. Most are professors who are firmly planted in the middle class. The vast majority certainly don't have the kind of wealth you'd need to buy a place like this."

"I was just thinking the same thing." He shrugged. "Maybe it's family money, or maybe he's sold some artifacts over the years."

"Archaeologists don't just sell what they find. They're not in this for the money, at least not the ones I know. But I guess there are always exceptions to any rule."

"Didn't you say you knew him?"

"No, I said I knew *of* him. I did a little reading on the flight over, but there really isn't much about him online. He's sort of a recluse."

"I guess we'll need to fill in the blanks when we speak to him." Zane checked the time on his phone—8:37. "Let's go."

As they exited the rental car and crossed the street, Zane took in their surroundings. The neighborhood was quiet, almost eerily so.

"What if he doesn't want to speak to us?" Amanda asked as they approached the wrought iron gate in front of Glaser's home. "I doubt the people in this neighborhood like nighttime visitors."

"He'll talk to us. He may not like us showing up unannounced, but I think most people are willing to listen if you tell them you have information that relates to their personal safety." Zane looked at her. "Maybe you should do the talking. You look a whole lot nicer than I do."

"I can do nice," she said with a laugh.

As Zane had suspected, the gate was unlocked. Most gates and walls in wealthy neighborhoods were decorative in nature and weren't meant to keep anyone out.

Inside the courtyard, a cobblestone path ran through the trees to the front stoop. As they started down the path, Zane noted a small lamp burning in the window to the right of the front door. Other than that, the house was dark.

"I predict he's not home," Amanda said as they climbed the front steps.

"It's a big house. Maybe he's in the back."

Zane pressed the doorbell, and a soft but distinct buzz sounded inside the house. They waited for a full minute, but no one responded. Zane tried a second time with the same result.

"He has an intercom." Amanda moved to the right of the door and pressed the button next to the speaker. "Mr. Glaser, are you home?"

Once again, there was no response.

"He's an old man," she said. "Maybe he's hard of hearing."

She balled her fist and banged it hard against the door. To their mutual surprise, it pushed open. The two exchanged a glance. A wealthy homeowner like Glaser wouldn't leave his door open at night.

Placing a finger to his lips, Zane made a gesture that signaled they were going in. He reached inside his jacket and drew his

Glock 17. Keeping it up, he pushed the door all the way open and stepped into the foyer. The space was dimly lit from the glow of the lamp in the other room. As Zane looked around, he noted three archways leading to other parts of the house: two on either side and one directly ahead. Beyond the one directly ahead was a hallway that he assumed led to the back of the house.

"His alarm system is turned off," Amanda whispered, nodding at a panel inside the front door.

"Turned off or disabled."

"Just seems odd."

After listening for several more seconds, Zane cupped a hand to his mouth and called out, "Dr. Glaser?"

There was no answer.

Amanda tried a few seconds later. "Dr. Glaser, are you there?"

"Okay, time to split up," Zane said. "You check the back, and I'll start up here."

"Roger that."

As Amanda walked off, Zane locked the front door behind them. The last thing they needed was to have someone show up unannounced.

Satisfied the door was secure, he stepped through the archway to the right. The tiny sitting room was sparsely furnished with several ornate chairs. The lamp they had seen earlier rested on a second small table in front of the window. Zane could tell it had been turned on to give the appearance that someone was home. Fearing he might be seen from the street, he drew the curtains shut then turned and surveyed the rest of the room. *Nothing.* There was nothing to suggest that Glaser spent any time here.

Zane reentered the foyer and was about to start on the other room when Amanda called out his name. He stopped. "Something wrong?"

"Just get back here."

Turning right, Zane entered the long hall that ran to the back of the house. Seconds later, he emerged into a cavernous room. On the left was an open kitchen, and to the right was Solomon Glaser's living room. Leather couches and chairs encircled a coffee table. Amanda stood on the other side of the table, facing a black couch that was set against the wall. Her flashlight was trained at something on the floor.

"What is it?" Zane moved in her direction.

She turned and looked back over her shoulder. "I think I found Dr. Glaser."

Zane's body tensed as he came up beside her. The beam of Amanda's flashlight illuminated the body of a heavyset man with a shock of gray hair. Even though the man was facing the other direction, Zane could see that he had a thick, bushy beard. Zane studied the man's attire. He wore a long-sleeve black shirt and a pair of old jeans. Zane shifted his gaze to the man's upper back. There was no movement to indicate he was breathing.

Just to be sure, Zane reached for the man's neck.

"I already checked his pulse," Amanda said.

Zane pulled back. "You sure it's Glaser?"

"No, but who else would it be?"

"His brother? A guest? In case you hadn't noticed, there are quite a few older men with beards in Jerusalem."

"Trust me, it's him."

Zane studied the man's position. He was lying against the bottom of the couch, his right arm resting on top of the seat cushion. It looked as though he had been trying to get up right before he died. There was no obvious sign of foul play, so why had he died?

Zane looked at Amanda. "Any idea how he—"

"He was shot," Amanda said. "It's hard to see without some light." She ran the flashlight beam across the dark shirt, revealing two wet stains. "Twice in the abdomen and once to the leg." She moved the beam down to his pants, illuminating a second stain behind the man's knee.

"Tortured," Zane said.

Amanda nodded.

Zane had seen a similar progression of wounds on several occasions. Victims with valuable information were often shot first in the knee, and if that didn't work, the perpetrator would move on to other more painful means of torture. Zane didn't see any damage to other parts of the body. No broken fingers. No broken fingernails. Had the attacker been interrupted?

He shifted his gaze to the stains on Glaser's shirt. Both rounds exited at the back of his lower torso. Neither shot would have killed him instantly. Maybe that was what the killer had used to make Glaser talk.

"Nine millimeter," Zane noted. "And no shot to the heart, despite being at close range. They wanted him to die a slow death."

"They needed information, or they wanted him to suffer." Amanda reached out for the man's shoulder. "I'm certain it's

Glaser, but let's have a look at his face."

Zane grabbed her arm. "Hold on a sec. Let's do this the right way."

"Copy that."

Zane walked to the kitchen and rummaged through the drawers until he found a small dish towel. After returning to the body, he used the towel to pull the man's right shoulder back until the face was revealed. Two glazed-over eyes stared into space.

"Yep, that's him," Amanda said.

Solomon Glaser had a round face, a ruddy complexion, and an unruly gray beard. Adding to the unkempt appearance were eyebrows that looked like they hadn't been trimmed in years.

Zane placed the back of his hand against Glaser's shoulder and held it there. "Interesting."

"What?"

"He's still warm."

Amanda's brow furrowed. "You think this just happened?"

Zane put the towel in his jacket pocket. "It's hard to say for sure." He looked around the room. "It's warm in here, which means the body would lose heat more slowly. Even so, I'd say this happened in the last hour or two."

Amanda's eyes narrowed. "You think the killer could still be here?"

Zane considered her question. The killer had abandoned the body suddenly. Was it possible he was still lurking somewhere in the house? Although he doubted it, he couldn't rule it out.

"Maybe he took off when we rang the bell," Amanda continued. "I mean, he could be gone, but he could also be hiding somewhere."

"The front door was open, so that's probably how he left," Zane said. "But it won't hurt to take a look around."

As Amanda looked behind the couches, Zane gazed at the French doors at the rear of the house.

Maybe the killer came in through the front then exited at the rear.

Zane walked to the doors and examined the locks. There was no sign of forced entry.

Sensing that was a dead end, Zane looked toward the kitchen, where a green light blinked on the counter. *An answering machine.* He went to it and examined the LED screen. A new message had been received, so he pressed the playback button. Following a loud beep, a woman spoke in accented English. "Dr. Glaser, this is Rachel. I hope everything is okay. I tried to call you twice. In case you're wondering about the final edits, I worked late and got them finished. Please call me when you get the chance, and I'll bring you up to date."

Amanda came over. "Play that again."

Zane pressed the button, and the message played a second time.

"It sounds like she works for him," Amanda said. "Maybe his assistant."

"If anyone might know what's going on, it would be her."

Amanda looked at him. "You think we should call her?"

"Why not? She sounded concerned, almost like she sensed something was wrong."

"Let me call her," Amanda said. "She might feel more comfortable answering questions from a woman."

"Sexist."

"Not hardly. Just a realist."

Amanda retrieved the caller's number from the screen. After saving it into her contacts, she and Zane discussed how best to handle the conversation that would follow. Once they agreed on the right approach, Amanda dialed the number and placed the call on Speaker.

After the third ring, a woman answered. "Hello."

"Is this Rachel?" Amanda asked.

"Yes, it is. Who's this?"

"My name is Amanda."

"Amanda?" There was a short pause. "I'm sorry, do I know you?"

"Well, no, you don't. I'm an archaeologist from the United States, and I came to Jerusalem to talk to Dr. Glaser."

"Well, if you're trying to find him, then I won't be much help. I've been trying to reach him for several hours."

"Actually, I *have* found him," Amanda said.

There was a brief pause. "I'm sorry. I don't understand. If you found him, why are you calling me?"

"Because something's happened to him."

Zane could hear the woman catch her breath on the other end.

"What do you mean?" Rachel asked.

"I hate to be the one to tell you this, but Dr. Glaser is dead."

Several seconds of silence were followed by soft sobs on the other end.

"I'm very sorry," Amanda said. She remained silent, giving the woman time to grieve.

A half minute later, Rachel pulled herself together. "What happened? How did he…?"

"I think we'd better discuss that in person."

"I knew something was wrong," Rachel whispered on the other end. "I just knew it."

"How did you know that?"

"He called me earlier today and said he wanted to meet with me. He said it was urgent and he would call me back to give me a time. I never heard from him, so I reached out several times."

"Did he say something was wrong?"

"No, but he sounded… Well, he sounded concerned. I thought it was about a deadline we've been trying to meet, but I realize now it must have been something else." There was a short pause. "Was he killed?"

Amanda paused for a moment then asked, "Why would you ask that?"

"Because of something he mentioned recently."

Amanda's frown deepened. "What did he say?"

There was a long pause. Rather than ask the question again, Amanda waited.

"He told me… he told me that some people were following him. I asked him why anyone would want to follow him, and he just said he had something they wanted."

"Did you know what that might be?"

"No, I don't."

Zane sensed Rachel was holding something back. They needed to push for more information, but they needed to do it in person. He leaned over and whispered some quick instructions in Amanda's ear.

"Rachel, my colleague and I came here to warn Dr. Glaser about something. Unfortunately, we didn't make it in time to help him, but with your help, maybe we can figure all of this out."

"What makes you think I can help you?"

"Don't you work for Dr. Glaser?"

"Yes, but—"

"Then you're best suited to interpret the information we have." Amanda waited a few seconds before continuing. "We also think you could be in danger."

"Me?"

"You said yourself that these people were looking for information."

"That's just what Dr. Glaser told me."

"Rachel, I don't know you, and I certainly don't want to scare you, but if they didn't get what they were looking for tonight, then you could be their next target."

It was a bold move, but Zane knew it might be the only way to get the woman's cooperation. At this point, she was likely their only hope of piecing everything together.

After a long pause, Rachel said, "Okay, I'll try to help if I can."

"Good," Amanda said. "You're doing the right thing. We're here at Dr. Glaser's home. You can come over here, or we can travel to you if that works better—"

"No, I'll come over there. I can be there in ten minutes."

"One more thing," Amanda said. "Don't call the police. We'll call them once we figure out what's going on."

CHAPTER FOURTEEN

AFTER THE PHONE call ended, Zane and Amanda made a quick search of the house. Even though his gut told him the place was clear, Zane wanted to be certain the killer wasn't hiding in one of the rooms. After all, the door had been ajar when they arrived, and Solomon Glaser's body was still warm.

Five minutes later, they returned to the living room without finding any evidence that the killer was still around. Zane noted a couple of rooms he wanted to search more thoroughly later. One of the rooms was Glaser's study. Zane had noted several unconnected USB cables on the desk, which seemed to indicate an electronic device had been removed. The study also had several large filing cabinets, which might contain documents related to Glaser's research.

He was just about to share what he had found when a sharp beep sounded from the kitchen. Zane turned and saw a red light blinking on a box affixed to the wall.

"It's the security system," Amanda said as she walked over to it.

"I thought you said it was disabled."

"I did say that." She stared at the screen. "It looks like there are two systems, one for the house and one for the front gate. This says the front gate was just opened."

"Rachel."

As if on cue, a soft knock sounded at the front door.

"I'll go get her." Amanda went down the hall.

A few seconds later, the sound of muffled voices came from the front of the house. The soft conversation continued for a while longer, then footsteps approached on the hardwood floors. Amanda emerged first, followed by a woman Zane assumed was Rachel. She was an attractive woman of medium height. Her dark hair was pulled back into a ponytail, and her dark-brown eyes peered at him through black-framed glasses. She looked to be in her early to mid-forties.

Her attire was casual. She wore a fashionable tracksuit that was paired with bright-white Adidas sneakers.

"Zane, this is Rachel Hammond," Amanda said.

He stepped forward and extended a hand. "Nice to meet you."

She shook the proffered hand. "It's nice to meet you too."

"Thank you for coming," Zane said. "I'm sure this can't be easy."

"No, it's not." Her eyes had a wet gleam. "I…"

Rachel caught her breath as her gaze fixed on something behind them. Zane turned and looked toward the circle of leather couches. The archaeologist's arm was still visible on the cushion. He had thought about lowering it out of sight but decided to leave the body the way they found it in case its position was significant. Maybe that had been a bad decision.

Rachel cried softly. Amanda put an arm around her shoulders and guided her toward one of the chairs. "Why don't you have a seat?"

"I want to see him," Rachel said.

"I don't think that's a good idea," Zane said. "Why don't we talk for a while, then if you're still feeling up to it, you can."

Rachel nodded as she wiped the corner of her eyes with the sleeve of her tracksuit.

"I'd offer you some water, but we're trying not to touch anything," Amanda said after Rachel lowered into the chair.

"I'll be fine."

Amanda sank onto a nearby couch, and Zane took a seat in the chair directly across from Rachel.

"So, I take it you've known Dr. Glaser for a long time?" Zane asked.

"No, I've only been working for him for a few months," she replied. "I know it seems crazy for me to be so distraught since I've only—"

"No, it's not crazy," Zane said. "I'm sure the two of you were close."

"He was a good boss and an even better person."

"What exactly did you do for him?" Amanda asked.

"A little of everything. I guess you'd say I was his personal assistant, but lately, I've been doing some light editing of a book he's writing. I studied languages in college and did a little writing when I was younger."

"How did you come to work for him?" Amanda asked.

"He and I have a mutual friend who works at a museum here in Jerusalem. A while back, he told that mutual friend he was overwhelmed with a new book he was working on." She paused a moment and wiped the corner of her eye again. "The friend suggested Dr. Glaser give me a call. I was really struggling with my finances at the time. I had just been laid off from another job, and my friend knew things were tight."

Despite the woman's fragile emotional state, Zane knew they needed to move things along. "I believe you told Amanda that Solomon Glaser thought he was being followed."

She nodded as her eyes moved back to the arm that was draped over the couch.

Zane needed to keep her talking. "When did this start?"

"Him being followed?"

Zane nodded.

"I don't know exactly when it all began. I guess a few weeks ago." She paused. "I don't want to be critical, but at the time, I didn't believe him."

Amanda frowned. "Why not?"

"I don't know. He sounded paranoid, which was not like him at all. He even thought someone had broken into the house."

Zane remembered the unconnected USB cables in the study. "What made him think that?"

"He said some things were out of place. Even though his office is extremely messy, he knew where everything was supposed to be. He was convinced that some papers had been moved around and that some drawers had been opened."

"Why would that be odd?" Amanda asked. "You were working here, too, right?"

"Not really. I came over here each day to pick things up and go over what he wanted me to do, but I mostly work out of my apartment."

"What made him think he was being followed?" Zane asked.

"He hated driving. He walked a lot, and he told me he had seen the same men passing by when he went out each day. They tried to hide what they were up to, but he believed they were watching him."

"Did he know why he was being followed?" Zane asked.

"He thought it might be related to a project he was working on."

Zane sensed they were getting closer to a motive. "Did he say what that was?"

"No. It wasn't anything I was involved with, so I assumed he wanted to keep it a secret." Rachel's expression seemed to indicate she had just remembered something important. "A while back, I did hear him say..."

She seemed hesitant to tell them something. Instead of pushing her to continue, Zane waited for her response. If she was trying to recall something, interrupting would only serve to stifle those efforts.

"I came into the house about a week ago, and Dr. Glaser was on the phone," Rachel finally said. "He always left the door open when I was supposed to come over. Anyway, I could hear him talking back here. I didn't want to interrupt, so I waited in one of the rooms up front."

"Were you able to hear what he was saying?" Amanda asked.

"Not at first. But while I was waiting, I decided to go to the bathroom."

Zane remembered seeing a door in the hallway just a few

yards away, which he assumed was a half bath.

"When I got to the bathroom door, I could hear him talking," she continued. "He sounded really excited about something. To be honest, I'd never heard him speak in that kind of tone before."

"What exactly did he say?" Zane asked.

"He said… it's hard to remember."

"Take your time," Amanda said.

"I think he said something like 'I found it. I know where it is.'"

Amanda's eyes narrowed. "Found what?"

Rachel shrugged. "I don't know."

"Maybe it wasn't anything important," Zane suggested. "Maybe he was just talking about something he misplaced around the house."

"No," Rachel said. "As I mentioned, his tone was different. I'd never heard his voice so animated before." She paused. "And there was something else. When he finally got off the call, he seemed to be uncomfortable around me. I think he heard me go into the bathroom and was probably wondering if I'd heard what he said."

"Is that all you remember?" Amanda asked.

Rachel nodded.

"Did he have any idea *who* might be following him?" Zane asked.

"He wasn't sure."

Zane was experienced at noting the tells that revealed a person's truthfulness, and while he felt Rachel was being honest, he also sensed that she was holding something back. "Is there something you aren't telling us?"

"I don't want to judge," Rachel finally said. "It's not really my—"

"It's important you tell us everything you know," Amanda said. "Remember, we're all just trying to figure out what happened here."

Rachel looked at her. "Well, Dr. Glaser had concerns about his son, Nathan."

"What kinds of concerns?" Amanda asked.

"They had had a falling-out some time back and weren't speaking, at least not very much. I think his son was angry at him for some reason."

Zane was having trouble putting all the pieces together. First, Rachel had said he thought someone was interested in his work. So how could that relate to his son? "So he thought the son was somehow involved in all this?" he asked.

"Dr. Glaser didn't know who was following him, but he believed his son was the only one who could have tipped these people off to whatever it was he was working on."

"Why did he make that connection?" Zane asked. "Was there anything concrete, or was it just conjecture?"

Rachel appeared to think for a moment then said, "His son doesn't live in Jerusalem, but Dr. Glaser said he'd seen his son's car driving past the house a few times. At least he thought it was his son's car. He thinks that's how these people were getting inside to look around."

Zane considered what she had just said. The disgruntled son learned about something his father had discovered, perhaps some important archaeological find. The son then decided to get more information and broke into the house. On some level, it made sense. On the other hand, who were the people he was working with? Had the son brought them in? Something didn't add up, but Zane wasn't certain what that was.

Rachel's eyes went to the arm again, so Amanda got up and grabbed a large pillow off the couch she was sitting on. She moved toward Glaser's body, and Zane could tell that she was going to cover it up with the pillow. She was trying to make sure there weren't any further distractions, which was the right thing to do.

Zane turned to Rachel. "So tell me what you know about the son. Does he live here—"

"Zane," Amanda called out.

Hearing the excited tone of her voice, he turned.

Amanda stood over the body, her eyes fixed on something.

"What is it?" Zane asked.

"I think we missed something."

CHAPTER FIFTEEN

ZANE RUSHED TO where Amanda was standing. She stood perfectly still, her eyes fixed on Glaser's hand. Was he holding something? He didn't seem to be. The archaeologist's fingers were smeared with blood, but they already knew that.

Sensing his confusion, Amanda turned on her flashlight and directed the beam at a point just beyond Glaser's hand. "See it now?"

Zane's gaze fixed on a large smudge of blood that he hadn't seen because it had blended with the dark color of the couch. As he studied the spot, he noticed a small object wedged between the two seat cushions. He leaned closer and saw what appeared to be the thin edge of a notepad.

"Looks like he hid it right before he died," Amanda said.

Zane had assumed the archaeologist was trying to pull himself up—perhaps a final attempt to get to his feet—but now it was clear he had used the last seconds of his life to hide the pad. And if he had hidden the pad, then it was likely significant.

"Let's have a look." He reached into his pocket and removed the dish towel he had used before. Moving carefully, he pulled the pad out of its hiding place. What appeared to be a hastily written message was scrawled across the top page.

Rachel leaned forward. "What does it say?"

"Let's get it into the light." He nodded toward the kitchen.

The three walked over to the round table. After turning on the overhead light, Zane set the pad down so they could all see the top page. Much to his surprise, there wasn't some cryptic message. Instead, there was simply an address: *102 David Yellin Street. FYEO.*

The three studied the message in silence.

"Strange," Amanda said.

Rachel's brow furrowed. "FYEO?"

"For your eyes only," Amanda said.

Hoping for more, Zane lifted the top page, but nothing was written underneath.

"Maybe he's trying to tell us who killed him," Amanda said after several seconds of silence.

Zane looked at her. "How so?"

"It's an address, so maybe that's where we'll find the killer."

"Then why not give us the name?"

She shrugged. "It's possible he doesn't have a name. He told Rachel there were people following him, so maybe he turned the tables and followed them to that address."

Zane stared at the note but said nothing.

"What do you think it means?" Amanda asked.

"I have no idea." Zane turned to Rachel. "Do you recognize the address? Maybe it relates to his work."

"I'm familiar with the street, but I have no idea who or what is at that specific address," she replied.

"Where is it?" Amanda asked.

"Not far from here, actually," Rachel answered.

Amanda removed her phone and began to tap the screen. "Let's see what comes up."

"You said you know the street," Zane said. "Is there anything special about it?"

"No," she replied. "It's just a street. There are lots of old apartment buildings and a café or two. I'm familiar with it because I used to live a couple of blocks from there."

"But you never heard Glaser mention it?"

"No, never."

Zane had no idea why Glaser would make that the last thing he'd written. Perhaps it was the address of someone they needed to talk to. And if that was true, then perhaps the intended recipient would know what Glaser had been working on.

"Got it." Amanda placed her phone on the table so that all could see. Displayed on the screen was a street view image from Google Maps. "Looks like some sort of store."

Zane leaned closer for a better look. 121 David Yellin Street was a nondescript two-story stone building. A small retail store occupied most or all of the ground floor. Flanking the entrance to the store were two carousels that seemed to be stocked with postcards and souvenirs. A white sign with black lettering was positioned above the entrance.

Zane pointed at the sign. "Can you enlarge it?"

Amanda used her fingers to zoom in.

Once the sign was visible, Zane could see that the lettering was written in Hebrew script. He looked at Rachel. "What does it say?"

"Makolet King David," she replied.

"Makolet?" Zane asked.

"Makolets are privately owned supermarkets," Amanda answered. "Some are like small grocery stores, and others are more like our convenience stores back in the States. I used them quite a bit when I was working here."

Zane stared at the image, unable to connect the dots. He couldn't even determine what the dots were. Why would Glaser direct someone to a store? What could it possibly have to do with the killer or his work?

Rachel looked at Amanda. "Any ideas?"

She shook her head. "No, but it does raise another question. Who did Solomon Glaser think would find the note? It's almost like he knew who would discover his body."

"It's possible it was meant for the police." Zane looked at Rachel. "Or perhaps his assistant."

Rachel's eyes widened.

"You said he wanted to meet with you tonight," Zane said.

"But the address means nothing to me," she said.

"You've never been to Makolet King David?" Amanda asked.

"I lived near there, so I stopped in a few times. But I don't remember anything about it."

Zane rubbed the stubble on his chin. "Maybe we've been looking at this the wrong way. Maybe Glaser confided in someone who works at the store."

"I suppose it's possible, but I'm really not sure we'll be able to figure it out right now," Amanda said. "We need to go there and—"

A loud beep cut her off. *The alarm.*

Amanda turned to Rachel. "Did you shut the gate when you came in?"

She shrugged. "I'm not sure. I don't think I did."

"Then it's probably just letting us know the gate was never closed," Amanda said. "I'll go take a look."

As Amanda disappeared down the hall, Zane's thoughts turned to Makolet King David. He looked at Rachel. "You told us you don't know anything about the store. But what about Glaser? Did he ever mention it?"

She shook her head immediately. "Never."

"Where did he buy groceries? Where did he pick up prescriptions?"

"He never told me," Rachel said. "He did like to walk, but I assume he did all his shopping close by. Even though it's not too far away, David Yellin Street wouldn't be easy to walk to from here."

She was right. People in compact cities like Jerusalem usually patronized businesses within walking distance of their homes. It wouldn't make sense for Glaser to go to this particular supermarket when there were probably a half dozen or more closer to his house.

Maybe they were grasping at straws. They would have to visit the place themselves.

Fast-paced steps sounded in the hall.

Amanda burst into the room, her eyes filled with alarm. "We've got visitors."

CHAPTER SIXTEEN

AFTER TURNING OFF the kitchen light, Zane followed Amanda toward the front of the house.

"What did you see?" he asked as they walked briskly down the hall.

"I'm not exactly sure." Amanda led him into the sitting room, which was now dark. "But the gate is closed."

"And?"

"The alarm gets triggered when the gate is opened."

"So someone else came in?"

"It would seem so." Amanda went to the front window and parted the curtains so they could both look out. "I didn't see anyone in the courtyard, but there's a lot of cover out there."

"I wonder if someone went out," Zane said. "Maybe they were hiding in the house."

"We searched the whole place. Remember?"

"We checked a dark house quickly." Zane thought for a moment. "It's also possible they were hiding somewhere outside."

Amanda spoke as she looked through the glass. "And if that's true, then they must have seen us arrive."

"We need to—"

"Wait a minute. In the courtyard. Ten o'clock."

Zane followed her gaze to a hedgerow about ten yards out. It took a few seconds, but he saw a head sticking up above the neatly trimmed foliage.

"There's another one," Amanda said. "Twelve o'clock, behind the tree."

Zane shifted his gaze to the right and saw the silhouette of a man crouched behind the trunk. He wore all-black attire and was holding what appeared to be a rifle.

As Zane continued to watch, he saw another man standing behind the one who was crouched. "There are two at the tree."

"That means three total."

"That we can see."

Zane recalled the old saying about roaches. If there were three in sight, then there could be as many as a dozen out there. It would be difficult enough to fend off three men with semiautomatic weapons, but facing three or four times that many would be impossible.

"It all makes sense," Amanda whispered.

He looked at her. "What?"

"The killer was here all along. He saw us and called in backup. Why else would they just show up?"

"Which means we need to get moving. This is a fight we can't win."

Amanda put a hand on his arm. "I have an idea. I've spent a lot of time in Jerusalem, and I've noticed there are cops everywhere. I'll call emergency services and tell them there are men walking around the neighborhood with guns. They take that kind of thing seriously over here. We'll hear sirens within a minute."

"We may not have a minute."

"We have pistols and the advantage of being inside the house," she countered. "I think we can hold them off until the authorities arrive."

"Then what happens?" Zane asked. "How do we explain our presence in the house of a man who was just shot to death?"

Amanda bit her lower lip. "I'll give them a different address, one that's a few houses away. Just getting them on this street should be enough to scare the attackers off."

Zane nodded. It was a good idea. The men outside the house were the type who operated in the shadows. The last thing they wanted to do was draw attention.

"Once they clear out," she continued, "we'll slip out right behind them."

Zane agreed, then the two quickly returned to the living room.

Rachel came toward them out of the darkness, her face paler than before. "Is someone out there?"

Zane nodded. "We need to get going."

"Who is it?"

He ignored the question. "We need to find a way out of here." He walked over to the French doors that led to the rear courtyard. He peered through the glass and saw a patio surrounded by tall bushes. It was impossible to see what was beyond. He turned back to Rachel. "Have you been out there before?"

She nodded. "Yes, a couple of times. We've had coffee out on—"

"Is there a gate?"

"Not that I know of. But there is a wall, and it's higher than the one in the front."

Zane swore softly. It wasn't what he wanted to hear. "What's beyond the wall?"

"An alley, I think. But I'm not sure."

On the one hand, the higher wall might prevent the gunmen from attacking the rear of the home. Then again, they might be waiting in the alley. But even if they were, escaping in that direction was really their only option. They had to hope the sound of approaching sirens would clear the way for them.

Turning to Amanda, he said, "Once we hear the sirens, we'll go over the wall. If there's an alley, we'll take it as far as we can then come around to our car from the other direction."

She nodded.

Zane took another look out the back. Seeing no movement, he said to Amanda, "Place the call."

She drew a burner phone from her jacket then dialed the number for emergency services. Even though the call wasn't on Speaker, Zane could hear someone answer on the other end. Amanda responded in flawless Hebrew. She used an alarmed tone, playing the part of terrified citizen.

She's good.

A half minute later, Amanda disconnected the call. "They're on the way."

Before Zane could respond, a scraping sounded in the foyer. Someone was picking the lock.

"What's that?" Rachel asked.

"It's our cue to get out of here," Zane said.

After grabbing Glaser's notebook off the kitchen table, he opened the French doors and listened. He heard the hum of distant vehicles but nothing else. He hoped there was no one waiting on the other side of the hedgerow. If there was, they would be caught in the middle of a tactical vise.

He pushed the door all the way open and stepped out into the cool night air. The ring of bushes limited their visibility, but it might also hinder the enemy's view of them. Regardless, they couldn't afford to wait for the sirens. They were too exposed at the back of the house.

Zane led them across the patio and through a gap in the bushes. Once on the other side, he saw the rear wall about ten yards away. Rachel was right. It looked at least seven or eight feet tall. They could scale it, but it would take some time.

Amanda tapped his shoulder and pointed at a tree that nestled against the wall. "Those limbs look low enough to grab onto."

As they moved in that direction, sirens screamed in the distance. Zane felt a jolt of encouragement, although it was tempered by the fact that the police were at least a mile out.

When they arrived at the tree, Zane told them what would happen next. Amanda would go over the wall first and make sure the alley was clear. If it was, Rachel would follow right behind her. That would allow the two Delphi operatives to cover both sides.

As the sirens drew closer, Amanda climbed the tree and dropped down on the other side of the wall. Several seconds later, she gave a low whistle to indicate all was clear.

"Which way?" Zane asked after he and Rachel joined her.

Amanda pointed south. "We go to the end of the alley then take a right. That should put us behind the car."

They had taken only a few steps in that direction when Zane heard the distinct crunch of gravel to their rear.

Someone was behind them.

"Go," he said sharply to Amanda and Rachel. "Stay along the wall to reduce your profile."

As they ran off, Zane turned in the other direction. A dark figure stepped into the alley. He lifted his rifle and fired twice in Zane's direction. Despite the short distance, neither round found its mark. Although the alley was dark, Zane was surprised he hadn't been hit.

Taking advantage of the opportunity, he dove to the ground and rolled over to the wall. He raised his pistol and squeezed off three rounds. He hadn't taken the time to aim carefully. The shots were simply designed to make the gunman seek cover.

Zane stood and fired two more shots before turning in the opposite direction. He sprinted down the alley, staying as close to the wall as possible. The sirens were close, perhaps a few blocks away, and the timing couldn't have been better. With the police closing in, the assassins would be forced to retreat.

After reaching the end of the alley, Zane turned right and followed the side road to Glaser's street. Their rental was parked just ahead on the left, and he could see the silhouettes of Amanda and Rachel inside.

When he arrived at the car, Zane slipped into the driver's seat and closed the door.

"You okay?" Amanda asked.

"Fine."

Leaving the headlights off, he started the car. He was about to pull out when he saw the attackers swarming out of the gate at the front of Glaser's house. They moved quickly to a waiting vehicle. Seconds later, tires squealed as the vehicle tore off.

Once the attackers had disappeared around a corner, Zane pulled out and drove in the same direction.

As they passed Glaser's house, Rachel gasped from the back seat.

Zane looked at her in the rearview mirror. "What is it?"

"See that white Range Rover?"

An SUV of that description was parked along the right side of the road. "What about it?"

"I recognize that car. It's Nathan's."

Nathan Glaser. Solomon Glaser's son.

CHAPTER SEVENTEEN

THEY ARRIVED AT the hotel at 10:52 p.m. After leaving Solomon Glaser's home, Zane had taken a circuitous route across the neighborhood where their hotel was located, doubling back several times to make sure they weren't being followed. One car had followed them through two different turns only to continue straight at the third. Only when he was certain they were free of tails did Zane drive to the hotel, which was located in the Emek Refaim district.

They decided that Rachel would stay with them for the time being. Zane was reasonably certain the killer had watched all of them arrive at Glaser's house, including Rachel. The group likely knew who she was since they had been watching the archaeologist for some time. Rachel had no knowledge of the archaeologist's secret project, but they didn't know that. That meant she could be a target.

Zane suggested they use Amanda's room since her windows faced the street. He was quite certain they had made it back undetected, but in their line of work, one could never be too cautious.

"You sure we weren't followed?" Rachel asked after they arrived on the third floor.

"I'm positive," Zane replied. "I do this for a living."

Amanda used her card to enter the room and make sure everything was clear before inviting them in.

Once they were inside, Rachel turned toward the two operatives. "Okay, I need to know who both of you are."

Zane and Amanda exchanged a glance.

Before either could respond, Rachel said, "I want to know everything. When I first spoke to you on the phone, you told me you had some information and had come to warn Dr. Glaser. Then when I show up, you don't share any of that information. Instead, you start asking *me* questions."

Amanda held out her palms. "We needed to find out what was going on. You were our only source of information."

"How do I know you aren't somehow involved in all of this?"

"Think about what just happened," Amanda said. "We're armed. You aren't. We could have taken you by force at any time."

"Maybe it was a ruse to keep me talking."

"Rachel, one of the men tried to kill Zane in the alley."

"Yes, and they also missed him."

She was right. The man had missed an easy target at short range. Zane assumed the miss was due to the darkness, but something about it still bothered him. It was possible the man had been under orders not to shoot Rachel, since she might possess information about Glaser's project, but any such orders wouldn't have included him.

Amanda looked at her. "Rachel—"

"Look, I just need to know who you are."

"I already told you. I'm an archaeologist."

"An archaeologist who carries a gun?"

Amanda pulled out her phone. "Look, I can show you my profile on the University of Texas website if that will help. I can give you the name of the dean of my department in case you want to call him."

Rachel waved her off. "I don't care what some website says. I saw what both of you did. I heard the things you said. You're professionals of some kind. So, I'll ask you one more time, who are you?"

The two operatives exchanged another glance, and Amanda gestured for Zane to respond.

"You might say we're private investigators," Zane said. "We're not spies, and we don't work directly for any government. We're a private organization that looks into sensitive matters at the request of others."

The response was one of several Zane used when asked about his work, depending on the situation. At times, he encountered people he couldn't trust. In those instances, he would simply lie about who he worked for. While some might think that was unethical, it was business as usual in the clandestine world in which they operated.

There were also times in which Zane trusted the person he was talking to but still felt the need for some level of secrecy. This was one of those occasions. Rachel had provided some helpful information, and so far, she seemed to be telling the truth about her relationship with Solomon Glaser. Even so, Zane knew almost nothing about her. So while he felt an obligation to answer some of her questions, he wasn't about to give her a complete picture of who they were. At least not yet.

"Everything we told you is true," he continued. "We do have some important information, and we did come here to warn your boss."

"Then tell me what you know," Rachel said.

Zane spent the next ten minutes giving her an overview of all that had happened, beginning with the attack at his condominium and ending with the discovery of Solomon Glaser's photograph on the assassin's phone. He took his time and chose his words carefully, an art he had mastered over the years. He provided a truthful outline of the story, but he also left out any details that might shed too much light on who they worked for.

"So you were able to find Dr. Glaser from a photograph?" Rachel asked after he was finished.

Zane nodded.

"How did you know it was him?"

"Facial recognition software," he answered.

"That sounds pretty sophisticated. Are you still telling me you don't work for a government agency or law enforcement?"

"Yes, that's exactly what I'm saying. Our organization isn't a part of any government, including the US government. Do we sometimes work on their behalf? Yes, but that's not the case here."

"You can trust us," Amanda said.

After a few seconds, Rachel gave her a slight nod.

As silence fell over the room, Zane stepped to the window and parted the curtains with a finger. All of the late-night activity seemed to be centered around the bar and café across the street. He studied the tables in front of the café, his eyes eventually landing on two men who were seated alone. In sharp contrast to the lively conversations around them, neither one spoke. One of them smoked a cigarette while the other sipped a drink.

Then Zane noticed something peculiar about the café's tables. Due to the small amount of space, most of the tables seated only two people, and all of the chairs were arranged so that each person faced up and down the sidewalk. All the tables except for one, which was the table where the two men sat. Its chairs had been moved so that one of the two men was facing the hotel. Was that a coincidence? Just to be safe, Zane noted the features of the man who was facing the hotel. Like many men in this part of the world, he had a Mediterranean appearance, with a shock of thick dark hair and a five-o'clock shadow.

As Zane watched, the man lifted his head and blew a plume of cigarette smoke into the air. His eyes seemed to fix briefly on the window where Zane was standing. Even though it was doubtful he could be seen through the thin break, Zane removed his finger and stepped back.

"What's up?" Amanda asked.

"A lot of drinking."

"I wouldn't mind a glass of wine myself."

Rachel took a seat on the bed then looked at Zane. "So why did these people attack you? What's your connection to all of this?"

"That's a question for which I have no answer."

"Surely you have some idea."

Zane considered how much he should say. "It may have something to do with one of my previous assignments over here. I didn't mention this before, but my partner and I helped authorities investigate the theft of an artifact at the Israel Museum."

Rachel's eyes widened. Did she remember the incident? Even though it predated her work with Glaser, the case had been widely covered in the news, both in Israel and abroad. Unless Rachel Hammond was a hermit, she probably knew the basic details. A lot of that information didn't make it into the news, but Zane decided to keep that to himself.

"So what's the connection?"

"The investigation took place here in Jerusalem and involved an expensive relic, so it's the only thing I can think of that would connect me to Solomon Glaser. At this point, there are more questions than answers."

"Did you ever meet Dr. Glaser when you were here for the investigation?" Rachel asked.

"Never," Zane replied.

"Zane and I discussed this before," Amanda said. "The perpetrator was caught, but there's always the possibility that there were others involved who weren't caught, perhaps even people associated with the museum."

"So maybe the same people who robbed the museum are the people we saw tonight," Rachel suggested.

Zane nodded. "Even though we found no evidence of a larger conspiracy, it's possible the person who was charged with the museum theft is part of a larger crime syndicate."

Amanda took a seat on the bed. "It could be a group that specializes in the theft of artifacts. Which brings us back to Glaser's mystery project." Amanda looked at Zane. "We need to go to the makolet tomorrow."

"I agree," Zane said, "although I still don't know what we're looking for."

"I think we know he was directing someone to the killer or to a confidant," Amanda said. "Whoever that person is, I believe they work at the store."

Zane looked at Rachel. "Are you sure you don't know what he might have been working on? You were with him every day. Anything might be important, even if it was just a passing remark."

"Everything he talked about was pretty mundane," she replied. "Other than the strange conversation I overheard, I don't recall anything that might hint at what he was working on."

"I'll get on the web tonight and see what I can find," Amanda said. "I know a few private forums where people discuss some pretty weird stuff in the world of archaeology. I can also place a few calls to people I know here in Israel. But I'm not holding my breath."

Zane parted the curtains and took another quick peek at the table across the street. The man with the five-o'clock shadow seemed to be staring at the hotel while his partner spoke on the phone. It was likely nothing, but something about the two men seemed out of place.

But if they were connected to Glaser's murder, how had they found the hotel so quickly? Zane was certain no one had followed them, but what if a tail hadn't been necessary? What if a GPS tracker had been attached to their rental? Zane regretted not checking the vehicle before coming to the hotel. If there was one, then it wouldn't do any good to take it off now. He made a mental note to check first thing in the morning.

"Do you mind if I stay here with you tonight instead of getting my own room?" Rachel asked Amanda. "I'd feel safer."

"Of course. In fact, I was going to recommend that you do."

"I'd also like to go with you tomorrow," Rachel said. "Who knows, maybe I'll recognize someone working there."

Amanda nodded. "That sounds good, but why don't we talk about that in the morning?"

"I think I'll head out," Zane said.

"Call me when you get up tomorrow morning," Amanda said.

Before leaving the room, Zane took one last look at the café across the street.

The men were gone.

CHAPTER EIGHTEEN

THE MAKOLET KING David looked just like the image on Google Maps, which had been taken about a year prior.

As they approached on foot, Zane couldn't help noticing it was a mundane building on a mundane block in a neighborhood that looked like all the other neighborhoods in this part of Jerusalem. He still found it hard to understand why Solomon Glaser had chosen to direct someone to what seemed like a random supermarket. It was so bizarre that he had begun to wonder whether that address had already been written on the notepad. Maybe it had nothing to do with the archaeologist's death. And if that was true, the whole outing would be an exercise in futility.

"I hadn't noticed something until now," Amanda said as they crossed the street. "It's a two-story building, and it looks like there are some apartments or offices on the second floor."

Zane followed her gaze. There were four windows on the second floor, and the style of the drapes suggested those more common in residential units. Zane had seen the second floor in the Google image, but he hadn't given it much thought.

"Maybe that's where Dr. Glaser wanted us to go," Rachel said.

"I'm not so sure," Zane said. "If those are apartments, then it's likely they have their own address."

Amanda nodded. "And it looks like there are at least two units. If he was directing us to one, then surely he would've specified which one."

"If he had time and if he remembered," Rachel said. "He was dying, after all."

It was a fair point.

"So what is the plan?" Amanda asked as they stopped outside the entrance.

"Let's talk to some of the employees first," Zane said. "If Glaser has a contact here, it's possible they'll be expecting us."

After going inside, the three went in different directions. Their goal was to talk to as many employees as possible without drawing too much attention. Amanda approached one of the cashiers, while Rachel went down a nearby aisle. Zane turned left into the produce section and immediately spotted a dark-haired teenager loading tomatoes into a vegetable bin. Before approaching, Zane made sure he had Glaser's photograph ready on his phone.

"Good morning," Zane said in Hebrew.

The man continued working without looking up.

Zane tried again, louder. "Good morning."

When the man finally looked up, Zane saw wireless earbuds protruding from each side of his head.

Realizing he was being spoken to, the teen reached into his pocket and turned off the device. "*Shalom*," he grunted.

Zane lifted his phone and turned the screen toward the teen. "Do you know this man?"

Frowning, the employee pulled the phone closer for a better look. His eyes widened ever so slightly.

He's seen Glaser before.

The teen let go of the phone and straightened. "I'm not sure—"

Zane pulled out his wallet and quickly flashed his Delphi ID, something he often used to lend an air of authority to his questioning. "This is part of an investigation, so you need to tell me if you have." Zane's statement was accurate, even though it wasn't entirely the truth. "I'll ask you one more time. Have you seen this man before?"

The employee's expression softened. "I think I've seen him around. But look, I don't know who he is."

As best Zane could tell, he was telling the truth. "Did he come to see someone who works here?"

"I don't know. I've just seen him in here. That's all I know."

Realizing he wasn't going to get any more out of him, Zane thanked the teen for his time then moved on. Over the next few minutes, he spoke to only one other employee, a girl stocking boxes of rice. She seemed to recognize Glaser, but like the other employee in produce, she didn't know anything beyond that. At least Zane knew one thing: Solomon Glaser had been in the Makolet King David before. But *why* had he been here? Had he come to meet one of the employees, or was he just a customer?

When they were finished, the three met at the rear of the store. Based on their expressions, Zane could tell the other two hadn't made any progress either.

"Nothing?" he asked Amanda.

"One of the cashiers knew him right away. Said he had come through once in a while. Apparently, she remembered him because of the huge beard and the fact that he came in late at night."

Late at night. Zane's brow furrowed. "That's interesting."

"Unfortunately, that's all she knew," Amanda said. "She never saw him speak to anyone on staff, nor did he do anything that might have aroused suspicion."

"Did any other employees recognize his photograph?" Zane asked.

Amanda shook her head. "Some thought he looked familiar, but I think they were just trying to be helpful. It seems like a third of the old men in Jerusalem look like Glaser."

Zane looked at Rachel. "What about you?"

"Nothing. I only talked to one person, and he said he'd never seen Dr. Glaser before." She looked around. "It's just a store. This whole thing seems pointless."

Zane thought for a moment. "We have made some progress. Unless there was a bad case of mistaken identity, we know he has been here more than once. We also know he was here at an odd time."

"Maybe we should speak to the owner," Amanda said. "This isn't a chain. It's locally owned. If Glaser knew someone who worked here, then I think it would almost certainly be the owner."

Zane nodded. "It can't hurt."

Amanda pulled out her phone. "Before we do that, let me see if I can find anything about him or her online."

As she tapped her phone, Zane noticed a young man entering the store. He wore headphones, and a backpack was slung over his right shoulder. Rather than heading down one of the aisles, he made a beeline in their direction.

He's not here to shop.

Seconds later, the man swept past them then disappeared through a doorway just beyond the frozen foods section. Above the door was a sign that read RESTROOMS in both English and Hebrew.

Hit with a thought, Zane turned to Rachel. "Do we know the store's hours?"

"I'm not sure," she replied. "Most of these places are open until eleven or twelve, although I think there are a few that are open twenty-four seven."

It was all he needed to hear. "I'll be right back."

As he walked off, Zane had a strange sensation that he had stumbled onto something important. While it was possible the man with the backpack had come in just to use the restroom, it seemed more likely he was there for some other reason. He hadn't stopped to ask for directions to the men's room, nor had he looked around for signs that would direct him there. He came in and walked straight to the back like he had done it a hundred times. Either he was an employee who had just arrived for work, or he was there for a different reason.

After pushing through the door, Zane found himself in a dimly lit corridor. To the right were the men's and women's restrooms. At the other end of the corridor was a glass door that opened into an alley. Was the man in the restroom, or had he exited into the alley?

Zane was about to go check the men's room when he noticed a red door to his left. A sign affixed to it read PRIVATE.

Zane stepped over and cautiously opened the door. A dark stairwell ran up to the second floor.

He drew his phone and called Amanda. "I need both of you to come to the back," he said when she picked up.

"Anything wrong?" she asked.

"No, but I think I may have found something."

After ending the call, Zane quickly checked the men's room. As he suspected, no one was inside. The man with the backpack had likely taken the stairs to the second floor.

Amanda and Rachel were waiting in the corridor when he came out.

Zane nodded at the red door behind them. "That leads to a stairwell that goes to the second floor. Someone just walked in and went straight up."

Amanda frowned. "So? We already knew there might be apartments up there."

"But I assumed there was a separate entrance. If you can access the units via the store, then that could mean they share the same address."

Amanda's eyes widened.

Rachel still seemed confused. "How would the residents get in at night when the store is closed?"

Zane pointed at the glass door at the end of the corridor. "If the store is closed, they can still come in at the rear of the building. My guess is there's coded entry there."

"Let's take a look upstairs," Amanda said.

Zane opened the door and led them up the dark stairwell.

On the landing was a hallway that ran back to the left. Two doors lined the hall, suggesting there were two units. Zane stopped at the first door and listened. Rhythmic trance music thumped inside. *The man with the backpack.*

Not wanting to make contact just yet, Zane continued on to the next door then pressed his ear against it. No sound came from within.

"What are you thinking?" Amanda asked.

"I'm thinking we need to see if anyone is home."

He knocked three times then waited. Hearing no response, he knocked again, harder. If someone was home, they had to have heard him.

"Shall we try the other door?" Rachel asked.

Zane shook his head. "No, let's take a look in this one."

Rachel looked at him. "You're going to break in?"

Zane reached into his pocket but said nothing.

Rachel tried again. "You sure this is a good idea?"

"Maybe, maybe not. I guess we'll find out."

Zane pulled out a specialty pocketknife then went to work on the door. Within seconds, the cheap lock succumbed to his efforts.

"Let me take a quick look first," Zane whispered.

He opened the door slowly and peered inside. The interior was dark, illuminated only by a sliver of light that came through the crack in the drapes. As his eyes adjusted, Zane saw a large room with an open kitchen to the left. On his right was a hallway that he assumed led back to the bedrooms.

Seeing and hearing no one, he gestured for the others to follow him in.

"I don't think anyone lives here," Rachel whispered.

As best Zane could tell, she was right. The only furnishings were a leather recliner and a mahogany desk and chair. Other than that, nothing else was in sight. No personal effects. No accessories. No paintings. Either the apartment was up for lease, or someone was just starting to move in.

Amanda pointed to the right. "It looks like someone moved out."

Zane followed her gaze. A thin coating of dust covered the floor, but there were large square patches that weren't covered at all. It looked as though furniture had been recently moved out.

"I don't think this is the place we're looking for," Rachel said.

Ignoring her comment, Zane clicked on his penlight and moved toward the desk that was situated against the far wall. Amanda and Rachel followed.

"Maybe the owner of the store uses this place as an office," Amanda said.

Zane opened the top drawer and directed the beam inside. The drawer was empty save for a few pens, a ruler, a letter opener, and a stapler. He was about to shut the drawer when Amanda grabbed his arm.

"Hold on," she said.

"What?"

She bent down and examined the side of the drawer. "Something's not matching up."

"I don't follow," Zane said.

"The drawer is at least six inches deep, but the bottom is only two or three inches deep," she said.

He looked at her. "A false bottom?"

Amanda removed the contents of the drawer, then took the letter opener and slid the tip into a visible notch on the right side of the particleboard bottom. Seconds later, the thin board popped out.

Zane trained his flashlight into the space below.

"What the…?" Rachel whispered.

Zane's neck muscles tightened. A passport and a matte black Sig Sauer P320 pistol were displayed in the cone of light. He wasn't sure what he had expected to find, but it wasn't this.

He removed the passport and read the lettering on the burgundy cover: EUROPÄISCHE UNION REPUBLIK ÖSTERREICH.

"Austrian," Amanda said.

Zane flipped it open and read the name printed on the center of the page. *Hans Schreiber.* It didn't sound familiar. He shifted the light slightly, illuminating the man's photograph.

Rachel caught her breath.

It was Solomon Glaser.

CHAPTER NINETEEN

"SO MY BOSS was a spy?" Rachel asked as the three stared at the picture in stunned silence.

Was it true? Was it possible that Solomon Glaser had been leading the double life of an agent? Zane had known many spies over the years—American spooks and others from around the world—and it was certainly true that many had a public face that camouflaged their clandestine activities. But an archaeologist? That seemed a stretch, but what else would explain the fake passport and the gun? As Zane saw it, there were really only two possibilities: either Glaser *was* a secret operative, or he was involved in criminal activity.

"He had secrets. That much is clear," Amanda said.

Remembering the passport's origin, Zane looked at Rachel. "Did he ever mention traveling to Austria?"

"No, never. He traveled throughout the Middle East, but I don't ever recall him going to any country in Europe."

"What about the name Hans Schreiber?" Zane asked. "Have you ever heard it before?"

She shook her head. "It doesn't ring a bell."

Amanda looked at Zane. "Why an *Austrian* passport?"

"I don't know."

"Maybe he was afraid of something," Amanda said. "Maybe he was planning to leave the country to get away from the people who were following him."

"But where would he get a fake passport?" Rachel asked.

"That's easy," Amanda said. "Anyone with enough money and the right connections can get one. Although I must say the Israelis have the tightest Customs in the world. Assuming the passport is a fake, he'd have trouble getting onto a plane here."

Zane flipped through the passport's pages. "Looks like he's been traveling quite a bit. United Arab Emirates. Jordan. Austria. Canada."

"Passport stamps can easily be faked," Amanda said.

"Why would someone fake stamps?" Rachel asked.

"To make the document look authentic," Amanda answered. "They say customs officials examine brand-new passports more closely."

"It's possible the stamps are fake," Zane said, "but it's also possible he's been using it to travel."

Two horns blew out in the street, followed by the sound of someone shouting. Amanda stepped over to the window and leaned toward the crack in the drapes.

Zane turned to Rachel. "You said Glaser took a couple of trips around the Middle East. To where, and how many times was he gone?"

"I remember he went to Saudi Arabia once." She paused for a moment. "There was another trip, but I can't recall where he went. I should also point out there were times when I didn't see him for a few days. Obviously, we had very little contact on the weekends. And I took a few days' vacation about a month ago."

Zane nodded then flipped through the passport again. He counted six international trips, but none had taken place within the last six months. Unless the stamps were fake, it seemed to rule out Glaser obtaining the passport to flee the country.

"Zane."

He turned at the sound of Amanda's voice. She was standing at the kitchen table.

"Come look at this," she said.

As he approached, he saw a thin laptop on the table. The device was black, which had made it hard to notice against the dark wood.

"Interesting that it's the only thing that was left out in plain sight," Amanda said as the other two joined her. "It's almost like he wanted it to be found."

"If there were more light coming through the drapes, then it would've been the first thing we saw," Zane said.

"Let's have a look." Amanda opened the laptop and pressed the power button.

As they waited, Zane looked around the apartment. Why would Glaser need a second place? Even if he was leading the double life of a spy, it didn't seem necessary. Encrypted messages could be read at home, and the passport and gun could certainly have been stowed somewhere in the house. None of it made sense.

A half minute later, a chime sounded as the laptop's home screen appeared. It had only three icons.

Amanda sank into one of the chairs and pulled the device closer. "Looks pretty bare."

"We'll find something," Zane said. "He left it out in the open for a reason."

Amanda double-clicked on the Outlook email icon then studied the contents. "Mostly spam."

"Open up his browser," Zane suggested.

Amanda closed the email manager then opened Google Chrome. "Nothing," she said after viewing the home screen and opening the bookmarks.

"Maybe he wiped it clean," Rachel said.

"Let me try one more thing." Amanda clicked out of Chrome then opened the documents section of the drive. "Bingo," she said after opening the sole folder. "Looks like he didn't delete everything."

Zane leaned closer. The folder contained two files. The name on the first one was a random series of numbers and letters, but the file extension indicated it was a video. "Open it," he said.

Amanda double-clicked on the file, and the device's media player popped up. The thumbnail preview showed Solomon Glaser sitting in front of the camera.

"He was sitting right here," Amanda said.

As Zane studied the image, he realized she was right. Glaser was seated at the very table they were gathered around. Apparently, he had used the laptop's webcam to film whatever they were about to watch.

Zane pointed at a few boxes in the background. "And now we can see what made the marks in the dust."

"At some point, he moved out," Rachel said.

"Play it," Zane said.

Amanda started the video. Glaser grabbed each side of the

laptop and adjusted it until his face was centered in the picture. He cleared his throat and began to speak.

> *"If you're watching this, then it means you're someone I trust with my life. I honestly didn't want to involve anyone else in this matter, but I was left with no other choice. The stakes are too high. Someone needs to carry on the work that's already started.*
>
> *"In case I didn't have the chance to speak to you first, let me explain what I'm talking about. Sometime back, I was visited by a man who called himself Amir. He told me he worked for the Israeli government, but he refused to tell me the name of the agency he worked for. He said he led investigations that were so sensitive that only a half dozen or so officials knew the details. Upon hearing that, it wasn't hard for me to guess which agency he worked for."*

Zane assumed Glaser was referring to Mossad. While other Israeli agencies also conducted clandestine work, Mossad was the most recognizable one.

> *"As you can imagine, I wondered why someone in this line of work would contact me. After all, I'm just an archaeologist. The answer became clear when he told me the reason for his visit. He had come across a tip that, if true, might lead to the greatest archaeological discovery of all time. But it wasn't just a historically significant discovery. It was one that could divide the world.*

"After sharing a few important details, Amir said he wanted me to take charge of the investigation. There were reports that others had learned about the discovery, and it was critical the State of Israel find it first. If they didn't, then the information might fall into the wrong hands. That or there could be an outbreak of violence because of the relic's significance.

"Amir assured me that I would be given everything necessary to succeed. In addition to a substantial fee, they would cover the entire cost of the operation. He assured me that I could get out at any time, although I had some doubt as to whether or not that was true.

"At first, I declined the offer, primarily because I doubted the veracity of the claim. After all, I get sensational leads all the time. But curiosity got the best of me, and when I checked the one piece of information Amir had given me, I quickly realized there might be something to it. Hit with a sudden urge of excitement and adventure, I told him I would help as long as he met a couple of conditions, one of which was to be given a place to carry out the work in secret. He promptly accepted.

"Given funding and a secure place to conduct my work, I began my own investigation. Unfortunately, I didn't make much progress. About three weeks in, the work took a very dark turn."

Zane noticed a change in Glaser's expression. He had fear in his eyes, the kind of genuine fear that was hard to suppress. The archaeologist retrieved a bottle of water that had been out of sight and took a long swig before continuing.

> "I began to notice that people were watching my home. They tried to disguise their activities, but I've always been someone who is aware of his surroundings. I notice everything. At first, I believed Amir had sent the people who were watching me. If true, it would be hard to blame the government for doing that. After all, there could be a legitimate concern that I might try to somehow profit from this endeavor. But if they were conducting surveillance, then they should have disclosed that up front. In light of that, I confronted Amir about sending people to watch me. His reaction wasn't what I had expected. He seemed genuinely surprised. He assured me that no one had been sent to watch my activities, and he repeated his claim that only a half dozen people even knew about his work. He told me he would look into the matter, and that I should limit my movements as much as possible.
>
> "He called me a day later. Up until that point, he seemed like the kind of man who wasn't fazed by anything. The prototypical Israeli spy. But when he called me, I noticed something in his voice I'd never heard before, and that was fear. Not a fear for himself but a fear for me. He said he believed he knew who was following me and that we needed to talk as soon as possible. We then arranged to meet at a local coffee shop, but he never showed. I tried to contact him several times

by phone but was unable to reach him.

"Hit with the real possibility that something bad had happened to Amir, I panicked. After all, I had lost my sole source of guidance and protection. It's not like I could show up at a government office in Tel Aviv and ask to speak to Amir. Not only that, but it was becoming quite clear that a dangerous group of people were following me. So dangerous that this hardened agent seemed to fear for my safety.

"So why am I telling you all of this? I'm telling you this because I need your help. I need you to carry out a small task so that someone else can carry on with my work. If this discovery gets into the wrong hands, then there could be horrible consequences.

"I know what you're thinking right now. You're probably wondering why I would expose you to the same danger I was in. After all, if you're watching this video, then there is a high probability that both Amir and I are dead. But that also means this group, whoever they are, likely believes that all parties with knowledge of the situation have been killed. In other words, they won't know that you're involved, nor will they know of what I'm about to ask you to do.

"Please help me if you can. Your task will be a small one, and once it's complete, you can go back to your life.

"If you're willing to help, then here is what I'd like you to do next. Find my colleague and give her this recording. She'll know what to do next. You can find her at Givat Ram."

Glaser paused for a moment, his eyes glistening with emotion.

"I can't thank you enough for helping me. If I'm right, then the entire world will thank you as well. Godspeed, and remember this very important thing—you were appointed for such a time as this."

After the video finished playing, the group sat in stunned silence, each person clearly trying to digest what they had just heard.

"Something doesn't make sense," Amanda finally said.

Zane looked at her.

"If he wanted the person watching this message to notify this mystery woman, then why not contact her himself?" she asked. "Why the intermediary?"

"That's a good question," Zane said.

"So what do you think his reason was?" Rachel asked.

"It's hard to say," Amanda answered. "I guess it was in case he died before being able to contact the person. Maybe he knew if he died, then the people Amir worked for—most likely Mossad—would find this apartment."

"I'm not so sure," Zane said. "I think it's safe to say this Amir was involved in a number of operations. Assuming he's dead, it might take his people some time to figure out who killed him." He thought for a moment. "But it's not just that. There's something about the message… It seemed like Glaser was speaking to someone he knew personally." He looked at Rachel. "Maybe he was going to deliver this message to you in person last night."

"So what do we do now?" Rachel asked.

Zane said, "We need to find the woman you were supposed to contact, the woman who lives on the hill of Givat Ram."

CHAPTER TWENTY

AFTER WATCHING THE video two more times, the three searched the rest of the apartment for anything that might shed more light on Glaser, his project, or the woman mentioned in his message. A search of the bathroom yielded a few personal effects: a tube of toothpaste, a towel, soap, and a half-used bottle of shampoo. Those items, coupled with the unmade bed in the bedroom, suggested the archaeologist had spent more time there than any of them had initially thought.

But despite going through every room thoroughly, they found nothing that might help them gain a better understanding of the archaeologist's activities. If there had been other items of importance, they were moved out prior to his death.

"We need to talk to this mystery woman as soon as possible," Zane said when the group reassembled in the kitchen.

"I know the name Givat Ram from somewhere." Amanda pulled out her phone. "If I'm not mistaken, it means *settlement* in Hebrew. Now we just need to figure out which one."

"In this case, it's not a settlement," Rachel said. "It's a

neighborhood right here in Jerusalem."

Amanda looked at her. "Yes, of course. How could I have forgotten that?"

"Well, that's helpful," Zane said, "but until we figure out who she is, it's going to be impossible to determine her address."

"No one actually lives in Givat Ram, at least not that I'm aware of," Rachel noted. "I said it's a neighborhood, but it's more like a district. It's where Israel's most important institutions are located. The Knesset. The National Library. The Supreme Court."

"Think Capitol Hill in DC," Amanda said.

Rachel nodded. "Yes, exactly."

"So she works for the government?" Zane asked.

"It's possible," Rachel said. "But there are so many places… where would we even begin?"

"We don't begin with the government at all," Amanda said. "We begin at the Israel Museum. It's located at Givat Ram."

"Solomon Glaser was an archaeologist, so that would make sense," Zane said.

"Here's the bad news," Amanda said. "The museum is a truly massive place. I'd guess there are at least a couple hundred employees and volunteers."

Zane looked at Rachel. "Who were Solomon Glaser's contacts at the museum?"

"There were a lot. He was in regular contact with a number of curators and their assistants."

"What did he speak to them about?"

"I'm not sure. I do know that he interviewed a number of them for his latest book."

"Can you get those names?"

"They were in the footnotes. Unfortunately, I hadn't started on those yet, so it may take me a while to sort through everything."

"We'll need to whittle that down," Amanda said. "Whoever he consulted with on his book isn't necessarily tied to this secret project he was working on."

Zane thought for a moment. "There is something we can do right now. We can put together a comprehensive list of all the female archaeologists who work at the museum."

"Then what do we do?" Rachel asked. "We can't just go in and start asking people if they were working on a secret project with Solomon Glaser."

Amanda nodded. "Once we narrow down the list of potential names, I think we can ask some discreet questions. But we do need to be careful. Whoever killed Dr. Glaser may have contacts at the museum. In fact, that might be how they became aware of what he was working on."

Zane spoke as he paced across the room. "The museum does seem to be the epicenter of all this. It's likely the place where Glaser's contact works, and it's also the place where I helped with a high-profile investigation."

"Which means you shouldn't set foot in there," Amanda said.

Zane turned around and came back toward them. "There's a lot we can do without actually going there. Once we have a preliminary list of female archaeologists, we can review their bios and try to narrow the number down even further by area of expertise."

THE CHAMBER

Amanda folded her arms across her chest. "It could still be a fairly large number if you include employees below the level of curator or assistant curator."

As silence fell over the room, Zane tried to recall the details of the investigation he had been involved in at the museum. He didn't remember Solomon Glaser's name coming up, nor could he think of anything that might link the theft of the artifact with the things they were looking into now. He made a note to contact Carmen to see if she could put the pieces together. It was always good to have someone who could provide a fresh perspective.

"Let's take another look at the video," Amanda said. "Maybe we missed something."

After taking a seat at the table, she opened the video file and played the entire message from start to finish. Once it was over, she replayed the last part of Glaser's message.

> *"Please help me if you can. Your task will be a small one, and once it's complete, you can go back to your life.*
>
> *"If you're willing to help, then here is what I'd like you to do next. Find my colleague and give her this recording. She'll know what to do next. You can find her at Givat Ram.*
>
> *"I can't thank you enough for helping me. If I'm right, then the entire world will thank you as well. Godspeed, and remember this very important thing… you were appointed for such a time as this."*

Amanda leaned back in the chair and put a hand on her chin. "He says the woman is a colleague of his. I think we need to focus on curators and assistant curators."

"I'll keep that in mind as I go through the footnotes," Rachel said.

"Once we're done here, we can take you back to your—"

"Wait a minute." Amanda leaned forward and played the last part of the message one more time. When Glaser finished speaking, Amanda looked at Zane, her eyes dancing with newfound excitement. "Did you hear that last part?"

Zane thought for a moment. "You were appointed for such a time as this?"

"Don't you recognize that?" she asked when he didn't continue.

"It sounds vaguely familiar, but I really don't—"

"It's a verse from the Bible," Rachel said.

Suddenly, the pieces came together. It was a story Zane had heard many times. "Esther," he said.

Amanda pulled out her phone and tapped the screen. "I should have that verse memorized." After a few more taps, she began to read. "For if you remain silent at this time, relief and deliverance for the Jews will arise from another place, but you and your father's family will perish. *And who knows, but that you have come to your royal position for such a time as this?*"

Rachel looked at Amanda. "So what are you saying?"

"I'm saying the person we're looking for could be named Esther."

"Sorry, but that sounds like a bit of a stretch," Zane said.

"Maybe, but we can check it right now." Amanda turned back to her phone. After a minute of searching, she broke into a broad smile. "Here you go." She handed the phone to Zane.

"Esther Navon. Curator of Dead Sea Scrolls."

Zane stared at the woman's image. Esther Navon had shoulder-length brown hair that was parted down the middle and pulled back over her ears. She had big green eyes that conveyed both intelligence and mystery.

Rachel leaned in for a closer look. "Curator of Dead Sea Scrolls."

The Dead Sea Scrolls. Even though he wasn't an archaeologist, Zane had some knowledge of the famous Jewish manuscripts. The ancient scrolls had been found in caves adjoining the Dead Sea, hence the name. The first scrolls were discovered in the mid-1940s by a Bedouin shepherd who was searching for one of his lost sheep. After that initial find, more scrolls were found in other caves at Qumran, the name given to the archaeological site. The subsequent discoveries resulted in a breathtaking collection of religious writing, including many sections of the Bible.

Amanda had often referenced the biblical texts found at Qumran. In particular, she liked to point out how the content of those texts supported the accuracy of the modern Bible.

Zane let his eyes run down to Esther Navon's bio. "Impressive credentials. A PhD from the Hebrew University of Jerusalem, and she teaches at the Martin Department of the Land of Israel Studies and Archaeology." He looked at Amanda. "Do you know her?"

"I met her briefly on a couple of occasions," Amanda said. "She's relatively new to the position of curator. The man who held that position before her is in his eighties and just stepped down early last year."

"Does she know who you are?" he asked. "That might be helpful in establishing communication."

"No, I doubt she remembers me," Amanda replied. "But I think my experience in the field might give me access to her."

Rachel looked at her watch. "Should we go to the museum now?"

"Let's reach out by phone first," Zane suggested.

Amanda took the phone back from Zane then asked, "What do you want me to say?"

"I'd keep it simple. Tell her that Solomon Glaser asked us to reach out to her in the event of his death."

"Do you think she'll even know he's dead?"

"I'm certain she does. I checked the news this morning, and local media is already reporting that he was found shot in his home after police responded to reports of armed gunmen."

Amanda pressed her lips together. "I hope she doesn't just take the message and cut us out of the loop."

Zane stroked his chin. "That's a good point. Be as cryptic as you can. Try to set up a meeting this afternoon or this evening, and make sure it's not at the museum."

Amanda dialed the number provided on Esther Navon's profile then put the phone on Speaker. The call was answered by a young woman who worked in the administrative offices of the Shrine of the Book, which Zane assumed was the wing of the museum that housed the Dead Sea Scrolls. The woman said Navon was tied up at the moment but offered to transfer Amanda to the curator's voicemail. Amanda told the receptionist she was with the University of Texas and had an urgent message for the curator. After some hesitation, the woman put Amanda on hold.

THE CHAMBER

Amanda looked at Zane and whispered, "Let's see if she takes the bait."

A half minute later, the woman came back on the line. "Please hold while I transfer your call."

Amanda winked at Zane.

A woman answered after the second ring. "Esther Navon."

"Dr. Navon, this is Amanda Higgs from the University of Texas. Thank you for taking my call."

"How can I help you? My assistant said it was urgent."

"I'm calling you on behalf of Dr. Solomon Glaser."

There was a long pause.

"Solomon Glaser is dead," Esther finally said.

"I know he is," Amanda said. "He reached out to me before his death."

There was another pause, this one even longer. "So what does that have to do with me?"

"He said that I should contact you. I believe the two of you were working together."

"He said the two of us were working on something together?"

"Dr. Navon, if we could meet in private, I'd be happy to go into more—"

"Miss Higgs, I believe you must be looking for someone else. I know Dr. Glaser, but I haven't been in touch with him for a long time. The Dead Sea Scrolls aren't his thing."

"I'm here with two colleagues. Can you just meet with us for a few minutes? I think if I explain—"

"I don't know how much clearer I can be. I haven't been in touch with Solomon for some time, and I certainly haven't been working on anything with him."

"Can you give me five minutes? That's all I'm asking."

"I'm very sorry, but I'm late for a meeting already."

Amanda opened her mouth to respond, but Esther Navon said goodbye and disconnected the call.

"Not a very pleasant woman," Rachel said.

Amanda set her phone on the table. "Back to square one."

"Maybe not," Zane said. "I think she's hiding something. She dismissed your request too quickly. Wouldn't she have wanted to know more?"

"She said she was late for a meeting," Rachel noted.

Zane was about to recommend they try a different approach when Amanda's phone flared with an incoming call.

She picked it up. "Unidentified caller."

"Answer it," Zane said.

Amanda placed it on Speaker. "Hello."

A female whispered on the other end. "Miss Higgs?"

Despite the lower tone, Zane recognized the voice immediately. *Esther Navon.*

"Yes, this is Amanda."

"I'm calling you from my cell phone in the restroom. Look, I'm sorry I ended the call so abruptly."

"That's not a problem," Amanda said. "I hope I didn't make you late for your meeting."

"There is no meeting."

Amanda frowned. "I'm confused. I thought you—"

"I've been expecting your call, but I couldn't speak on a public line. I think they're watching me, listening to me."

"Who is watching you?"

"I don't have time to explain. Can you meet me tonight?"

CHAPTER TWENTY-ONE

ESTHER SUGGESTED THEY meet at seven o'clock at her apartment on George Washington Street. Since she suspected she was being watched, Zane parked on a street that ran parallel to hers. The group then followed a series of connecting alleys that brought them to the rear entrance of her building.

As they entered and took the elevator to the third floor, Zane couldn't help noticing the luxurious trappings. It seemed odd that Solomon Glaser and Esther Navon—who worked in a field not known for high incomes and wealth—were both able to afford such upscale accommodations. Amanda believed Glaser's lifestyle could be explained by several best-selling books the archaeologist had published. Esther Navon's wealth was still a mystery.

After arriving at the door, Amanda knocked twice.

A moment later, the peephole darkened, then the door swung open, revealing the dark silhouette of a woman.

"Esther?" Amanda asked.

The woman nodded. "Yes, please come in."

After brief introductions, Esther led them down a short

hallway that opened into a spacious living room. Not surprisingly, most of the room's accessories looked like relics that had been recovered from an archaeological site. Vases, oil lamps, and ceremonial weapons were placed on every surface. Across the room, two statues of Greek gods flanked either side of a big-screen television.

Zane studied their host for the first time. Esther Navon looked almost identical to the photograph on the museum's website. She was an attractive woman, albeit in an academic sort of way. She had expressive almond-shaped eyes, and her lips were the color of a French rose.

Even though he couldn't point to any reason for it, Zane felt uncomfortable in the woman's presence. It might be nothing, but he had learned to pay attention to his intuition.

"I assume you weren't followed?" Esther asked.

Zane shook his head. "Not unless they're watching the rear entrance of your building."

Esther nodded. "Can I get any of you something to drink?" After all three politely declined, she gestured toward a white sectional. "Please."

As everyone took their seats, Esther went to a white recliner and sat down. A half-filled wineglass sat on the coffee table between them.

"Thank you for agreeing to meet with us," Zane said. "We felt like a face-to-face meeting would be best."

"It would be too risky for me to meet in public right now." Esther looked at Amanda. "I believe you told me you were a professor of archaeology at the University of Texas?"

"That's correct."

"I hope you don't mind, but I did some poking around online, and it seems you don't spend much time in Texas anymore." Her statement had a slightly questioning tone.

"I still teach when I can."

"When you can," Esther said with a half smile. "I took a great deal of risk by inviting three strangers into my home. So now I need you to level with me. Who are you?"

"That's a fair request," Zane said. "Let me tell you who we are and how we got here."

Esther settled back into the recliner. "Thank you."

Over the next several minutes, Zane gave her the same information they had given Rachel the night before. Although there was still something about the curator he didn't trust, Zane knew he really had no choice but to cooperate. Despite knowing almost nothing about them, she had invited them into her home. It was also clear she was the person Glaser had referenced in his message. And if Glaser trusted her, then so should they, at least for now.

"You said Solomon left a video message indicating you should contact me?" Esther asked after Zane had finished.

"He told us where to find you," Amanda said. "I think he wanted to be somewhat cryptic in case the video got into the wrong hands."

Esther lifted her wineglass and took a sip. "And how do I know this video didn't get into the wrong hands?"

"I guess you don't," Zane admitted. "We believe Rachel was the intended recipient, but none of us knows for sure. But we're here, so we'd like to work together if we can."

Esther sat forward. "Tell me exactly what that message said."

"I'll do better than that." Zane took out his phone. "I'll let him tell you in his own words."

After finding the file, Zane hit Play then set the phone on the table. Sitting forward on the recliner, Esther listened to the entire message then asked him to play it again. After hearing it a second time, she sat back and stared off into space, as if her mind was consumed by the haunting words.

A half minute later, she looked at Zane. "Thank you. And I'm sorry if I sounded a little suspicious earlier."

"I think all of us are a little on edge."

She smiled. "Now there is something I need to show you."

Without going into further detail, she stood and walked down a nearby hall. Moments later, Zane heard drawers opening and closing in quick succession. An angry sigh of frustration followed.

Zane and Amanda exchanged a glance.

Footsteps sounded in the hallway.

A moment later, Esther emerged, a pistol clutched between two trembling hands.

Zane reached for the gun that was tucked into his coat pocket.

"I wouldn't do that if I were you," Esther said, pointing her weapon at him.

Zane could draw a gun as quickly as any in the business, but even he didn't dare attempt it with the muzzle of a pistol already pointed at his chest. All she had to do was pull the trigger, and he would be dead before his fingers closed on the grip of his pistol.

He held up his hand in submission. "Easy."

"Did you think I was stupid?" Esther said through clenched teeth.

"What are you talking about?" Amanda asked.

Esther stepped farther into the room, her eyes lit with rage. "I know you took it. You called me at work just to make sure I wasn't here, didn't you?"

"Wait a minute," Zane said, his hands still in the air. "Let's talk through this. Are you saying something was taken from you?"

She swung the gun back in his direction. "Yes, and it just happened to have been taken on the same day I hear from all of you."

Zane lowered his voice even more. "Think about what you just said. If we have whatever it is you're referring to, then why would we come back?"

Esther paused as she considered his logic. "Maybe you realized you needed more information. Those pictures don't tell the whole story."

Pictures. What pictures was she talking about? Zane would have to come back to that later. For now, he needed to talk her off the ledge. "Listen to me. I have a pistol in my coat pocket. If we came here to get something from you, I'd have it already."

The first hint of understanding crept into her eyes.

"We came here because Solomon Glaser told us to," Amanda said. "You heard him yourself."

Esther stood perfectly still. Her hands still trembled, but she seemed to have calmed a bit.

"Keep your gun out if you must, but let's talk about what was taken from you," Zane said. "Maybe we can help you figure it all out."

After a long silence, Esther finally sat down in the recliner and set the gun on the table. She rubbed her face with her hands. "I'm sorry."

"It's okay," Amanda said in a comforting tone.

Zane exhaled for the first time in almost a minute. The most dangerous gun was the one held by someone not used to wielding it.

Amanda scooted forward in her seat. "Esther, tell us what happened. Tell us about these photos."

Esther stopped rubbing her face and returned her gaze. "Solomon gave me a box several weeks ago. He told me not to open it unless he told me to or unless someone came with a message... the one you played for me tonight."

"And that box is gone now?" Amanda asked.

She nodded. "I put it in my nightstand."

"Are you sure that's where it was?" Rachel asked.

"I never put it anywhere else." She rubbed her cheeks. "I know, I was dumb not to lock it up somewhere."

"Did Dr. Glaser give you any idea what was in it?" Amanda asked.

Esther looked up at her. "No, but he didn't have to. I opened the box last night."

CHAPTER TWENTY-TWO

"SO WHAT WAS in the box?" Amanda asked.

"It contained several photographs that were taken in a cave or cavern."

Amanda pulled out her phone and began typing in notes.

"Each image depicted different views of a large archway," Esther said.

Amanda looked up from her phone. "You say it was a large archway. How large was it?"

Esther exhaled. "It was tremendous. I'd say it was as tall as a two-story building. You could easily drive a tractor-trailer through it."

Amanda's eyes widened.

Although the structure sounded impressive, Zane still couldn't see the significance of a giant entryway. "What else did the photographs show?"

"That's it," she replied. "There were several different shots of the same thing, this ancient archway."

Zane found it more difficult to trust Esther with each passing moment. Earlier, she had claimed that someone had broken into her apartment, and yet there had been no sign of forced entry at the front door, which was the only way in. Then there was the pistol she had pointed at them. Zane didn't know much about firearm laws in Israel, but he had been told it was difficult for the average citizen to get a permit. And even if she had a permit, why did an archaeologist feel the need to own a gun?

But those weren't the only things that had aroused Zane's suspicions. He also found it strange that Glaser would pass along a photograph of an archway without telling the recipient what the significance was. Were there other photographs that Esther wasn't telling them about?

"Was anything else in the box?" Amanda asked.

"Yes, there was something else," Esther said. "He also included a binder with several pages of what appeared to be a genealogical record of some kind."

Rachel frowned. "He sent you a family tree?"

Esther nodded. "That's what it looked like."

"Whose family tree?" Amanda asked.

"I don't know. I opened the box late last night and spent most of my time studying the photographs. I was going to start on the genealogical record tonight."

"Anything else?" Zane asked.

"Yes, there was one last thing," Esther said. "There was a map of Jerusalem."

"Just a map?" Zane asked.

"Yes…" Esther stared off into space as though she was only vaguely aware of the question.

Zane frowned. "And?"

"Is something wrong?" Amanda asked.

Esther stood abruptly. "Sorry, I just remembered something." She turned toward Amanda, her eyes lit with excitement. "The map. I read it in bed just before going to sleep last night. I think I might still have it."

She turned and went down the hall again.

Zane felt a rush of excitement. If she did have the map, they would finally have something to work with. He also wondered if that was a sign she had been telling the truth all along. If she was trying to hide the contents of the box from them, it wouldn't make sense to bring up the map.

Esther returned a moment later, a folded piece of paper clutched in one hand. "I put it in the book I was reading last night." She sat on the recliner, unfolded the map, then spread it out on the table between them. "It's a satellite view of Jerusalem."

"Does it show the location of the archway?" Amanda asked.

Esther shook her head. "I wish it was that easy. As with the genealogical record, I couldn't make any sense of it. I was drowsy when I looked at it last night, and I obviously didn't want to take it to work with me."

"Maybe some fresh eyes will help," Amanda said.

"There were a couple of things that caught my attention." Esther pointed at a spot on the map. "He highlighted this building in the Jerusalem Quarter."

Zane scooted forward in his seat and stared at the map. The highlighted structure was in the tightly packed tangle of buildings to the west of the Temple Mount. *The Jewish Quarter.* He had been to that maze of pedestrian streets and alleys many times.

"Do you know what's in that building?" Amanda asked.

"That's what makes the whole thing so confusing. It's not what I expected at all." Esther set her phone on the table and brought up a note-taking app. "I looked on Google Street View and figured out it's a place called Café Nehemiah. As best I could tell, there isn't anything special about it."

Amanda nodded. "You said there were a couple of things that caught your attention. What's the other?"

Esther pointed at another place on the satellite image. "He wrote the number fifteen hundred here."

Zane noted the digits were written in black ink just to the right of the highlighted building.

Amanda frowned. "I wonder if that's the address of the café?"

"That was my first thought as well, but it's not a match. In fact, the number doesn't match any address within a quarter mile of that location."

Zane wondered what the number might mean. Was it some random scribble, or was Glaser trying to communicate something?

Esther looked at Amanda. "Any thoughts?"

"No, the whole thing is strange," she said after a short pause. "I would assume the map is related to the underground archway, but if that's the case, then what's the connection?" She paused, a frown forming on her face. "Unless he wasn't marking the café. The buildings in that part of the Old City are tightly packed together. It would be nice to go there and try to see if he actually meant to mark another place."

"It certainly couldn't hurt," Zane said.

"But we still need to look at the café," Amanda said. "Maybe there is something inside that will become clearer if we go there ourselves."

"At least the people who broke into your apartment don't know about the map," Rachel noted.

Zane remembered something he'd wanted to ask Esther. "You said you were concerned that someone was watching you even before the break-in. What made you think that?"

"There were several things," she said. "It all started about a month ago when I started hearing some strange *clicks* on the landline in my office. I originally wrote it off as a bad connection, but then I realized it was happening too often. So I asked a couple of colleagues if they were experiencing the same thing, and they told me they weren't."

"Anything else?" Zane asked.

"I also noticed some things in my office had been moved around. A drawer was left open, which is something I never do. I'm a little OCD about that. I even noticed a few papers had been shuffled around, like someone was going through them. I know my office, and I know when things aren't where they're supposed to be."

Amanda looked at Rachel. "That's the same thing Solomon Glaser told you."

"Who else has access to your office?" Zane asked.

"No one, really. I leave it unlocked while I'm at the museum, but I seriously doubt someone would risk going through my things during working hours. And I *always* lock my door when I leave each night."

"Who else has a key?" Zane asked.

"The cleaning staff, but obviously, they couldn't care less

about what might be on my desk. I don't keep anything of value there." She was quiet for a moment. "The security team also has access to all offices in our building."

"That's not unusual," Amanda said. "Most large organizations give security personnel access to private offices unless there's a good reason not to. Security has access to my office at the university, which is why I keep my important papers locked up in a cabinet that only I have access to."

"There is something else," Esther said. "I know this sounds crazy, but I've caught a member of our security team watching me a few times lately. At first I thought it was just harmless flirtation. But I soon realized that wasn't it. He was keeping an eye on me, almost like he suspected me of doing something."

Zane had worked closely with the museum's security team when investigating the theft of the relic. Was it possible he had met the man Esther was referring to? "What's his name?"

"Robert Lecompte. He's one of our top security people. A man was fired in the wake of the heist, and I believe Robert was promoted to take his place."

While the name didn't ring a bell, that didn't mean Zane hadn't met him. "Do you have a picture of him?"

Esther shook her head. "No, I don't."

"What about photos on social media?" Amanda asked.

"Probably not. I seriously doubt he keeps an online profile. Unless…" She thought for a moment. "The museum has a Facebook page, and I remember we put up a large gallery of photos from our most recent gala. I can see if he's in one of them."

As she pulled out her phone, Zane wondered if they might

have stumbled onto something important. If this man was watching Esther, it was possible he was connected to the group that had killed Solomon Glaser.

"Here he is," Esther said after searching for several minutes. "It's not a very clear shot, but that's probably about as good as we're going to get."

She slid the phone across the table to Zane, who examined the image carefully. Two men and a woman dressed in formal attire stood next to an hors d'oeuvre table, talking while they sipped champagne.

"Look behind them," Esther said.

A tall man in a dark suit was just visible behind the three. He was standing so that only his profile was in view. Zane noted the man had short dark hair, a square jaw, and a beak-like nose. A tiny headset protruded from his left ear.

Zane believed he had met the man before, although he couldn't remember anything about him. Even so, they had at least made a clear connection between the two cases. The man he had contact with months ago was the same man who had been watching Esther Navon.

Amanda leaned in close and pointed at something in the image. "What's that on his neck?"

Zane zoomed in for a better view of the dark smudge just above the white collar of Lecompte's dress shirt.

"It looks like a dragon-head tattoo," Amanda said.

Zane's pulse quickened as a memory flashed in his mind. He remembered the body of the lead assassin sprawled on the floor of his condominium. Just like Lecompte, that man had a dragon tattoo.

Zane briefly considered sharing the connection to the assassin then decided against it. He would tell Amanda once they were alone, but he wouldn't tell Rachel and Esther until he knew he could completely trust them.

"It looks like the head of a dragon." Amanda paused for a moment. "Which is interesting because there's thought to be a criminal enterprise that operates in this part of the world. They're known as the *Drachen*, which is German for dragons. Some say they're responsible for a number of high-value heists and killings in the Middle East."

Zane thought it strange that the name hadn't come up during the museum heist investigation. "I've never heard of them."

"That's not surprising," Rachel said. "There's never been any proof of their existence. Most people believe they're a myth."

Zane looked at Amanda for a response.

"She's actually right. Their existence is controversial. Some law enforcement agencies believe the *Drachen* are behind some of the largest unsolved crimes across the region, while others think the group only exists in the minds of conspiracy theorists."

"What's the evidence for their existence?" Zane asked.

"Initially, it was simply the eyewitness reports of people who were present at the scenes of crimes," Amanda said. "A number of them noted that the perpetrators had dragon tattoos."

"I've seen quite a few dragon tattoos over the years," Zane said.

"Which is why the theory is controversial." Amanda paused. "But tattoos aren't the only thing people point to. There was also a case in Italy that added more fuel to the fire. A group of thieves tried to steal the Shroud of Turin several years ago, and only one of them was caught. While awaiting trial, he told another inmate that he was a member of the *Drachen*. As it turned out, the other inmate was an informant. He took copious notes of their conversation and passed the information along to Italian authorities. According to those notes, the man not only admitted to being a member of the group, but he also spoke fearfully of some woman who supposedly leads the order. He said she was the most evil person he'd ever met."

"So what happened?" Zane asked. "Did they investigate the claims?"

"The suspect hung himself in jail," Esther interjected. "The police believe he realized his cellmate was an informant."

"Which in turn fueled more conspiracy theories," Amanda said. "News of what the man said was leaked to the press, which is why some believe he committed suicide."

Zane said, "I don't understand."

"Some said the man preferred killing himself to facing this mystery woman."

"And there were also some who believed the man didn't actually hang himself," Esther said. "They believed the *Drachen* had him killed."

"How could they possibly do that?" Zane asked.

"The *Drachen* supposedly have moles in many places, so it's believed they sent someone in to kill the man and make it look like a suicide."

"So what do you think?" Zane asked. "Do you believe they're a real group?"

"Although there isn't a lot of hard evidence, I'd be foolish to dismiss it all out of hand. I have a friend who works in law enforcement, and he told me that some of the witnesses who described the tattoos were totally unaware of the controversy about the *Drachen*. Then you have an informant who takes some pretty detailed notes." She shrugged. "It's hard to ignore all that evidence, although none of the proof is conclusive."

"It's possible the accused man lied to the informant," Amanda noted.

"Yes, it's possible he was lying," Esther admitted. "But what purpose would it serve? And why kill himself right after that? He was relatively young, and he probably wouldn't have gotten more than five or ten years with good behavior."

Zane couldn't explain why the man had killed himself, nor could he shake the feeling that something dark was lurking beneath the surface of this case.

Amanda said, "We have a map, a number, and a man with a tattoo." She looked at Zane. "I say we go to the Old City and take a look at the café."

"Tonight?" Rachel asked.

"What about tomorrow afternoon?" Esther asked.

"I think we need to move as quickly as possible," Amanda said. "If you're not comfortable going—"

"No, it's not that. I've been thinking about the number fifteen hundred that was written on the map." She pointed at it. "We all thought it might be an address, but what if it was a time?"

"Three o'clock?" Amanda asked.

Esther nodded. "Solomon served in the IDF years ago, so it wouldn't surprise me if he still used military time."

"But why even put a time on the map?" Zane asked.

"Maybe he's supposed to meet someone at the café," Esther said. "We know the number isn't an address. Nothing else makes sense."

"Surely they would know Solomon Glaser is dead," Rachel noted.

"Not necessarily," Esther said. "There was one initial report, then it seems coverage was shut down. If Mossad is involved, they may have asked the media to suppress the story until they get their arms around what's going on."

It was probably the best hypothesis, but Zane still wasn't convinced the number denoted a time. Why tell them about a meeting when they didn't know who he was meeting with? Not only that, but they didn't have a date. He looked at Esther. "How do we know the meeting is tomorrow?"

"We don't. I think it must be some sort of regular meeting, perhaps with someone who has information about his project."

"Maybe he's meeting with the person who took the photographs," Amanda said.

Zane thought for a moment. "It certainly won't hurt to be there tomorrow at three."

"I'd like to go with you," Esther said.

While Zane still didn't trust her, her knowledge of archaeology might be helpful. "Of course."

"There is one other thing I forgot to mention," Esther said as they all stood. "I got a voicemail from Solomon's son Nathan this morning. He said he wanted to talk to me. Should I let him know what's going on? Maybe he's the one the video message was meant for."

"No, don't call him," Rachel said. "We have reason to believe he may be working with the people who killed his father."

CHAPTER TWENTY-THREE

ZANE STEPPED OUT into the cool night air. He was going to get the car ready while Amanda and Rachel stayed behind to help Esther pack a few things. The archaeologist was certain her apartment was being watched, so Zane had suggested she get a hotel room until the danger passed. If these men tried to torture information out of Solomon Glaser, they wouldn't hesitate to do the same thing to her.

As he entered the alley behind Esther's building, his mind was besieged by a whirlwind of thoughts. First and foremost was the possibility that the fabled *Drachen* were behind all of the current intrigue. Did the group really exist, or had the whole thing been cooked up by conspiracy theorists in the law enforcement community? In modern times, conspiracy theories had permeated the political world. That being the case, it certainly wasn't a stretch to think such theories might have infiltrated law enforcement as well. The *Drachen*—assuming they were real—had everything a conspiracy theorist would love: they committed crimes and were never caught; they had a cruel and dark leader who struck fear in the hearts of men; and they had tentacles in government. The latter was compulsory in any good conspiracy.

But that wasn't the only thing that troubled Zane. He also couldn't figure out what was so important about an underground archway. Was it the entrance to an underground city? Esther had posited that theory right before Zane left. Did the archway lead to some breathtaking relic? Whatever was on the other side had drawn the attention of the Israeli government. It had also driven a group to torture and kill a prominent archaeologist.

For now, they would simply follow the clues they had. They would visit the building Glaser had highlighted on the map and try to figure out what the archaeologist was pointing them to. Was it the café or something else close by? If he was directing them to the café, they needed to figure out why. Esther told them it was possible there was a hidden entrance to the tunnels and caverns beneath Jerusalem. She said Glaser had mentioned the network of passageways several times in the weeks leading up to his death.

Although Esther's theory was logical, Zane wanted to see the café for himself. He found it difficult to believe that a secret entrance was there. If there was, why hadn't the Israeli government sealed the area off until it was found?

Zane emerged on Abraham Lincoln Street and turned north. About halfway down the block, he saw a Muslim woman coming toward him out of the darkness. She wore a navy robe and burqa. Her eyes stared straight ahead as the two passed. Zane thought it odd that she was out alone at this hour but then immediately questioned himself. Why wouldn't she be out at this time of night? Maybe she had gone to pick something up, although he hadn't seen her holding anything.

As he neared the car, he took in his surroundings. A block away, an old man in a fedora walked his dog. Across the street, a dark-haired woman walked briskly down the sidewalk while talking on the phone. Other than that, the neighborhood seemed mostly quiet.

Seeing nothing of concern, Zane opened the driver's-side door and slipped inside. The night air was cold, so he decided to warm up the vehicle's interior before looking at the map on his phone. He wanted to park as close to the Old City as possible in order to limit the distance they would have to travel on foot.

As he reached for the heat controller on the console, he froze. A series of words had been scrawled in the thin layer of dirt on the windshield. He frowned. He didn't remember seeing the writing before, although it was possible the nearby streetlight had illuminated it for the first time.

Leaning forward, he read the words, which appeared in reverse from his side of the glass. *Erase after reading. She can't be trusted. Ask*

The letter *k* trailed off, suggesting the writer had been interrupted. Perhaps it had been the man in the fedora, Zane thought. Or perhaps the man in the fedora *was* the writer.

Suddenly, he remembered the Muslim woman he had passed a minute before. The timing certainly fit. If she had stopped and walked away when he emerged from the alley, that would have put them together at just the right time.

Then Zane remembered something else. A Muslim woman wearing a dark-blue burqa had been in the lobby of their hotel when they first arrived in Jerusalem. She had been sitting in one of the chairs, talking on the phone. Was it the same person? Many women wore hijabs in Jerusalem—in some places, it was hard to walk a block without seeing one—but burqas were a rare sight, even in the city's Muslim quarter.

A question surfaced: Why would a Muslim woman have written the note on the windshield? *Maybe the person underneath the burqa wasn't a Muslim.* Zane knew that Muslim head coverings were sometimes used as a disguise, even for men. The eye slits on burqas were small, making it almost impossible to determine the sex of the person underneath.

Realizing he wouldn't be able to solve the mystery right then, Zane turned his thoughts to the message itself. Assuming it was meant for him, who was the "she" the writer had warned him about? Esther? That would certainly line up with his suspicions. What about Rachel? While Zane didn't trust her completely, she hadn't done anything that had aroused his suspicions, at least not yet.

Zane glanced at the time on the dash and realized the others could arrive at any moment. Whoever had written the message on the windshield had asked that the words be erased, presumably to keep the person referred to as "she" from reading them. For the time being, Zane would follow those instructions and keep the message between Amanda and himself.

He removed his phone and snapped a few pictures using his flash. He'd take a closer look later on the off chance he had missed something.

Satisfied he had captured several good images, he turned on the wipers and spray, erasing the message forever.

CHAPTER TWENTY-FOUR

AN UBER DRIVER dropped them off in the Old City around half past two the next day. The plan was to set up outside Café Nehemiah and watch for anyone who went in alone. Esther would also look for the arrival of anyone known to be a part of the archaeological community. If Solomon Glaser was meeting with someone, it was possible they had some connection to that field of study.

After thinking about it overnight, Zane still couldn't get comfortable with the theory that Glaser was pointing them to some meeting. The whole thing was too complicated. If he wanted them to know about a certain individual, then why not provide more direct clues, as he had with Esther?

Then again, he knew better than to dismiss the idea completely. He operated in a world in which questions often had unusual answers. The number 1500 did seem to correlate to a time, and Glaser might have been cryptic in his message to throw off any unintended recipients. And even if the theory of a meeting was incorrect, they could still use the time to learn more about the café.

After briefly consulting Google Maps, Esther led the others

into the Jewish Quarter. Tourists packed the pedestrian streets, drawn by the perfect weather. The group had to push their way through the throngs in several crowded intersections.

As he took in the familiar surroundings, Zane realized the Old City never changed. A perpetual cloud of cigarette smoke hung in the air, offset by the delicious smell of roasted lamb and fresh bread. An endless procession of colorful shawls, hats, and cheap souvenirs filled the kiosks that lined both sides of the narrow alleyways. Interspersed among the shops were myriad restaurants and cafés offering coffee, bagels, and kosher food.

Ten minutes later, they arrived at Café Nehemiah, which was located at the intersection of Ya'ara and Gilboa Streets. It was slightly more upscale than the other cafés Zane had seen, making him wonder if the theory about a meeting might be true. They certainly weren't going to find an archaeological relic or an entrance to the underground Jerusalem at such a place.

"Should we go in and get a table?" Amanda asked as they stopped near the entrance.

"Let's stay out here for now," Zane said. "We don't know where they'll seat us, and we need to have eyes on the front. It's possible our target might not go in if he or she doesn't see Glaser inside."

Amanda peered through the window. "True, but what if our target has already arrived? I can't see all the tables from here. I think at least a couple of us should go in and get a table."

Zane looked at his watch. It was 2:37. Although he doubted the mystery person had arrived yet, it still made sense to have eyes on the inside. "I'll stay out here while the three of you go inside and check things out."

"Do you want me to wait out here with you?" Esther asked.

Zane was already concerned that there were too many of them watching the front entrance. "No, it's going to be easier for one person to blend in." He looked at Amanda. "I'll let you know if anyone goes in alone."

She nodded then led the others toward the entrance. Once they were inside, Zane stepped over to the gift shop across the street. He positioned himself behind a carousel of magnets depicting scenes of Jerusalem. From there, he would watch the café entrance while pretending to browse for souvenirs.

Over the next half hour, seven people entered Café Nehemiah: one group of three, another group of two, and two women who entered by themselves. Zane sent Amanda a quick text when the two women entered by themselves, but neither turned out to be who they were looking for. One picked up a coffee to go then left. The other joined several friends who already had a table at the back.

As time passed, Zane began to sense that they were wasting their time. In fact, his mind was already transitioning to the next logical step of the investigation, which was to focus on museum employee Robert Lecompte. There was a good chance Lecompte was connected to the group that had murdered Solomon Glaser, and if they could somehow find out where he lived, it might provide the break they were looking for.

Zane glanced at his watch. *3:11.* It was time to wrap things up. There was no meeting, and there was no mystery person. After drawing his phone, he fired off a text telling the group inside to meet him out front. He knew Esther wouldn't be happy about the decision, but they needed to turn in another direction.

As he put his phone away, Zane saw a man exit the café. Instead of walking off, he paused for a moment, his eyes scanning the throngs of people passing by. Zane felt the muscles in his neck tighten. The man seemed to be making sure no one was watching him depart.

Zane studied the man's appearance. An inch or two under six feet tall, he had wavy brown hair that was partially covered by a black *kippah*, the traditional Jewish head covering. He also had a close-cropped beard that looked a shade darker than the hair on his head.

As Zane's eyes moved lower, he saw something that grabbed his attention. A small badge was pinned to the chest of the man's shirt. *He's an employee.* That was why they hadn't noticed him before. Apparently, his shift had just ended.

Zane's pulse quickened as he realized the time correlated with the time written on the map. Was that a coincidence? Maybe Glaser hadn't set up a meeting after all. Maybe Glaser had been watching the man, tracking his movements.

Suddenly, he turned in Zane's direction. Their eyes locked briefly. Zane shifted his gaze to the carousel, but he didn't think it had been quick enough. In all likelihood, the man had made him.

After pretending to browse for a few more seconds, Zane glanced toward the entrance to the café. The man was gone.

Zane stepped out into the street and looked left. *Nothing.* Turning in the other direction, he saw a black kippah bobbing in the crowd about twenty yards away. Zane couldn't see who was wearing it, but he didn't need to. It was him.

At least he's not running.

Zane drew his phone and dialed Amanda's number.

She answered on the first ring. "We're just coming—"

"Where are you?" Zane asked.

"As I said, we're coming out. I just left some money on the—"

"I found our guy."

She hesitated. "What are you talking about?"

Zane picked up his pace to keep the kippah in sight. "The person we were trying to find. He works at the café."

"How do you know?"

"I don't have time to explain. When you come out, turn left down Ya'ara Street."

"We're outside now." She paused. "I think I can see you. We're on the way."

Zane disconnected the call then looked ahead. A throng of Japanese tourists was gathered in the middle of the street, blocking his view of the target. Afraid he might lose him, Zane pushed his way through the crowd. One of the men shouted at him in Japanese.

After coming out on the other side, Zane scanned the street ahead. He could see the man, but he was thirty or forty yards away. Zane picked up his pace. He needed to keep the target in sight. The Jewish Quarter was a maze of streets and alleys, which meant the man could disappear in a matter of seconds.

A minute later, the man took a right turn about thirty yards ahead. Throwing caution to the wind, Zane sprinted the remaining distance. After taking the turn, he came to a stop. A large outdoor market opened in front of him. The market was filled with rows of kiosks that stretched on for about a hundred yards. After scanning the crowd, Zane came to a troubling realization—the man was gone.

Amanda and the others joined him seconds later. All three were out of breath.

"See him?" Amanda asked.

"No."

"How far ahead was he?" Amanda asked.

"Not that far. I closed the distance pretty fast just before the last turn."

"Then he may still be close by." Amanda scanned the crowd then looked back at Zane. "Did he know you were following him?"

"I think so," Zane said. "We locked eyes outside the café, then he took off." He gestured toward the aisles of kiosks. "Let's split up and cover this place from one end to the other." He then gave them a brief description of the man and what he was wearing.

"So what do we do if we find him?" Esther asked.

"Just let us know then keep an eye on him until I get there."

Zane took the aisle on the far right. As he worked his way through the crowd, Esther's question echoed in his thoughts. What *would* they do if they found the man? Zane doubted he would cooperate, particularly if he considered Zane a threat. They could try to tell the man that they were connected to Solomon Glaser, but there was no guarantee the man would believe them.

Zane considered another possibility. What if the man was a danger to them? What if he was somehow connected to the group responsible for Glaser's murder? Slight of frame, the man appeared harmless. But Zane also knew that many of his toughest adversaries hadn't been physically imposing.

Despite scanning every face on his aisle, Zane reached the other end of the market without seeing any sign of the man. Esther and Amanda were already there waiting, which meant they probably hadn't either.

"Nothing?" he asked.

Amanda shook her head. "Then again, I was just searching based on your description."

"I think he's gone," Zane said.

Esther nodded. "There are crossing streets on each side of the market. All in all, I'd guess there are at least a half dozen ways out."

Zane frowned. "Where is Rachel?"

"I haven't seen her," Amanda said.

Zane drew his phone and dialed her number. The call went straight to voicemail. "Strange. Her phone is turned off."

Amanda's brow furrowed. "That *is* strange. Particularly since you told us to keep them on."

"I saw her check her phone before we set out," Esther noted.

"Let's check the aisle she was working," Zane said.

Rachel had been working the side opposite Zane's. The three took their time, examining every kiosk along the way. But despite the thorough search, they saw no signs of her.

"Do you think she's in danger?" Amanda asked when they reached the other end.

"I don't think so," Zane answered. "I'm hoping she's following our guy and decided to turn off her phone."

Amanda nodded but said nothing.

"What now?" Esther asked.

"We find somewhere to sit and wait for her to call," Zane said. "At this point, it's about all we can do."

Esther nodded. "I know of a quiet little deli a few blocks away."

"Quiet would be perfect," Zane said.

Esther led them through the market and turned in to a narrow alleyway behind a kiosk that sold Turkish rugs. As they continued through several turns, Zane couldn't shake the feeling that something significant was behind Rachel's disappearance. He hoped he had been right about her following the man, but that still wouldn't explain why she had turned her phone off. Zane had never heard its ringtone, so he assumed she kept it on vibrate.

Something was wrong. Very wrong.

Hearing the other two stop, Zane looked up. About ten yards away, a man stood in the alley. He held a pistol with both hands, and the muzzle was pointed in their direction.

Zane thought back to how quickly Esther had offered to lead them to a deli. Had she taken this route on purpose? Was she working with the gunman?

The man came toward them with his weapon extended. He was bald and wore jeans and a black leather jacket. The darkness of the alley made it hard to discern his features, but something about him seemed familiar to Zane.

Then it hit him.

He knew who it was.

***

Zane recognized Nathan Glaser from the photographs he had studied online. He had the kind of appearance that wasn't easily forgotten. His bald head was tanned by years spent in the sun. His dark, piercing eyes were topped with the thick eyebrows of his father. Zane also noted the man's distinctive nose. It was bent to one side, possibly the result of some injury he had suffered in the past.

And there he was, brandishing a gun at them.

"Let me see your hand," Nathan barked.

Zane realized his hand was inside his jacket. He had instinctively reached for his weapon. He removed it slowly and held it in the air. "See, no gun."

Once Zane's hand was visible, Nathan pointed the pistol at Esther. "Who are you?"

"Why don't you put away the gun so we can talk this through?" Zane asked.

Nathan ignored him. "What's your name?"

"My name is Esther."

"Esther Navon?"

She nodded.

Zane held his hands up. "Look, we're not here to hurt you."

Nathan lowered the pistol. "And I'm not here to harm you either." He paused for a moment. "I'm here to warn you that you've been working with the person who killed my father."

That wasn't what Zane had expected him to say.

"She's been right under your nose the entire time," Nathan added.

Zane looked at Esther. Her hands trembling, she took a step back.

Maybe I was right all along.

Apparently sensing the confusion, Nathan said, "Not you.

I'm talking about Rachel Hammond."

Zane thought back on the events of the last half hour. Was that why Rachel had gone missing? In a way, it all made sense. Assuming Nathan was right, Rachel had probably worked closely with them in order to draw on the expertise of Amanda and Esther. And now that she had found the man Glaser referenced in his message, she didn't need to keep the ruse going.

Zane wondered whether his suspicion of Esther had simply been misplaced. Maybe he had misinterpreted his own gut. While that might be true, he would continue to watch Esther. Something about her concerned Zane, something he couldn't quite put his finger on.

Anxious to learn more, Zane looked at Nathan. "So why should we trust the man who just pointed a gun at us?"

Nathan slowly slid the pistol into his pocket. "It's dark here in the alley, so I needed to be sure she hadn't rejoined you."

"I appreciate that, but it still doesn't tell me why we should trust you. We've heard a lot of things about you, and most of those things aren't good."

Voices carried down the alley. People were approaching.

"Why don't we find a place where we all feel safe," Nathan suggested. "Once we're there, I'll tell you my story. If you believe me, then maybe we can work together. If not, then we can go our separate ways."

CHAPTER TWENTY-FIVE

AFTER SOME DEBATE, they decided to question Nathan Glaser at the hotel. Finding a restaurant or bar would have been quicker, but they needed to get away from all the noise and distractions. A half dozen questions swirled in Zane's mind as the four took the elevator up to his room. First and foremost, he wanted to know how Nathan had found them. Did he have help, or was he working on his own? How much did he know about the people who killed his father?

"I have one request before we get started," Nathan said once they were gathered in Amanda's room. "I need a drink. A strong drink."

The request didn't surprise Zane. He had watched the man's countenance on the way back and could tell he was under a great deal of stress. His father had been brutally murdered, and it was plausible that Nathan could become a target as well.

"Good idea," Zane said. "I think I'll have one myself." He looked at Amanda and Esther, who were taking seats at the small table in the corner. "Care to join us?"

Esther waved him off. "I'm fine. I'm running on adrenaline."

"A water, please," Amanda said.

As the others took seats at the table, Zane opened the tiny refrigerator and looked inside. The hotel had stocked it with beverages for every taste: two bottles of mineral water, two bottles of Goldstar beer, a bottle of a California Chardonnay, and a half dozen mini bottles of M&H whiskey.

Zane tossed Amanda a bottle of water then removed two mini bottles of whiskey. Nathan wanted strong, so strong it would be. Clutching both in one hand, Zane retrieved two courtesy glasses off the top of a nearby dresser then sat down at the table.

He filled one glass with whiskey and slid it to Nathan.

"Thank you."

Zane poured himself a glass then took a slow sip, enjoying the faint burn at the back of his throat. Nathan tilted the glass back and drained half of the contents in one pull. Zane would have to monitor the man's intake. They wanted him to talk, but they also needed him to answer their questions accurately.

"Feel better?" Amanda asked.

After setting the glass down, Nathan wiped his mouth with the back of a hand. "Not yet, but this will help."

Zane wanted to dive right in with a few questions, but he didn't know whether their interviewee needed a moment to gather himself.

Not as patient, Amanda turned to Nathan. "I'm confused by something. You saw us with Rachel at the market, so how did you know you could trust us?"

Nathan took another sip of M&H before answering. "To be honest, I still don't know if I can trust you, at least not yet."

"You're here," Amanda noted.

He nodded. "It took me a while to figure things out. I guess it goes back to that first night. When I arrived at my father's house, I saw the killers when they came out. They were dressed in black and were carrying guns, so I knew what had happened." Nathan's eyes had a wet gleam. "It took me a while to gather myself, but eventually, I realized I had to go inside. Maybe Dad was still alive. And if he was, then maybe he could tell me who did it."

"So did you go in?" Amanda asked.

"I was about to open my door and get out when I saw the two of you get out of your car. I had no idea who you were, but I didn't believe you were connected to the men who killed my father since they were already gone."

"So you just waited and watched?" Zane asked.

He nodded. "I saw Rachel arrive about an hour later. That's what made me really confused. My father had told me he was convinced she was connected to the people who had been following him. At the same time, my gut told me you two weren't involved in any way." He took another sip of whiskey then set the glass on the table. "At some point, I made the decision to sneak up to the house to see what was going on, and that's when the killers came back."

He fell silent, his eyes fixed on his whiskey glass.

Amanda tried to coax him along. "So what happened next?"

"I heard gunshots, so I knew they must have come back to kill you. The fact that you were attacked by the same people who killed my father confirmed my belief that you weren't working with them. At that point, the only wild card was Rachel. I didn't know what to think." He looked at Amanda. "I didn't learn the truth about her until today, when I followed the four of you. That's when all of the pieces fell into place."

Zane frowned. "How did that clear things up?"

Nathan took a sip of whiskey then set the glass on the table. "When the four of you split up at the market, I decided to follow Rachel. I wanted to keep her in sight because I knew she might recognize me." He paused. "Then something strange happened. Once she was out of sight, I saw her speaking into her wrist."

"A mic," Amanda said.

"I knew it was some sort of communications device, and I also knew she wasn't using it to talk to you. I surmised she was communicating with other people in the area."

"Is that all you saw?" Amanda asked.

He shook his head. "At some point, she caught sight of the man you were looking for, the guy from the café. While she watched him, I used the opportunity to get close. I needed to see if I could hear what she was saying into the mic. She was standing in front of a row of oriental rugs, so I was able to come up behind her and listen. That's when I heard her tell someone she had found the person they were looking for. A minute later, two men showed up, then the three of them followed the man through the market. At one point, one of them seemed to look at me, so I was forced to turn off."

"Did you lose them?" Zane asked.

Nathan nodded.

"What did the men look like?" Amanda asked.

"I don't remember. To be honest, they just looked normal. They were dressed a little nicer than most people, but that's about the only thing I remember."

Zane recalled a question that had bothered him for some time. "Let's go back to the night your father was killed," he said. "How were you able to find us after that?"

"I followed you."

Zane felt a sense of dread wash over him. That was the one thing he didn't want to hear. He was certain they hadn't been followed, and yet apparently, Nathan had pulled it off.

"Well, I didn't exactly follow you all the way."

Zane's brow furrowed. "I don't understand."

"After you drove past me, I waited until you were a couple of blocks away, then I pulled out with my headlights off. I actually did a pretty good job of keeping you in sight, but then I lost you when we entered the Emek Refaim district. Once we got there, you doubled back on me, forcing me to turn down a side street to avoid detection. I came back to the spot a minute or two later, but you were long gone."

Zane felt relieved that his evasive maneuvers had worked. Still, it didn't explain how Nathan had found them. "So how did you track us down?"

"I got lucky. You were driving a rental car, so I figured you weren't from Jerusalem. In fact, I could tell from the way you were dressed that you weren't even from Israel. That meant you had likely rented a room. And if you had rented a room, then I figured it might be near where you lost me."

"Emek Refaim," Esther said.

Nathan nodded. "I know it sounds crazy, but I spent the entire evening driving past every hotel, hostel, and Airbnb in the area." He looked at Zane. "I found your hotel a little after three the next morning."

Zane was impressed. He had employed the same tactic many times before. Yes, a lot of luck was involved, but sometimes it worked. Zane had new respect for Nathan Glaser. "So were you the one who wrote the message on the windshield?"

"Yes, that was me."

Another piece of the puzzle snapped into place. Nathan must have been the one walking away from the car when Zane walked out. He was the man disguised in the Muslim garb.

Frowning, Amanda stared at Zane. "What message are you talking about?"

Zane gave her a quick description of what happened when he went out to the car, including the message written on the windshield.

"You should've told me," Amanda said.

"I was going to as soon as we were alone." Zane turned to Nathan. "I want to ask you about something else. Rachel said you had a falling-out with your father. I assume that was a lie?"

Nathan exhaled. "No, actually, that's true. We did go through a rough patch some time back."

"Anything we need to know about?" Zane asked.

"About a year ago, I learned something that shocked me to my core." He paused for a moment then looked at Zane, his eyes filled with emotion. "I discovered I had a half sister named Nina."

"So you never knew about her?" Zane asked.

Nathan shook his head. "No, and I wouldn't even know now had she not contacted me." He paused. "Once she told me, I confronted my father. It wasn't pretty. I blew up at him, and he blew up at me. At one point, he even threatened to take me out of his will. He said Nina was going to be his sole beneficiary."

"I'm sure that must have been traumatic," Amanda said.

"It was, but I also realize I overreacted," Nathan said. "Dad's side of the family is very particular about appearances, which is why he didn't want his secret revealed. I've met his family. They're very rigid, so I understand why he wouldn't want that to get out."

"So the two of you stopped talking?" Amanda asked.

"For a while, but eventually, he reached out to me. He apologized for not telling me and for making the threats about my inheritance. He seemed sincere, so I accepted his apology."

"And things got better after that?" Amanda asked.

"Yes, but it took some time for things to get back to normal. I had to heal, and he was also dealing with this project all of you are looking into."

"Let's talk about that," Zane said. "What did he tell you about his work?"

"He told me the government had asked him to look into something. He said he couldn't share any details, but he did say it related to his work as an archaeologist. I assumed he was asked to look for something... perhaps a valuable relic. As I'm sure you know, archaeology can be a political hot button here in Israel. Certain groups don't like it when things are found that contradict their view of history." Nathan drained the last of his whiskey then set the empty glass on the table. "Anyway, that's also when he told me that he was being watched."

"Did he know who was watching him?" Zane asked.

"No. At first, he thought the man who had hired him had sent some people to keep an eye on things, but at some point, he dropped that idea."

"Did he explain what changed his mind?" Amanda asked.

"Eventually, he began to believe there was an implicit threat behind the surveillance. It's why he asked me to come from Haifa to meet with him two nights ago. I think he realized his life was in danger and wanted to tell me everything he knew."

A thought entered Zane's mind. "This may sound strange, but how did he communicate all of this to you?"

"We talked on the phone a couple of times," Nathan replied. "But most of the time, it was by text. Why?"

"Everything Rachel shared with us seems to align perfectly with what you told us tonight. That means she must have found your father's phone and all of those texts." Zane looked at Amanda. "When she met with us, she simply placed herself in Nathan's shoes. She played the role of trusted friend while painting him as the villain."

Amanda nodded. "And she was able to use the father-son conflict to add an element of truth."

Zane had to admit that Rachel had played her cards well. Based on his experience as an operative, he knew it wasn't easy to pull something like that off, especially with so little time to prepare.

"So what now?" Esther asked.

"We find the man who works at the café before Rachel and her friends do."

CHAPTER TWENTY-SIX

AFTER THEY FINISHED questioning Nathan, Zane returned to his room and called Brett Foster. Zane asked Delphi's chief technology specialist to find out who the mysterious café worker was. Even though Zane could only provide a place of employment and a general description, Brett felt certain he could dig something up.

Zane had expected Brett to call back in the morning, but instead his phone buzzed an hour later, just as the operative was sliding under the covers.

"Avi Yosef," Brett said by way of greeting.

Zane sat up in bed and turned the nightstand lamp on. "That's his name?"

"I was able to get into Café Nehemiah's payroll system."

"You sure you got the right guy?"

"Yes, I'm certain. It's a small operation with thirteen employees, nine females and four males. Only one fits the description of your guy."

"How do you know what they look like?"

"Fortunately, the company keeps copies of each employee's

ID in the system as a way of proving their eligibility to work."

Zane opened the top drawer of the bedside table and pulled out a pad and pen. "Outstanding. Give me what you found."

"It seems Yosef gave the café a post office box as his address."

"What about a phone?"

"Yes, there was a contact number on file."

After Brett gave him the number, Zane asked, "What else?"

"Actually, that's all I have."

Zane frowned. "That's it?"

"I conducted my usual search and came up empty. He's a ghost."

Zane felt a pinch of concern. Brett was a master of digging up online information. Over the years, he had found people even the FBI couldn't locate. If he couldn't come up with anything on Avi Yosef, there might not be anything to find.

"There is something about this guy that's really strange," Brett continued. "Twenty-three years old and he has no online footprint whatsoever. No Facebook. No Instagram. No Snapchat. I assume he has an email address, but I haven't even been able to find that."

Assuming Brett's statement was true, it was bizarre that a twenty-three-year-old had managed to stay out of the digital world. Every young person had an online presence of some kind. If Avi Yosef didn't, then that probably meant he was operating in the shadows. And if he was operating in the shadows, that in itself was significant.

"Keep looking," Zane finally said. "In the meantime, we'll call him."

Brett laughed. "Good luck with that. I highly doubt he's just going to answer his phone and start sharing information."

"No, but we can always leave him a voicemail or send him a text. And if that doesn't work, then we'll show up at the café."

"He won't be back. Whatever he's involved in is much more important than that minimum wage job."

"You're probably right. Anyway, let me know what you find out."

"Roger that."

After ending the call, Zane's thoughts moved back to Solomon Glaser. Why had he directed them to this Avi Yosef? Were the two connected, or had Glaser simply targeted him for some reason?

As Zane considered all the possible answers, sleep overcame him.

***

As it turned out, Brett was right. The ghost had disappeared. Avi Yosef was gone. Zane tried calling him the next morning, only to discover the number had been disconnected. He guessed it was probably a burner Yosef had given the café at the time he applied for the job.

Unable to reach Yosef directly, Zane asked Esther to call the café and ask to speak to him. At first, the girl who answered the phone refused to give out information on an employee's schedule. Esther then told the girl that she was Yosef's aunt. She said she was trying to reach him because of a family emergency. The girl then disclosed that Yosef had taken an extended leave of absence.

Zane took the news with a small measure of comfort. If Avi

Yosef had requested a leave of absence, at least it meant he was alive. At the same time, the girl might have just made that up in order to get Esther off the phone.

Hit with a dead end, Zane immediately turned his attention to Robert Lecompte. After a long discussion by the group, they finally decided they would break into his home. Desperate times called for desperate measures. A man's life was on the line, and there were really no other options.

Esther placed a discreet call to a colleague at the museum in order to learn the security officer's schedule. As fortune would have it, Lecompte would be working at a special donor banquet that night. Based on her experience with similar events, Esther estimated the museum's head of security wouldn't be home until well after ten o'clock.

Zane doubted Lecompte was holding Avi Yosef at his home, but it was certainly possible they might find information helpful to the case, including communications between Lecompte and those he worked with.

Despite the dangers, they were going to have to break in.

CHAPTER TWENTY-SEVEN

ROBERT LECOMPTE LIVED in the Germany Colony, a neighborhood that was settled by members of the German Temple Society in the second half of the nineteenth century. The quiet, upscale district was characterized by beautiful homes and expensive apartments.

Brett had located the address in less than an hour. He started by checking Jerusalem's extensive online real estate records. Even though they weren't available to the public, he had no trouble hacking his way through the log-in screen from his desk at Delphi headquarters in Arlington.

Although the break-in would take place that night, they decided to scout Lecompte's home during the day. Zane and Amanda agreed it would be helpful to see everything in good light, a preparatory act that would hopefully help them avoid any potential surprises.

Amanda turned onto Lecompte's street at half past three. The block seemed quiet, consistent with the neighborhood's reputation. Other than a woman walking her dog, Amanda saw no signs of activity.

"It should be the third house down on the left," Zane said.

Amanda slipped the car between large sport utility vehicles that were parked along the right side of the street. After cutting off the engine, they took in their surroundings. Even though each home had a slightly different design, Amanda noted that all of them had several things in common: stone block exterior, red tile roof, and a walled courtyard in front. The homes were tightly packed together, which would make the break-in more difficult.

"You want me to come with you?" Amanda asked as Zane put on a pair of aviator sunglasses.

He shook his head. "I'm just going to make a quick pass in front of the house then circle around through the alley behind. I'll probably take that route tonight, so I want to get a feel for what's back there."

"We'll keep our eyes open," Amanda said.

Zane put on a baseball cap and reached for the door. "Be back in fifteen."

Amanda watched as Zane exited the car and crossed the street. She hoped no one would notice him walking around. Based on her experience, most blocks had a resident busybody or two, one of several reasons she didn't like working in residential neighborhoods. A man walking down a street probably wouldn't draw anyone's attention, but a tall, longhaired man moving down an alley might.

"I think we have trouble," Esther said.

Pulled out of her thoughts, Amanda looked over her shoulder. "What?"

"The gate."

When Amanda faced forward again, her stomach tightened. The black gate in front of Lecompte's house was slowly swinging inward. Zane had just walked past it moments before.

"Is he coming out?" Nathan asked.

Ignoring the question, Amanda stayed focused on the scene across the street. After the gate stopped moving, the tail end of a black BMW appeared.

Amanda looked at Esther in the rearview mirror. "I thought you said he would be at work all day then at the banquet tonight."

"That's what I was told."

"Maybe it's not him," Nathan said. "Maybe it's a girlfriend or roommate."

"Nope, it's him," Esther said as the car eased out into the street. "That's Robert."

Amanda dialed Zane's number. "Did you see the car?"

"Yes, but I didn't turn around because I thought it might look odd."

"It's Lecompte. Get out of sight."

Amanda watched as Zane sprinted to the corner and turned left. He disappeared about the same time that the BMW finished backing out into the street. She hoped he had managed to get out of sight in time.

Amanda looked over her shoulder at the two in the back. "Get down. He's coming our way."

As they lowered out of sight, Amanda kept her phone pressed against her ear. One person sitting in a car wouldn't look out of place on a residential street, but three people might.

Seconds later, the BMW raced past them. The fact that

Lecompte hadn't slowed down to take a look inside their car made Amanda feel a little better. She spoke into the phone. "Zane, you still there?"

"Yes."

"Where are you?"

"In the alley behind the house. It's all clear. I'm going in."

Amanda's eyes widened. "You're joking, right?"

"No, I'm not. Lecompte is gone, which is exactly what we were waiting for. I just need to make sure Brett is ready to take down the security system."

"In case you hadn't noticed, it's broad daylight."

"You know how these things work. If we wait until this evening, then something else will come up. It's pretty clear that Esther's colleague wasn't right about him being at work this afternoon. And if they were wrong about that, then they might be wrong about tonight. We need to strike while he's gone."

"Zane—"

"I need to call Brett. I'll send you a text if and when I go in. Let me know if he comes back."

Before she could respond, he disconnected the call.

***

Robert Lecompte was always aware of the world around him. It was, after all, his job. As head of security for one of the world's most prestigious museums, he made it a priority to learn the location of every relic and work of art on display. And in order to protect those treasures, he needed to know the buildings in which they were housed—the air ducts, vents, and pipes. If there was a way for someone to break in, he knew about it.

But Lecompte's skills were even more important on his *real* job, the one the public didn't know about. Robert Allen Lecompte was also a member of a secret order that operated in the shadows. Most public figures denied the order's existence, and it was Lecompte's job to keep it that way. If law enforcement believed the group was a myth, it was unlikely they would ever peel the layers back far enough to uncover the group's leadership.

One of those layers had almost been pulled back during the museum heist some months before. The *Drachen* had almost been exposed. Fortunately, Lecompte and others had minimized the damage, and he would make sure that door would never be opened again.

Due to the nature of his work, Lecompte had to watch his back at all times. His enemies never slept, and he couldn't either. He even kept his own neighborhood under a microscope. He knew every person who lived on his street. He knew which ones minded their own business and which ones didn't. He knew which people stayed home during the day and which ones didn't. His scrutiny was so meticulous that he even knew of two affairs going on behind closed doors.

But Lecompte didn't just track the people who lived around him. He also tracked their mode of transportation. He memorized every vehicle on the block, from the Kawasaki motorcycle owned by the teenager across the street to the Cadillac Escalade owned by a member of the Knesset two doors down.

Therefore, it was no surprise that when Lecompte backed out of his driveway at 3:42 in the afternoon, he immediately noticed the white Hyundai parked a half block away. Using his peripheral vision, he studied it closely as he swung out into the street. None of his neighbors drove a white Hyundai, nor did any of the visitors who came on a regular basis. It wasn't supposed to be there, and Robert Lecompte didn't like it when strange vehicles were parked so close to his home.

Even so, he probably would have dismissed the sighting were it not for what happened next. After coming out of the gate, he had noticed three people sitting inside the car: one female in the front and two people in the back. But when he drove toward the Hyundai, only the driver was visible. Where were the others? If they had gotten out, he would still be able to see them.

That left only one other possibility—they had lowered out of sight.

Lecompte had tried to get a clear look at the driver as he drove past. Unfortunately, the blond-haired woman had a phone pressed to her ear, and it was positioned in a way that hid the details of her face. That wasn't a coincidence, he thought.

As Lecompte drove off, he was hit with an undeniable truth. Strangers had entered his neighborhood, and they had come to watch him.

Immediately, he began to review all of the pertinent facts. He had seen three individuals in one car. Were there others?

The man who was out walking.

As he'd backed out into the street, Lecompte had caught a glimpse of a man in his rearview mirror. The view had been too quick to note any details, but he *had* seen the man turn down the next street.

Lecompte realized what was going on.

He's going to the alley.

His body trembling with excitement, Lecompte drove to the end of the next block and parked along the side of the street. He reached inside the glove compartment and removed the Glock 17 and matte-black suppressor that were hidden there. He then screwed the silencer into the muzzle and tucked the pistol into his coat.

It was time to remove an unwanted visitor.

***

Zane entered the alley cautiously. Save for a few trash cans, there was nothing in sight. It was also quiet, eerily so. Since it was late afternoon, he had at least expected to hear children playing in the distance. But he wasn't about to complain. Silent solitude was what he had hoped for.

Confident no one was around, he continued on. He counted houses as he went and stopped at the fourth one down on the left. As with the other properties, a sand-colored wall marked the back of Robert Lecompte's lot. The wall, only four feet high, allowed Zane to catch a glimpse of the house through the maze of bushes and trees. The vegetation was actually beneficial because it likely obstructed the view of any cameras that might be aimed at the alley.

There was an iron gate, but Zane decided to climb over the wall at a point that was concealed by a large tree with thick foliage. That should keep the cameras out of play.

After taking a last look around, Zane started to mount the wall when his foot caught a stray bottle, sending it bouncing loudly down the alley. A dog barked from a nearby yard.

Cursing under his breath, Zane continued over the wall and dropped down on the other side.

Staying low, he crawled over to the tree and sat against the trunk. As the dog's barks died down, he drew his phone and dialed a number from his contacts list.

Brett answered after the first ring. "Zane? I didn't expect to hear from you so soon."

"Our plans changed, and I need your help. Where are we at on the security system?"

"There's good news and bad news. The bad news is this security system is a modified version of a commercial system we run into a lot."

"I assume you mean it was modified to make it more difficult to penetrate," Zane said.

"Precisely. This thing is a bear. Whoever set it up knows what they're doing."

"So what's the good news?"

"The good news is that I'm even better than the person who built the firewall, so I should have everything taken care of in a half hour or so. In other words, we'll be ready to go tonight."

"I need you to take it down now."

"I'm confused. Why would you want me to take it down now?"

"Like I said, things have changed. We were scouting the house and saw the subject leave. According to the information Esther received, he wasn't supposed to be here right now. He may have just come home to grab something, or it could mean the information we got wasn't accurate. Whatever the case, we know he's gone now, and we can't wait to see what may or may not happen tonight."

"You don't know that house is empty," Brett noted. "He could have a wife or girlfriend inside."

"The same would be true tonight. Besides, I'm going to take a quick peek before going in."

"You're talking about breaking into a house in broad daylight. I've seen the satellite views of this street. Those places are packed together like sardines. No telling how many eyes are out and about."

Zane didn't have time to debate the merits of the plan. He was going in one way or the other. "You can't do a workaround?"

There was a long pause on the other end. "I have access to the power company's grid," Brett finally said. "I can take the power out to his house, which will cause the system to reset. There is a battery backup, so you'll need to disable that when you get inside."

"No problem. Just tell me how."

After giving him quick instructions, Brett said, "Just realize you'll have about three minutes to get that done."

"Stay on the line," Zane said. "Let me get to the door before you take everything down. I want to see how hard it's going to be to get in."

Zane removed two wireless earbuds that would allow him to move without holding his phone. After inserting them, he stood and moved through the trees.

The dog barked twice then fell silent.

After coming out of the trees, Zane crossed the patio to the set of French doors at the back of the house. He examined the locks. They wouldn't be a problem. Apparently, Lecompte relied on his state-of-the-art security system to keep his home safe. That, and he probably had a small armory of weapons inside.

Before asking Brett to cut the power, Zane took a peek through the crack in the drapes. The house was dark. There could be someone upstairs, but Zane's gut told him Lecompte lived alone.

"The lock isn't going to be a problem." Zane looked up at the roofline. Cameras hung at each end of the house. "But we do have at least two eyes back here. Can you erase the footage after this is over?"

"Yes, that won't be a problem."

"Good. Take it down, then."

"Okay, hold." After a half minute, Brett came back on the line. "You're good to go. By the way, the controller and the battery backup should be in a closet room just off the kitchen."

"Copy that."

After disconnecting the call, Zane removed his lock pick and went to work. It took him less than a minute to disable it and slip inside. Fortunately, the system's components were exactly where Brett said they would be. Zane disconnected the battery backup from the controller with a minute to spare.

Now free to operate, he started his search in the kitchen. Seeing no electronic devices on the counters, he moved quickly into the living room. As he did, the neighbor's dog barked several times. The animal's nerves were still probably on edge.

Finding nothing in the living room either, Zane stepped through a doorway that opened into a large room that ran to the front of the house. The shades were drawn, making it difficult to see. As he waited for his eyes to adjust, the dog began barking again. Zane frowned. What had caused the outburst? There was no way the animal could hear him. Zane guessed the dog had been aroused and was barking at every little noise. At least he hoped that was what it was.

As Zane's pupils dilated, he noticed a series of bookshelves lining the wall on the left. Casting his gaze around, he saw a desk on the far end of the room. Sitting on top of the desk was a laptop. A shot of adrenaline entered Zane's bloodstream. Electronic devices were at the top of his list.

After crossing the room, Zane took a seat at the desk and turned the laptop on. A soft whine sounded as the device started up. He hoped to find something of value on the drive. Perhaps there would be information linking Lecompte to Rachel and the group that had murdered Solomon Glaser. Perhaps they would find something that would lead them to café worker Avi Yosef, assuming he had been kidnapped.

A loud chime drew Zane out of his thoughts. The laptop's home screen was up, but Zane was disappointed to see that the device wasn't password protected. There was little chance Lecompte would save valuable information on an unprotected device. Still, even small pieces of information might be helpful.

The dog's barks continued unabated.

Zane pulled out the special USB drive he had brought with him and snapped it into the port. Seconds later, a small box appeared. He entered a password, activating Trojan malware that would vacuum up every file on the device's hard drive.

As the software began its work, Zane's eyes were drawn to a large piece of paper spread out on the desk. He leaned closer for a better view. It was a map of Jerusalem with words scribbled in various places. A red circle was drawn over a section of the city, although it didn't seem to be the café.

His heart beating faster, Zane pulled out his phone, enabled the camera's flash, then began taking pictures. Once he was satisfied that he had photographed the entire map, he slipped the phone into his pocket.

Then, as he turned his attention back to the laptop, he heard a creak in another part of the house.

***

Hidden behind a row of bushes, Lecompte studied the windows at the back of his house. From what he could see, the interior seemed quiet, but he knew that was misleading. The intruder was almost certainly inside.

A minute later, that thought was confirmed when a shadow crossed by one of the windows. It lasted for only a second, but it was there long enough to confirm someone was walking around inside.

Lecompte seethed. The man had invaded his private space, and that meant he had to be punished. If the opportunity presented itself, Lecompte would take him alive and make him suffer before finally putting a bullet in his head.

But Lecompte also knew he needed to proceed with caution. The man inside his house wasn't some random burglar. Lecompte believed it was the man they had targeted in the United States. The same man who had made the team of assassins look like fools.

Yes, the hit team had been sloppy. But after reviewing all

aspects of the operation, Lecompte had come to realize that the man they had targeted was an elite killer, a skilled professional of the highest order. Not only had the man turned the tables and killed two of the mercenaries who were sent into the building to kill him, but he had also tracked down and killed the others as well.

With the benefit of hindsight, Lecompte wished he had taken on that job himself. The American might be good, but Lecompte was better. He had once been a hired assassin in Eastern Europe, and he had never once failed to complete a job.

And he wouldn't fail today either.

After taking a final look around, Lecompte came out from behind the hedges and sprinted to a door at the side of the house. After removing his pistol, he turned the knob and opened the door, which creaked on its hinges.

Lecompte froze, wondering if the noise had been heard.

Erring on the side of caution, he waited two minutes. Hearing no sound of anyone approaching, he slipped into the utility room. He moved past the washer and dryer to a door that led to the rest of the house. The door was ajar, allowing Lecompte to look down the hall that led to the kitchen. Lecompte had seen the intruder walking toward the other end of the house, but he couldn't be sure the man hadn't turned and come back.

As he waited, Lecompte thought he heard something in the distance. It sounded like voices, but he couldn't be sure. Was the man talking on the phone? Was he calling the others in?

Lifting his pistol, Lecompte slipped out of the room and into the hallway. As he went into the kitchen, the voice he had heard before was more distinct. Following the sound, he passed through the kitchen and turned down the hall that ran to the front door. As best he could tell, the voice was coming from the half bath on the left.

Careful not to make a sound, Lecompte crept up to the closed bathroom door. The muffled voice continued on the other side. Could the man really be that sloppy? Lecompte sensed something was wrong, and yet he also knew his ears weren't lying.

He considered his next move. Should he allow the man to come out in order to get a better shot? While it was always good to put eyes on one's target, it could also give that target the opportunity to fire back. That might prove even more risky, since the man inside the bathroom was both crafty and skilled. Lecompte had already decided against taking him alive. Instead, he would kill the man at the first possibility.

Lecompte decided to take the less risky path. There wasn't much space in the tiny half bath, which would make hitting him a near certainty. Any shots fired at chest level should find their mark. Lecompte also didn't need to worry about running out of ammunition. The Glock 17's magazine carried seventeen rounds, plus there was one in the chamber. That gave him eighteen total shots—more than enough. He would fire five bullets at chest level then lower his aim and fire five more times in case the man was sitting on the floor. Even after all of that, he would still have eight rounds left to defend himself should the man somehow miraculously survive.

Careful not to make a sound, Lecompte positioned himself in front of the door. He wouldn't be able to torture the man who had caused them so much trouble, but he would at least take pleasure in killing him.

After visualizing where the target was standing, he lifted the gun and fired.

CHAPTER TWENTY-EIGHT

THEY ARRIVED AT the hotel at dusk. They couldn't be sure how much of their mission might have been compromised, so Amanda entered the room first to make sure all was clear. It was probably overkill, but she wasn't taking any chances.

After swiping her card, she stepped into the dark entryway. Feeling around on the wall, she found the light switch and turned on the two bedside lamps. Soft light filled the space as she moved farther into the suite. No one was waiting, and as best she could tell, no one had been there while they were out. As was her custom when staying in a hotel, she had positioned her belongings so that she could tell if they had been moved even the slightest bit.

"All clear," she said.

Esther and Nathan came in and took seats at the table, while Zane went straight to the fridge and removed a bottle of water.

"I'll take one of those," Nathan said.

Zane offered Esther a bottle, but she shook her head.

Amanda was still trying to process all that had transpired over the last hour. She had been sitting silently in the car when Zane scaled the wall and came running toward them. He had taken her completely by surprise. Once they were out of the neighborhood, Zane told them that Lecompte had somehow figured out what was going on and returned to the house. To buy them some time, Zane had placed a radio in the bathroom and turned it on.

At first, the whole thing seemed like a complete disaster. But then Zane told them that he had been able to retrieve what might be valuable information. He said he would fill them in once they were safely back at the hotel.

Amanda tossed her key card on the dresser then sat on the edge of the bed. "Okay, so what did you find?"

"A couple of things." Zane took a seat on the table then held up the USB drive. "First, I was able to download a few files from Lecompte's laptop. Unfortunately, I don't think it's going to be that helpful."

"Why not?" Esther asked.

"For one, I had to stop the download when he came in, so I'm sure I missed some files. Two, the drive looked pretty bare. I think he just used the laptop to pay bills and email family members."

"Okay, so what's the good news?"

"I found a map of Jerusalem." He held a hand up. "But before you ask, it's not the same one Esther received from Solomon Glaser. Lecompte or someone else wrote on it, so we'll need to figure out what's going on." He looked at Amanda. "Do you have your laptop handy?"

"Yes." She stood and walked over to her luggage.

"I took some photos of the map, and I'll forward them to you right now."

Nathan watched Amanda pull the laptop from a suitcase. "I thought you were professionals. You guys just leave your devices lying around the room?"

"If someone stole this, they'd be awfully disappointed." Amanda came over and set the device on the table. "Any unauthorized attempt to gain access will result in the hard drive being wiped clean. Besides, I really just use it to analyze things we find in the field. Like the photographs Zane's about to send me."

"You should have them," Zane said.

Seconds later, a soft chime sounded as the message hit Amanda's email account. After opening the attachment, she turned the screen so that all could see it.

"There are eight photos total," Zane said. "The first is a view of the entire map. Let's start with that one."

Amanda opened the attachment labeled 001.JPG. As Zane had indicated, it was a satellite map of Jerusalem. Several words and symbols were scrawled on the surface in red ink.

Zane pointed at the image. "As you can see, he drew a circle, and he made some notes as well. Let's look at the circle first."

Amanda used the bar at the bottom of the image to zoom in.

"It's right over the Temple Mount," Nathan said as that part of the map enlarged.

"Actually, it's the Western Wall Plaza," Esther noted.

Amanda looked inside the circle. Esther was right. It more or less encompassed the plaza that abutted the Western Wall, one of four walls built by King Herod to support and expand the Temple Mount in 19 BCE.

"So he circled the Western Wall Plaza," Zane said. "How

does that relate to the photograph of the arch?"

"It's an underground gate, so perhaps it's located underneath the circle," Nathan said. "In fact, there's a famous tunnel at the site." He placed his finger on the northern edge of the plaza. "It starts here and runs north for quite some distance."

"A little over four hundred meters," Esther said.

"I've heard of that tunnel, but I've never been," Zane said. "What's down there?"

"People call it a tunnel, but it's really just a passageway that was covered up over the centuries as things were built over it," Amanda said. "There are all sorts of archaeological goodies down there. Warren's Gate is one of the first things that comes to mind. It was one of four gates that gave access to the Temple Mount in ancient times. Even now, many Jews pray there because it's the closest point to the Holy of Holies."

"There's also the Narrow Passageway, which is a stretch of the tunnel that has glass floors," Esther said. "Visitors can look down and see the massive stones that were hurled there by the Romans."

Amanda nodded. "They were the same stones that Jesus Christ predicted would one day be thrown down."

"I thought the tunnel was more of a tourist attraction," Zane said.

"It is," Amanda said. "Which means it's probably not related to Glaser's work. Every square inch of that space has been studied, photographed, and cataloged hundreds of times."

"Let's look at the other writing on the map," Esther said.

"I couldn't make any sense of it, but maybe you can," Zane said.

Amanda turned back to the screen. Remembering that the writing was to the south and east of the Temple Mount, she used the cursor to drag the map to the left. Once the red scrawl came into view, she enlarged the area and read what was written there: *AC 68*.

It was an odd combination. The letters looked like someone's initials, but she had no idea what the number might represent. After looking at it again, she noticed a slight gap between the numbers, so it was possible the person wrote six and eight rather than sixty-eight.

"AC sixty-eight," Esther said softly.

Nathan pointed at the writing. "That's not sixty-eight, it's six *dash* eight."

Amanda leaned closer. He was right. Between the two numbers, a dash had been written over a line on the map, hiding the mark.

"See, it makes no sense," Zane said.

"AC seems like someone's initials," Amanda said. "Or maybe it's shorthand for something."

Nathan nodded. "And if it is, then it's probably something only the writer would know."

Zane cupped his chin. "I wonder if it has to do with the area it's written over."

Amanda looked again. The letters and numbers were written across the southern slope of the Mount of Olives, an area known for its cemeteries and tombs.

"I guess it's possible," Esther said. "But I really just think he wrote it on a light part of the map. If he had written it anywhere else, it would be hard if not impossible to see."

Zane nodded. "That's a good point."

"But if we can't figure out how it relates to the circle, we can always consider that later," Esther said.

"Maybe it's an appointment," Nathan said. "What if Lecompte was supposed to meet someone with the initials AC between six and eight o'clock? Maybe they were meeting at the Western Wall Plaza."

Zane shook his head. "That wouldn't make sense. Why would a man intimately familiar with Jerusalem need to circle a place that half the people on the planet would be familiar with? That would be like the mayor of Washington circling the Jefferson Memorial because he had a meeting there."

Nathan shrugged. "Just throwing it out as a possibility."

Zane seemed to realize his words had sounded condescending. "No, that's just the kind of thinking we need. We need to brainstorm every possible—"

"Wait a minute." Esther looked at Zane. "What did you just say?"

"I said several things."

"The example you used about Washington."

"I said it would be like the mayor of Washington circling the Jefferson Memorial because he had a meeting there."

"That's it," she said. "I know what all this means."

CHAPTER TWENTY-NINE

"LET ME GET this straight," Amanda said. "You're saying all of this somehow relates to Washington, DC?"

Esther shook her head. "No, that's not what I'm saying at all. There's a festival going on at the Western Wall Plaza right now. Everyone at the museum has been talking about it." She looked at Zane. "You mentioned the mayor of DC, and that made me remember something I read about the festival. There's a series of speakers tomorrow night, which is the final night. And guess who's giving the keynote address?"

Zane smiled. "The mayor of DC?"

Esther returned his smile. "No, the mayor of *Jerusalem*."

"Ariel Cohen," Nathan said. "AC."

The initials on the map.

The letters fit, Amanda thought. But what about the numbers? "Okay, let's assume you're right about the mayor's initials," she said. "What does the six-dash-eight stand for? Is that the time the mayor is supposed to speak?"

Esther stared at her phone. "I'm looking for that right now." After searching for several more seconds, she said, "The festival hours are from eleven in the morning until ten tomorrow night, and get this. Several dignitaries will be speaking from six to eight."

Amanda felt something stir inside of her. Three connecting pieces of information seemed like more than a coincidence.

"That has to be it," Nathan said.

"You said there's more than one speaker," Zane noted. "When does the mayor speak?"

"It doesn't say, but since he's giving the keynote address, I think it's safe to assume he'll go last."

"So what's this festival all about?" Amanda asked.

"It's called the Coming Light," Esther replied. "It's a celebration of the coming Third Temple."

Zane lifted a brow. "The coming Third Temple?"

"Yes," she replied. "As you probably know, the Jewish people—in particular certain sects of Orthodox Jews—have long wanted to rebuild the Temple. The celebration was started several years ago, and its purpose is to build momentum for the construction of the Temple on the Temple Mount."

"So rebuilding the Temple is really a thing?" Zane asked.

Esther nodded. "Absolutely, and it seems to gain momentum every year."

"Some Christians, including me, also believe the Temple will be rebuilt in the not-too-distant future," Amanda said.

Zane frowned. "What does the Jewish Temple have to do with Christians?"

She nodded. "The Bible teaches that a future temple is going to be built. That's in both the Old and the New Testaments."

Zane thought for a moment then said, "I assume you're

talking about Revelation. Isn't that an allegorical book, a series of apocalyptic stories that were just meant to encourage the early church?"

"No, it's not allegory," Amanda said. "All you have to do is read what John wrote in the book itself. In the first few verses, he tells the reader that Jesus is about to show his servants a series of events that will soon take place. Then later in the fourth chapter, an angel tells John they're going to talk about events that are clearly tied to the end of the age. John even calls the book a 'prophecy' in two different places—in the first chapter and in the last. It's like he bookmarked the entire letter, declaring it a prophecy from God."

"So is the rebuilt Temple described in Revelation?" Zane asked.

"Actually, the best description of the third Temple is in the book of Daniel. In fact, Daniel is another proof that Revelation isn't allegory. Many of the same events described in it are also described in Revelation."

"So when is it supposed to be built?"

"I'm sure you're aware that some Christians believe there will be a seven-year period at the end of the age called the Tribulation. It's the point at which grace ends and God pours out his wrath on an unrepentant planet. Daniel tells us that in the middle of the Tribulation period, the Antichrist will set up what Daniel calls an 'abomination that causes desolation' in a wing of the Temple. The Antichrist is basically declaring himself to be God and insisting that the world worship him. Even Jesus mentioned this event. He called it the 'abomination of desolation.'"

Zane nodded. "So if this future Antichrist desecrates the Temple, then that means one would have to be rebuilt prior to the Tribulation."

"Exactly."

Zane turned to Esther. "So what does the rebuilding of the Temple have to do with our investigation? I just don't see a connection to any of the things we've been looking into."

"I do see a connection, although I don't claim to understand it entirely." Esther paused for a moment. "The purpose of rebuilding the Temple is to restart the biblical sacrifices. The Jews hope those sacrifices, if done properly, will bring about two things. They hope they will bring the presence of God—the Shekinah Glory—back to the Holy of Holies, and they also believe they will usher in Messiah."

Zane gave her a blank stare.

She explained. "In order to restart the work of the Temple, the priests will need a large assortment of items, from vessels to garments to animals. Interestingly, there are groups who have already produced many of those things."

"The Temple Institute is one such group," Amanda said.

Esther nodded. "They are. But here's what I believe might connect everything. There are some Orthodox Jews who believe some of the actual vessels that were used in the previous Temple will need to be found and utilized in order for *true* sacrifices to take place. The Menorah, the Showbread Table, and so on."

"So what does this have to do with the arch in the photograph?" Zane asked.

"I think it's possible that this gate may lead to the location of some of these implements," Esther said.

Zane nodded. "That makes sense. But what about the mayor? How does he fit into all of this?"

"That's the part I don't understand. He's obviously a big supporter of the Third Temple movement, but it's hard to know specifically why the *Drachen* would be interested in him."

"Maybe he knows the location of the gate," Nathan suggested.

"I suppose that's possible," Esther said, "but as far as I know, Ariel Cohen has no connections to archaeology or to any groups like the Temple Institute."

Amanda looked at Zane. "So what now?"

"We show up at the festival tomorrow night and see what happens."

CHAPTER THIRTY

ZANE STOOD SILENTLY at the periphery of the crowd, his eyes fixed on the temporary stage in front of the Western Wall. The second of three speakers had just finished, and the host announced that Mayor Ariel Cohen would begin his keynote address promptly at seven fifteen.

Zane and Amanda had been at the festival since three that afternoon. After arriving, they split up in order to cover more ground. Zane took the north end of the plaza and Amanda the south. The two operatives had no specific information to act on, so they decided to simply look for anyone or anything that seemed out of place.

Zane hadn't noticed anything that might be a concern. He was beginning to wonder if they had somehow misinterpreted the notes Lecompte made on the map. Even though the initials and the numbers seemed to line up with their hypothesis, Zane found it hard to figure out what the mayor's role was in all the intrigue. Was he working with Mossad? Did he have some connection to the photographs that ended up in Solomon Glaser's possession?

As the crowd moved off, Zane's thoughts turned to the break-in. How had Lecompte known he was there? Had he seen Zane walking in front of his house? Had he seen the others in the car across the street? *What about Esther?* If she was connected to the *Drachen,* she might have realized the potential damage that could be done if Zane got inside and searched the house. She could have easily sent a text to Lecompte from the back seat of the rental car.

Zane checked the time on his phone. *6:41.* Ariel Cohen wouldn't take the stage for another half hour, which meant there was time to conduct one last sweep of the plaza. He spoke into his headset. "Amanda, you there?"

Seconds later, her voice crackled in his earpiece. "Yes, I'm here."

"Cohen goes on a half hour from now. Has he arrived yet?"

She was positioned at the southern end of the Western Wall Plaza, where limos and SUVs were dropping off the speakers and other important people. It was the only side of the plaza with vehicular access.

"Negative, although I heard someone say his motorcade was on the way. Where are you?"

"I'm still near the stage, but I'm getting ready to take one final walk through my end."

"Want me to join you?" Amanda asked.

"No, stay put for now. I want eyes on the mayor when he gets here."

"Copy that."

A stiff breeze kicked up as Zane walked south toward the maze of booths, kiosks, and tents that crowded the main section of the plaza. Some of the booths were educational in nature, providing short video teachings on the Tabernacle and the two previous Temples. Other booths sold books, DVDs, and tiny replicas of the vessels that were used in the Temple.

As he continued on, Zane studied the mannerisms, attire, and actions of the people around him. More specifically, he was looking for someone who looked out of place. Unfortunately, it was like finding the proverbial needle in the haystack. Several hundred people were crammed into the plaza, and the number seemed to be growing by the minute.

It's the perfect place to blend in.

Ten minutes later, Zane approached a large tent sponsored by the Temple Institute. Having already checked it an hour before, he continued on. As he went around the corner, he saw a woman about thirty yards away. He stiffened. She wore a burqa. A *navy* burqa.

His pulse quickening, Zane stepped behind a nearby kiosk and watched as the woman came toward him. It was the third time he had seen someone wearing a head covering of that color since he arrived in Israel. Could that be a coincidence?

Nathan. Even he had chosen that color as part of his disguise. Was there a connection? As Zane thought back on that night, he realized he had never asked Nathan about the disguise.

Zane drew his phone and called Nathan, who was with Esther in a coffee shop a few blocks away. Since both of them could easily be recognized by the *Drachen*, Amanda had suggested they wait somewhere else in order to ensure their safety.

"Hey," Nathan said by way of greeting. "I have a question

about the night you wrote the message on my windshield. What color was the burqa you wore that night?"

There was a long pause.

"Are you there?" Zane asked.

Nathan laughed. "Is this a joke?"

"Of course not."

"Why are you asking me about a burqa? I think you must have forgotten that I'm male, and I'm a secular Jew."

Zane's face twisted into a frown. "Weren't you wearing a disguise that night?"

"No. Why would you think that?"

Zane realized he had been operating under a false assumption. He remembered thinking it was odd that a Muslim woman—if it was a woman—was walking around late at night in a predominantly Jewish neighborhood. There wasn't anything wrong with that, but it did seem a bit out of place. Something else was going on.

"But you're not going crazy," Nathan said. "It seems like I saw a woman wearing some sort of head covering that night. I thought it was a hijab, but it might have been a burqa."

Zane peered around the corner of the kiosk. The woman was only about ten yards out.

"Zane?"

"You've been very helpful. I need to run."

"If you need Esther and me to—"

Zane disconnected the call before Nathan could finish. Instead of putting the phone away, he moved it back to his ear as though he was still engaged in a conversation.

As the woman drew near, he could see her eyes through the

slit at the front of the burqa. They were black as night. He could also see that her robe was large and bulky.

Big enough to hide a gun or suicide vest.

The woman swept past him and continued north toward the stage.

Zane waited for several seconds then fell in behind her.

CHAPTER THIRTY-ONE

"WE'VE GOT a big problem," Zane said.

Seconds later, Amanda's response came through his earpiece. "What's wrong?"

"Something is about to go down."

"How do you know?"

"I know this is going to sound weird, so stay with me. I'm watching someone right now who is wearing a burqa. And here's the thing. I don't think the person wearing it is a Muslim, and I don't think they're a woman."

"So it's like some sort of disguise?"

"Correct."

"How could you possibly know some man is wearing the burqa if you can't see his face?"

Zane launched into a two-minute recital of how he had seen the same garb on three different occasions, including the time outside Esther's apartment building.

"There are burqas and hijabs all over Jerusalem," Amanda said. "This is the Middle East."

"Even at a predominantly Jewish event?"

She paused. "Okay, I'll give you that."

"Besides, hijabs are common in Jerusalem but not burqas."

There was another pause, this one longer.

"Amanda?"

"Sorry, I was just thinking about something. I may have seen someone wearing a burqa earlier. They were far off, and their back was facing me. At the time, I just assumed it was a Catholic nun or a Muslim woman wearing a hijab."

"When was this?"

"About twenty minutes ago."

"What color was it?"

"I think it was blue."

Zane wondered if there could be more than one person using the disguise. If that was the case, something big was about to go down.

"Has the mayor arrived?" he asked.

"As a matter of fact, he just got out of the limo and is heading toward the tunnel right now."

She was referring to the tent tunnel that had been erected so speakers could travel to the stage without having to wade through the throngs of people. The tunnel began at the southern end of the plaza, where the dignitaries were dropped off, and ran north along the east side of the plaza.

"Do you want me to come to you?" Amanda asked.

Zane glanced at the person in the burqa. They were standing still about twenty yards away.

"Yes. Just make sure he gets safely into the tunnel then head my way." Zane gave her directions. "I'll let you know if I have to move."

"Copy that."

As Zane waited for Amanda to arrive, he turned his attention to the person in the burqa. They were moving toward a covered area that had been set up for people to eat their food. After taking a seat, the person placed a phone against their ear. Zane studied the hand that held the device. It seemed to be the large hand of a Caucasian male.

He's probably communicating with others who are hidden in the crowd. And if that was the case, it was possible something was about to go down. Zane considered what that *something* might be. Esther had suggested they were going to make an attempt on the mayor's life. She speculated that Cohen had somehow learned about the group's plans, and while she could be right, a crowded festival seemed like a bad place for an assassination attempt. For one, the place was crawling with police officers. And two, it would be difficult to get out of the plaza once the killing took place.

Five minutes later, Zane saw Amanda coming toward him.

"Where's our target?" she asked by way of greeting.

Zane nodded in the man's direction. "He was just on the phone for several minutes."

"*He?*"

"I saw his hands. There's no doubt it's a man."

"That confirms we have a problem," she said.

Zane was about to suggest they find a table near the man when he stood up abruptly. "He's on the move."

Before leaving, the man pushed his chair in then looked in their direction. Zane turned away, as did Amanda. Had he seen them?

A few seconds later, Zane stole a glance toward the covered dining area. The man was gone. "Let's go."

The two hurried over to the table area and scanned the crowd. There was no sign of a navy robe or burqa.

"Did you see which way he went?" Amanda asked.

Zane nodded at the stage. "No, but I'd be willing to bet that's where he's headed."

The two moved in that direction. The throng in front of the stage was growing larger by the minute, which meant if they didn't find their target soon, they might never find him at all.

As they neared the back of the crowd, Amanda pointed to the left. "There."

Following her gaze, Zane saw a navy burqa slipping through the crowd. The man was on the move. A few seconds later, he came to a stop at the north end of the plaza.

"Let's move around behind him," Zane said.

The two slipped through the crowd until they were positioned about fifty yards away from the man. After gesturing for Amanda to follow him, Zane moved behind several Orthodox Jewish men who were talking among themselves. He hoped the move would give them a little cover in case the man looked in their direction. If he had spotted them earlier, he might still be looking for them.

"So what are we going to do?" Amanda asked. "We don't have guns."

Each guest had to pass through a metal detector, which had forced Zane and Amanda to come in unarmed. For the time being, Zane had asked Nathan to hold his pistol off-site.

"We watch and wait," Zane answered. "Not much else we

can do. The good news is that he doesn't have a weapon either."

"I wouldn't be so sure."

"Good point."

"The mayor is here," Amanda said.

Zane turned toward the front. Ariel Cohen had just stepped onto the stage, followed by four men in dark suits. It looked more like a presidential entourage than that of a city official. Zane had seen security details for mayors in large cities like New York but never for a town the size of Jerusalem. *It comes with the territory.*

Cheers broke out as Cohen turned and waved at the crowd. Zane stepped slightly to his right to get a better view of the man in the burqa. He was still in the same spot, and he was using his phone again.

"I think something's about to happen," Zane whispered.

Another man appeared on the stage—the host, Zane assumed. After shaking hands with the mayor, he stepped to the podium and began to speak in Hebrew. Zane didn't understand what the man was saying but guessed he was introducing Ariel Cohen.

As the host continued to speak, Zane noticed their target was hiking up the side of his robe. As the fabric came up past the man's waist, Zane saw what was hidden underneath.

"He's got a gun," Zane shouted.

The man raised a pistol in the air and fired twice. At the same moment, other shots rang out at various points around the plaza.

Pandemonium rippled through the crowd. Screams and shouts filled the air as people tried to get as far away from the stage as possible.

Although the view was blocked, Zane rushed toward the place where he had last seen his target. Most people were moving in the opposite direction, forcing him to push his way through. A minute later, he arrived at the spot. Amanda came up beside him.

"Where is he?" Amanda shouted.

"He didn't pass me, so he must be between here and the—"

"Follow me," Amanda said.

"Do you see him?"

She didn't answer.

As they sliced a path through the crowd, Zane saw where she was leading him. Just ahead, the robe and burqa lay on the ground. The man had thrown off his disguise before running away. It was a genius move. Witnesses would undoubtedly tell police about a gunman disguised in Muslim garb. Not only would that put the officers on the wrong track, but once word got out, it also might even set off a riot.

Catching movement in his peripheral vision, Zane looked toward the stage. Ariel Cohen's security detail was moving off the north side of the platform, the side opposite the tent tunnel. That made sense. If they went back the way they came, they would be moving in the same direction as the crowd, potentially exposing the mayor to one of the shooters.

Cohen's security detail was clearly trying to get the mayor onto one of the narrow pedestrian streets that crisscrossed the area north of the plaza. That was probably the first step in their contingency plan—move the mayor to a safe zone until reinforcements arrived.

Now off the stage, Cohen's entourage came toward Zane and

Amanda. Eight security guards were running with the mayor, four on either side. It was a tight formation but probably not tight enough to prevent Cohen from being shot.

As Zane watched, the mayor and his team moved toward the security checkpoint at the northwest corner of the plaza. He knew where they were going.

"They're headed for Al-Wad Street," he told Amanda.

"You follow them," she said. "I need to check something out real quick."

He hesitated. "Check what out?"

"It will only take a second. I promise." She nodded at the mayor's team, which was moving off quickly. "Go."

Zane didn't like splitting up, but there wasn't time to argue. She was right—they needed at least one set of eyes on Cohen.

As Amanda ran off in a different direction, Zane turned just in time to see the mayor's entourage run through the checkpoint and disappear down Al-Wad Street.

Fearing he might lose them, Zane sprinted in that direction, passing through the exit and onto the crowded cobblestone street beyond.

After several minutes of pushing his way through the throng, Zane finally saw Cohen and his security team just ahead.

As he hurried to catch up, he noticed something peculiar about one of the guards.

CHAPTER THIRTY-TWO

ARIEL COHEN HAD eight guards protecting him, and Zane noticed they were all dressed in similar attire. They wore charcoal suits and crisp white dress shirts, all of them save for one man at the back, who wore a white turtleneck.

Was that one exception a coincidence?

Zane guessed a private security firm was providing the mayor's protection, and it was obvious they had a dress code for their employees. And if that was the case, why was one of the men dressed differently? Was it simply because he didn't have a white shirt available? That was possible, although it seemed unlikely. Those companies were generally flush with cash and could supply as much attire as needed.

A more sinister possibility entered Zane's thoughts. What if the man wearing the turtleneck was trying to hide something? What if he was trying to conceal a tattoo? Zane remembered the words of the gang leader in Bulgaria. Just before passing away, he'd said the organization that hired him had tentacles everywhere. If that was true, they could certainly place someone in the mayor's inner circle.

Zane's thoughts shifted back to the present. He would have to sort through all the details later. For now, he had to assume the mayor was in danger.

After traveling a short distance down Al-Wad Street, the security team took a left then two more turns before finally emerging on a cobblestone street that ran west. Based on Zane's knowledge of Jerusalem, they were moving toward the streets with vehicular traffic. That meant an armored limousine was probably waiting to whisk the mayor to safety.

Would the impostor make a move before then? Zane considered his options. Should he try to warn the mayor and his team? He doubted they would listen. In fact, they would probably assume *he* was the one who presented a threat. For now, Zane would simply follow and attempt to thwart the man should he make a move.

Five minutes later, Cohen's entourage slowed to a walk. The security team probably preferred to keep running, but it was clear the mayor was gassed. Zane was surprised that Cohen had made it as far as he had. The politician was apparently in good shape, an attribute that might have saved his life.

Zane looked around. They were in the Muslim Quarter, which seemed deserted. Only a few people were out and about. Zane vaguely remembered hearing a news report that most of the Muslim-owned businesses had shut down in protest of the festival.

If the impostor was going to try something, now would be the time.

As they continued on, Zane spoke into his headset. "Amanda, are you there?"

It was the second time he had tried to reach her, and once again, he got no response. He was angry at her for striking off on her own, and he was also angry at himself for letting her. Even though she hadn't said what she was doing, Zane guessed she was following the man who had been wearing the burqa. He hoped she had just turned off her comms so as not to be distracted, but he couldn't help thinking something might be wrong.

Unable to reach Amanda, Zane dialed Nathan.

"Zane? What happened over at the—"

"No time to explain. I need my pistol, so I need the two of you to come to where I am."

"Which is where?"

Zane gave him the name of the street and the approximate location.

"You're in luck. We're only two blocks away."

Zane frowned. "I thought you were in the Jewish Quarter?"

"The police told everyone to evacuate and go west."

"I'm following the mayor, and it looks like they're headed toward the Tower of David Museum."

"We're on the way."

After disconnecting the call, Zane sent Amanda a quick text giving her the same information. He didn't tell her about the suspicious guard, but he did say to drop whatever she was doing and come his way.

Zane put away his phone then came to a stop. There was a bend in the street, and the mayor's team was no longer in sight. He sprinted forward until he came to an intersection. All three options had bends that made it impossible to see more than about thirty or forty yards.

Zane cursed under his breath. They had probably started running again, which made it impossible to know which route they had taken.

As he considered his options, the distinctive staccato of automatic gunfire sounded in the distance. Zane's blood ran cold. The guard had sprung his attack.

The shots seemed to come from somewhere ahead, so he sprinted forward. Two minutes later, the street opened into a long, rectangular plaza. Zane expected to see some sign of the gun battle, but instead, the plaza was empty. Had he taken the wrong route? Perhaps the echo of the gunfire had played tricks on his mind.

He was about to turn back when he saw a flicker of movement in his peripheral vision. Turning to his left, he noticed something was moving just beyond a decorative fountain. He hurried in that direction. As he came around the fountain, a horrific sight came into view. The bodies of Cohen's security team were strewn across the cobblestone pavement. Only one of them was alive.

After rushing to his side, Zane knelt and assessed the man's condition. His suit coat was open, revealing at least four bloodstains on the white shirt. Zane studied the location of each wound. None of them were centered over the heart, but they were close enough to create a massive loss of blood.

He wouldn't live long.

As Zane reached out to unbutton his shirt, the man began to mumble. Zane leaned closer. The man mumbled again, but the words were garbled by the blood rising in his throat.

"Don't talk," Zane said softly. "I'm going to call an

ambulance. You're going to be fine."

He didn't necessarily believe that, but he had to do everything he could to keep the man from giving up.

The man lifted an arm as if trying to point at something beyond the fountain. Zane stood and looked in the direction where he had been pointing. On the far end of the plaza was a street, but no one was there. He wondered what the man was trying to tell him. Had Cohen and his abductor gone that way? If so, they had probably been picked up by a vehicle.

Crouching again, Zane placed his hand on the man's arm to comfort him. He used his other hand to remove his phone. He needed to call an ambulance. With the festival only a mile or two away, it was possible one was close by.

But as Zane unlocked his screen, a final wheeze of breath escaped the man's mouth. Zane moved his hand up to the man's wrist and felt for a pulse. *Nothing.* He was dead.

"There he is," someone called out from the other side of the fountain.

Zane turned in that direction. Two people came toward him out of the darkness. *Esther and Nathan.*

The two came to a stop when they saw the bodies.

"My heavens," Nathan whispered.

"It's Cohen's security team," Zane said. "None survived."

Esther came closer. Her face was white as ash. It was obvious she had never seen such carnage before. Few people had.

She looked at Zane. "What happened?"

Zane gave them a brief recounting of all that had taken place over the last twenty minutes. He also told them about Amanda striking off on her own.

"I don't understand," Esther said after he had finished. "How did he do it? How could one man kill—"

"It probably wasn't as difficult as it seemed. By the time they got to this plaza, they probably felt safe. The impostor probably held back and waited for a time in which he could shoot all of them in the back at once. It was an automatic weapon, so it would have only taken seconds to complete the task, particularly if the group was bunched up."

"So the mayor is dead as well?" Esther asked.

"No, I think he's still alive. This was a kidnapping, not an assassination attempt."

"Oh, thank heavens," she said.

"So why would they do this?" Nathan asked.

Zane shrugged. "Probably for the same reason they wanted to talk to Solomon Glaser. They believe he has information—"

"I know why they would do that," someone said.

Zane wheeled around at the sound of the voice. A man and a woman stood about ten yards away.

The man stepped closer, his hands in the air as if to indicate he meant them no harm.

When the man got within a few feet, Zane's eyes widened in surprise. It was the last person he had expected to see.

CHAPTER THIRTY-THREE

AMANDA MOVED QUICKLY down the street, making sure she kept the suspect in sight. He occasionally looked back, forcing her to step behind a group of people or duck into an alcove. So far, she believed she had managed to escape detection.

Initially, the sheer number of people flooding out of the event had allowed her to follow without fear of being noticed. But as they got farther away, the crowds began to dissipate, making the task more difficult.

Amanda believed the man in front of her was the same man who had worn the burqa disguise. When he had lifted his robe, she had seen he was wearing a pair of black stonewashed jeans and black sneakers. Later, she saw a man wearing similar attire following Cohen's entourage as they rushed toward the exit. She'd had only a brief glimpse, but she was certain he was the same man who had fired the shots.

She thought he might attempt to assassinate the mayor right there in the plaza, but instead, he turned off onto a narrow cobblestone alley. Either Cohen had been too well guarded, or the man was instituting another plan.

After parting with Zane, Amanda had followed the man as he crossed Al-Wad Street and continued in a westerly direction. He moved with both speed and purpose, which told her he must know where the mayor was going. Had he somehow obtained prior knowledge of the mayor's contingency plan? Was a mole operating within the mayor's inner circle?

Amanda thought about turning her comms back on and updating Zane but decided against it. Her target was moving quickly, and she needed to make sure she didn't lose him. Keeping him in sight was her first priority.

Just ahead, the man ducked under the awning of a closed shop and pulled out his phone. As he did, he glanced down the street, forcing Amanda to step behind two people who were walking next to her. Had he seen her?

Amanda prayed the call would be quick. If it wasn't, she would be forced to walk right past him. Now that she thought about it, maybe that was the very reason he had stopped. If he suspected he was being followed, that was one way to determine who was behind him.

She had only seconds to come up with a plan.

Think, Amanda. Think.

If she continued on, she would have to travel for quite some distance before returning again. If she stopped, that could mark her as the person the man was looking for. It seemed as though she was damned either way.

Amanda had just made the decision to duck into an alcove on the right when the man put his phone away and continued on. Even though she could now continue to follow the target, Amanda was concerned about the fact that he had stopped to place a call. Had he realized she was following him and called in backup? If so, then she might have to worry about getting caught in a trap. From this point forward, she would need to be more aware of her surroundings.

A minute later, the man turned left into an alley. That presented Amanda with yet another dilemma. If she turned as well, it might be obvious she was following him. Just to be safe, she continued past the place where the man had turned. She traveled to the next block then turned and sprinted back to the alley. To her surprise, the man was nowhere in sight. The alley intersected with a street on the far end, but she didn't think he could have made it that far in such a short time.

Maybe he'd entered one of the buildings on either side.

She slowly made her way down the alley. About halfway down, she found a door on the right. It was cracked open, revealing only darkness beyond. She hesitated. Why would a door be open? She stepped closer and listened, but no sound came from within.

The more she thought about it, the more it was obvious the man had gone inside. Should she go in? If the *Drachen* had kidnapped the mayor, they might be holding him in the building. Then again, it was also possible the man had set up a trap.

After weighing her options, Amanda decided to split the difference and take a quick look inside. If there was no sign of the man, she would come back out and do her best to catch up. She knew he had been traveling west, so it might still be possible to find him.

After pushing the door all the way open, she slipped inside

then took several quick steps to the left so that her silhouette wouldn't be framed by the light coming in. She remained in place, her back against the wall. So far, she saw no signs of an ambush. As her eyes adjusted, rows of pallets and boxes came into view. It looked like some kind of storage facility, and she could tell that it hadn't been used in quite some time.

Amanda reprimanded herself for what looked like a bad decision. There was nothing of interest here. The man was likely a quarter mile away by now.

Letting out a sigh of frustration, she moved toward the door. As she did, she heard the quick *thump* of footsteps. Someone was moving toward her with speed. Before she could turn, a strong arm wrapped around her midsection. She tried to wrestle free but stopped when a sharp point pressed into her back.

A deep male voice spoke in her ear. "Got ya, you little bitch."

CHAPTER THIRTY-FOUR

EVEN THOUGH IT was dark in the plaza, Zane had recognized Avi Yosef immediately. The slight frame. The short, wavy brown hair. The close-cropped beard. It seemed odd that the same man who had fled from them before was marching boldly toward them.

Something had changed.

Concerned about a possible attack, Zane studied Avi and his companion. As best he could tell, neither was armed, nor did they appear to have bad intentions. Even so, he would monitor their movements carefully.

"Do you know who I am?" Avi asked.

"Of course," Zane said.

The girl who had accompanied Avi stepped forward. She was petite. Perhaps an inch or two over five feet with a slender build. Her red hair was braided into two ponytails that fell on either side of her chest. She wore large blue-framed glasses that gave her a nerdy appearance.

Avi nodded at her. "This is my friend Maya. She let me stay with her while I was on the run."

As the five made quick introductions, Zane noticed that Maya said almost nothing. He assumed she didn't speak English very well.

Avi turned to Zane. "As I said before, I know why they want to kidnap Mayor Cohen."

He was about to continue when sirens sounded in the distance. They sounded like the sirens used by police and not emergency responders. Had there been time for someone to report the gunfire? Even though the area seemed deserted, there were probably people close enough to hear.

"I think we need to go," Avi said.

"I think you're right," Zane said.

"Follow me," Avi said. "I know a place where we can talk."

Before leaving, Zane took a moment to examine the fallen guards. He doubted any of them had survived, but he couldn't depart without making sure. If they needed medical attention, he would do what he could to help them, even if it meant being there when the police arrived. Unfortunately, they were all dead.

As the sirens drew near, Avi led them down a nearby street. After several turns, they emerged in another plaza. The restaurants and cafés were all closed, so they found an outside table underneath an awning.

After they sat down, Zane looked at Avi. "Before we get to the mayor, I have a question. How did you know you could trust us?"

"It started in the market. I could have easily gotten away from you, but I was overcome by curiosity. I needed to know who you were."

"So you hid there?" Zane asked.

He nodded. "I saw the three women join you." He looked at Esther. "I know who you are, and I knew you were a person of reputable character."

Esther's brow furrowed. "Do I know you?"

"We've never met, but anyone who knows a little about archaeology knows who you are."

"So if you trusted Esther, then why didn't you reveal yourself to us?" Zane asked.

"Because there was another woman with you that I didn't trust, the one who wore glasses."

"Rachel," Zane said.

He nodded. "My people…" He stopped abruptly, as though he might have said something he shouldn't have.

Maya spoke to him in Hebrew.

Avi turned to the others. "She's right. How do you say in English? Put cards on the table?" He paused as if searching for the right words. "I'm a part of a secret organization. We don't know much about this woman Rachel, but we do know that at some point, she became aware of our existence. We know that because she began inquiring about someone in our organization. No one is supposed to know we even exist." He took another quick pause. "Anyway, she began following one of our people, and he was able to take a few discreet photographs of her. Those photographs were then circulated within our group."

Esther nodded. "So that's what caused your confusion in the market."

"Yes, exactly," Avi said. "Since I knew you had an impeccable reputation, I figured the other woman must have somehow gotten you to help her without revealing who she really was."

"You said there were a couple of things that led you to trust us," Zane said. "What was the other?"

"Well, that came in the last hour or so. Maya and I were at the festival, and we happened to see you and the blond woman standing near us as Mayor Cohen was being introduced. So we saw how you reacted when the shooting began. You were truly surprised by what was happening, which told me you weren't connected to those who did this thing."

"You told us you were a part of a secret Jewish organization," Esther said. "What group were you referring to?"

"As I said, it's secret, so I can't—"

Maya whispered something to him in Hebrew. The two conversed in low tones for a full minute before Avi finally turned toward them again. "She's right," he said. "If we're going to trust one another, then I need to be honest about everything."

Zane nodded. "And we'll do the same."

"Our group is known as the Temple Guardians."

Zane heard Esther catch her breath. The name meant nothing to him, but it obviously had great meaning to her.

"We have been in existence for two millennia," Avi continued. "We come from three families of pure Jewish lineage. Our origins are related to a group known as the Essenes." He looked at Esther. "As curator of the Dead Sea Scrolls, I know you're familiar with the Essenes."

"Of course." Esther nodded at Zane and Nathan. "But I'm not sure about them."

"I know the basics," Zane said. "They were an ancient Jewish sect that existed around the time of Christ. If I'm not mistaken, they left Jerusalem and established a community at Qumran on the shores of the Dead Sea."

"That's correct," Esther said. "We believe the Essenes organized around 200 BCE and existed for about three hundred years."

"And didn't they produce the Dead Sea Scrolls?" Zane asked.

"That's where it gets interesting," Esther said. "Some scholars believe the Essenes established the Dead Sea community of Qumran and produced the scrolls. Others believe the group that established Qumran was actually an offshoot of the Essenes."

"We believe the Essenes produced the scrolls at Qumran," Avi said. "Now was it the main group of Essenes or a smaller group related to the Essenes? I guess no one knows for sure, but at this point, it's really not that important."

"I agree," Esther said.

Avi paused before continuing. "In addition to producing and protecting the scrolls, the Essenes also held a very important secret. They knew the location of the sacred Temple vessels, which were lost when the Romans destroyed the Second Temple in 70 AD."

"Wasn't the location of the vessels described in the Copper Scroll?" Nathan asked.

Amanda had taught Zane quite a bit about archaeology, and he remembered her mentioning the Copper Scroll on several occasions. While the scroll's content was still a mystery, she believed it contained directions to the place where all the Temple treasures were held.

"We believe the Copper Scroll does give the location of *some* Temple vessels but not all. The location of the most important Temple treasures couldn't be written down. Instead, that location was entrusted to us."

Silence fell over the group as the incredible revelation sank in. Zane looked at Esther to see her reaction. While she seemed open to the information Avi had provided, she didn't appear to be completely convinced. Zane guessed she had more questions.

"So where are the Temple vessels?" Zane finally asked.

Avi and Maya whispered again. A half minute later, Avi turned to the others. "I don't want to go into any specifics right now, but I will tell you this. The treasures are located underneath our great city. They're in what you might call a vault or chamber."

"I think there is a connection to what we've been looking into," Esther said. "Do you know Solomon Glaser?"

Avi nodded. "Yes, of course."

She gave Avi a brief overview of all that had happened so far, including a description of the box Glaser had given to her.

"One of the things in that box was a photograph," Esther said, "and I think it may be the entrance to the place you're describing."

"Do you have a copy I can see?" Avi asked.

"Yes, I have a digital copy." After finding it on her phone, Esther handed him the device. "Here it is."

Avi held the screen so that he and Maya both could see it. After studying the image, Avi's eyes had a wet gleam. He seemed overwhelmed with emotion.

"Is that it?" Esther asked.

"Yes, it is." He handed the phone back to her. "But I must say it makes me sad that you even have this picture. I believe it's how this whole thing started."

"What do you mean?" Zane asked.

"Several months ago, around the same time this woman Rachel became aware of our existence, our elders made it clear to me and a few other trusted individuals that our mission was in danger of being compromised. They suspected that one of our own had copied some of our documents. Despite the betrayal of trust, the elders believed this man's intentions were good. Supposedly, he believed the Israeli government was better able to safeguard the Temple treasures than we were. Obviously, he was wrong about that. And now, it seems our precious secrets are getting into the wrong hands."

"At some point, the Israeli government asked Solomon Glaser to discreetly look into the matter," Zane said. "The *Drachen* are said to have people in high places, so we think that's how they learned about it as well."

"They have a mole in Mossad?" Avi asked.

"We assume so."

"Let's go back to the man who betrayed your group," Esther said. "If you knew about him, then why didn't you try to stop him?"

"We did cut him out of the group before he could determine the location of the underground chamber. That person has now gone missing, so we fear he may have been killed by the *Drachen*."

Esther frowned. "I don't understand," she said. "If he was a member of your group, then he should have known the location of this chamber."

"Only our six elders know the precise location of the Temple treasures. The rest of us are assigned to do other things such as maintaining an inventory of the Temple vessels and keeping the genealogical records of our group."

"Which reminds me of something I forgot to mention to you," Esther said. "There was a genealogical record in the box Solomon gave me. It wasn't long, but it may have contained the names of individuals who were involved in the Temple Guardians."

"That must be how Glaser found Avi," Zane said.

"And if the *Drachen* obtained some of the genealogical records, that's probably how they learned the mayor was one of our elders," Avi added.

"If they tortured my father, then they won't hesitate to torture the mayor," Nathan said.

"We need to figure out where they're taking him," Esther said.

"I believe my partner was trying to track one of the men who fired shots at the festival. I've been trying to reach her with no success."

"So what now?" Esther asked.

Zane looked at Avi. "Do you think the mayor would give up the location of this secret chamber?"

Avi shook his head. "We all took an oath to keep that secret, even if it means losing our own life." His expression darkened as if hit with a disturbing thought. "But I do know Ariel has two daughters, and if…"

He never finished, and he didn't need to. It was obvious the Temple Guardians took their mission seriously. And Zane had no doubt any of its members would endure torture and death to keep the location of the sacred vessels a secret. But he also knew there were few people who would allow their children to suffer or be killed for any cause, no matter how important.

Zane leaned forward and put his elbows on the table. "Even though it may not have happened, we need to assume the *Drachen* know the chamber's location. And we need to be there to stop them and save the mayor." He looked at Avi. "You need to call one of the elders and warn them that the treasures may be compromised."

"I can do that, but they won't take action. We're sworn to nonviolence. Even if we could somehow prove to them that the chamber was being violated, they would only alert authorities. Throughout the centuries, our job has been to keep a very important secret. Once that secret gets out, our mission dies."

"Then tell them to give *us* the location," Zane said.

"They won't give it to me."

Avi and Maya looked at each other. Some unspoken communication was going on between the two, but Zane couldn't figure out what it was.

"I can take you to the gate," Avi said.

Zane frowned. "I thought you said you didn't know the way."

"I don't know the way." Avi nodded at Maya. "But she does."

Esther looked first at Maya then at Avi. "And how does she know?"

"Because her father is one of our elders."

CHAPTER THIRTY-FIVE

"SO MAYA'S FATHER shared the chamber's location with her?" Esther asked.

Avi laughed. "No. That would be a violation of his oath. But he did make a mistake."

Avi and Maya conversed in low tones. Zane guessed he was asking her how much he could share. Zane didn't really care about how she got her hands on the information. They could discuss that later. Right now, they needed to focus on getting there before the *Drachen*.

Avi finally turned and addressed the group. "About six months ago, Maya came home from work to find her father rushing out of the house. Her mother had just been in an automobile accident, and her father was going to meet her at the hospital. Maya insisted on going, but her father said it wouldn't be necessary. She was just a little shaken up, and they were simply checking her out as a precaution. He asked Maya to stay home to clean up the house and start dinner so that her mother wouldn't have to worry about that.

"So that's what she did. She cleaned the house and prepared

a few simple dishes for them to eat. After that, she went to her father's study to work on some things for school and found his laptop open to… I don't really know the word in English. It's like a secure website that only some people have access to."

"A portal?" Esther asked before taking a sip of tea.

He nodded. "She realized it was a map of some kind, along with a set of instructions. She didn't know what it all meant but took some pictures to show me. Of course, the minute I saw them, I knew what it was." He held Maya's gaze for a moment then looked back at the others. "I know it sounds like she was a bad person, but at the time, she didn't realize how important it was. Her dad is an adventurer, so she thought it was some sort of a treasure hunt."

They needed to keep things moving. At this point, *how* she came to acquire the map wasn't important.

"So does she still have all the information?" Zane asked.

"Yes, we both have copies on our phone."

Zane looked at the time on his watch. "Then we need to get moving."

"Before we leave, I must tell you something," Avi said. "The map shows two different ways to get to the system of caves underneath Jerusalem. One of those routes is through a large building. If the *Drachen* go in, then I believe that's the one they'll take."

"Which means we should probably take the other one," Zane said.

Avi nodded. "The alternate route just happens to be closer to where we are now."

As they all stood, Zane removed his phone and noticed he

had a text from Amanda. *Finally.*

He wondered if she had been following the man who had fired the first shots at the festival. If so, she might know where they were taking the mayor.

Zane looked at Avi. "I need to respond to this. I'll be with you in a moment."

As the others talked among themselves, Zane unlocked his phone and read the text.

> *hey… it's me. thought I had something but turned to dead end. where are you?*

After Zane finished, he was hit with the distinct sense that something was wrong. The message had been hastily written, with no capitalization and two missing words. Having worked with Amanda for a long time, he knew she typed out her texts like an English professor. The word at the beginning of each sentence was always capitalized, and her grammar was always flawless. They were the opposite of his, which were usually written with a complete disregard for spelling and punctuation.

Still, it didn't necessarily mean something was wrong. She might have typed it while walking, or she might have used voice typing to save time.

Until he could be certain her phone hadn't been compromised, Zane decided to conceal what was truly happening on his end.

> *we're at a plaza near tower of david. are you close? lost sight of mayor but believe he made it out ok.*

Zane hit Send then waited for a response. In the event someone had taken Amanda's phone, he wanted them to assume he had given up on finding the mayor and was no longer a threat.

A half minute later, his phone buzzed with the response.

i'm only about ten minutes from you. send me your precise location and i'll head your way.

Zane typed out his reply and sent it.

i'll call you. easier to explain over the phone.

The response came seconds later.

too loud where I'm at. text me directions.

Zane felt a sliver of suspicion run through him. Each exchange seemed to reinforce that it wasn't Amanda on the other end. Even if it was loud, she could have moved to a place where it wasn't.

He considered his next move. There was really only one way to settle the question of who was in control of her device. He would ask the question that Delphi operatives posed to one another if it was believed someone's device had been compromised. He typed it out carefully using the precise verbiage specified by organization protocol.

Can you confirm you're safe?

If a Delphi operative was using the device, the only correct response would be: *Copy that. Delphi 428.* The 428 stood for the section of the Delphi manual that dealt with such situations.

Zane sent the message. Regardless of the answer he received, they would need to get moving. If Amanda gave the proper response, he would simply tell her to rendezvous with them at the entrance to underground Jerusalem.

A half minute later, his phone buzzed. As he read the incoming text, a chill ran down his spine.

> *yes, I'm safe and as far as I can tell I'm not being followed.*

CHAPTER THIRTY-SIX

"PUT HER IN there," said the man who had grabbed her earlier, the same man who had used the burqa disguise.

"Move it," the second man growled.

A hand roughly shoved Amanda toward a door on the left side of the hall. Caught off guard, she stumbled forward and fell, her shoulder slamming into the concrete floor. Pain rippled across her upper torso, adding to the ache that came from the large knot on her forehead.

Despite the circumstances, she felt fortunate to be alive. After following the man into the dark building, she remembered being grabbed and held at knifepoint. The next thing she remembered was waking up in the back seat of a car. Her wrists were bound with plastic ties, and she had a throbbing knot on her head.

Soon thereafter, the car pulled up at the back of a nondescript building. Amanda assumed they were still in Jerusalem but couldn't be sure. Two of the men yanked her out of the vehicle while the third had driven off. Once inside, Amanda was taken through a long corridor that ran down the back of the building. On one occasion, she heard voices down a hall to her right. Was that where they had taken the mayor? She made a mental note of the location in case it could be of use later.

"Get up," a male voice said, bringing Amanda back to the present.

Strong hands grabbed her under each arm, yanking her into the air. Her right shoulder, which had borne the brunt of the impact, felt as though it was being ripped out of its socket. Amanda grimaced but managed to suppress the groan that rose up in her throat. She wasn't about to give her captors the satisfaction of hearing her verbalize the pain.

One of the men walked off as the other pushed her inside. Amanda thought he was going to shut the door, but instead, he came up behind her and placed his cheek against the side of her head. His breath smelled rancid.

"The boss lady said not to harm you," he whispered softly in her ear. "Said we need to keep you alive in case we need a bargaining chip down the road."

Amanda stepped forward to get away from the foul stench, but the man moved along with her.

"But you know what? She also told me that once this was all over, I could have you to myself."

"I doubt that," Amanda said.

The man laughed. "You won't doubt it when the time comes." He pushed his nose into her hair and sniffed. "You even smell good."

"You don't."

The man laughed again. As he turned and headed for the

door, Amanda knew she needed to make something happen. If she was left in a locked room with no light, her chances of escape would drop precipitously.

Hit with an idea, she called after him. "Wait."

He turned around with a smile. "You miss me already?"

"I need to go to the bathroom."

He turned back toward the door. "You'll be fine. Just find a nice corner."

"You won't like dealing with me later if I have an accident."

The man stopped again as if considering what she had just said. If he planned on assaulting her, then her ruse might work.

He turned, came back to her, and grabbed her arm, making her wince. "You try one smart move and I'll kill you." He shook her arm again. "You hear me?"

"Yes. I just need to go, and I'll make it quick."

"And don't think I can't hurt you," he said. "I can always say you attacked me first."

"I understand."

"I'll give you two minutes, and that's it."

Amanda nodded but said nothing.

Apparently satisfied with her response, the man led her out of the room and down the hall. A minute later, they turned right. No one else was around, although Amanda could hear voices in the distance.

So far so good.

The man grabbed her arm as they neared a door on the left. Before letting her in, he opened the door, turned on the light, then glanced around inside. "Two minutes."

After the door shut behind her, Amanda looked around the

small bathroom. A small sink and mirror were affixed to the wall on her right. The stained sink looked like it hadn't been cleaned in a decade, and hair strands were scattered across its surface like miniature snakes.

Amanda moved past the sink to the toilet. It seemed even dirtier than the sink. Fortunately, she didn't really need to use it.

She swept her gaze over every square inch of the cramped space. There had to be something she could use to initiate her plan. Her eyes stopped on the toilet paper holder. She studied the metallic piece for a moment then looked at the toilet seat. Would it work? It might, but she would have to move quickly. She would also have to hope that the man didn't decide to barge in before she was done.

As if on cue, the man beat his fist on the door. "Hurry up in there."

CHAPTER THIRTY-SEVEN

AFTER MAKING A quick stop to purchase flashlights, the group took an Uber to the synagogue Beth Sholom Central Jerusalem, which was located just east of Bloomfield Park. Under protocol, if an authorized member of the Temple Guardians wanted access to the chamber, they would have to arrange a meeting with the synagogue's Hakham, or wise man. The Hakham would then escort the person to a hidden door, which in turn led to a system of tunnels underneath Jerusalem.

According to Maya, the secret door could only be opened with a code. Fortunately, that code was included in the information she had taken from her father. What they didn't have was the authority to meet with the Hakham, who was also a member of the Temple Guardians. That meant they would need to break into the synagogue and use the code to pass through the secret door. The break-in would almost certainly trigger an alarm, but Zane doubted there would be a police response in light of all the chaos at the Western Wall Plaza.

"Are you sure this is the place?" Zane asked as they entered the dark alley that ran down one side of the towering white building.

"Yes, I sure," Maya said in broken English. "The instructions very clear."

Zane had learned on the way over that she did speak a little English. She had probably pretended not to be fluent to avoid being questioned. Now that she trusted them, she seemed to have opened up.

A minute later, they came to the rear of the building and found a steel door barring their way.

"Can you get us in?" Avi asked.

Zane studied the locking mechanism. "It won't be a problem."

A single light hung above the entryway, a cheap security measure meant to deter would-be burglars. Zane reached up, unscrewed the bulb, then tossed it into the bushes. It probably wasn't necessary, but he didn't like being exposed in the light.

It took him three minutes to pick the lock. Once he was finished, he readied his pistol, opened the door, and stepped inside. He stood perfectly still, listening for any sound that might indicate the building was occupied. While Avi felt certain the *Drachen* were going to use the other entrance, they still needed to proceed with caution.

Hearing nothing, Zane gestured for the others to come in.

As his eyes adjusted, he could tell they were in a small utility room. Through a door on the opposite side, a long hall ran toward the front of the building. There was a soft glow at the other end, which provided just enough illumination for them to make their way forward without using their flashlights.

"Interesting," Avi whispered.

Zane turned to see him staring at a panel on the wall. "Something wrong?"

"The security system. We use the same one at our synagogue, and I can tell that this one has been turned off."

"Isn't that a good thing?" Nathan asked.

"Theoretically, yes," Avi said. "But if the system is turned off, then it could mean someone got here before us."

"That or perhaps the staff forgot to turn it on when they left," Zane said.

"Do you think the *Drachen* are here?" Maya asked.

"We haven't heard anything yet," Zane said. "If they are here, then they're probably down in the tunnels already."

Just to be sure, Zane listened for another minute. Hearing nothing, he led them down the dimly lit hall. There were a couple of doors on the right, but he decided to keep going. There wasn't time to clear the entire synagogue. They needed to keep moving.

A minute later, the corridor opened into the sanctuary. Zane had been inside several Jewish synagogues before. This one looked similar, only it was larger and more ornate. At least two dozen rows of pews stretched to the far end, encircled by a portico that ran around the perimeter of the room. Two lights were on underneath the portico.

After referring to the instructions, Avi led the group across the transept. To their left was a set of wide stone steps that ran up to the chancel. Zane saw the dim shape of a table at the top. Based on his previous visits to synagogues, he knew that a set of Torah scrolls was usually kept there.

As they neared the end of the transept, Avi stopped abruptly, his eyes focused on something directly ahead. Maya came up beside him then caught her breath. Gripping his pistol tightly, Zane pushed past them and saw the body of an elderly man sprawled out on the marble floor just ahead. He wore a dark suit and a crisp white dress shirt. He had gray hair and a long, shaggy beard.

"The Hakham," Avi whispered.

Stepping closer, Zane saw a single bullet wound in the center of the man's forehead. There were no signs of torture, and it was clear the man had died instantly. Shifting his gaze, Zane noted a dark stain had spread out from underneath the body. The blood glistened in the soft light, suggesting the shot had been taken within the last few minutes.

He frowned. If the Hakham had just been murdered, then that meant the killers…

A dark figure rose out in the pews.

"Everybody down!" he shouted.

As everyone hit the floor, Zane went down on one knee and lifted his pistol.

The hooded figure took aim with a rifle. Fortunately, his silhouette was framed by the light under the portico. Zane squeezed off two shots. The gunman clutched his chest and dropped out of sight.

Like some macabre carnival game, another hooded figure rose and managed to get off several shots. Zane returned fire then dove to the floor. He peered down the rows of pews. About twenty yards out, a shadow moved.

The shooter.

Taking aim at the legs, Zane fired once. The man cried out, which gave Zane the opportunity he needed. He stood and sprinted down the left side of the sanctuary, looking down each row as he went.

About halfway back, he saw the gunman attempting to get up. Zane fired three times. The man twitched violently then slumped forward.

Concerned there might be others, Zane continued down the rest of the rows. Fortunately, the rest of the sanctuary was clear. He was thankful for that, but at the same time, it didn't make sense. Why were there only two gunmen? Had the *Drachen* left them behind to cover their rear flank? Zane didn't think so. With the Hakham dead and the security system disabled, a rear guard wouldn't be necessary.

The more he thought about it, the more he believed the two men had been sent over as scouts. Rachel probably wanted them to confirm there was an alternate route in case the other one fell through.

Returning to the front of the sanctuary, Zane found the others crouched in a dark corner to the right of the chancel. To his surprise, Esther was holding a pistol. He frowned. "Where did you get that?"

"Off one of the mayor's guards," she said as they stood.

"Why didn't you tell me you were armed?"

"Because I knew you wouldn't like it." She nodded at the others. "There are five of us. We need more than one weapon."

Zane didn't like the fact that she had kept him in the dark about taking the gun. It added to his growing suspicions about her intent, but he didn't have time to question her further. And she was right about one thing. An extra pistol might come in handy later. "Let's go before more show up."

"Surely they aren't the only ones here," Nathan said. "There could be others waiting at the tunnel entrance."

"I think these two were sent over to scout the synagogue as an alternate route."

"I hope you're right," Nathan said.

Using the directions on Maya's phone, Avi led them down a hall that seemed like a mirror image of the one they had taken to the sanctuary. They passed several offices on the right. Zane watched the doors closely, but they encountered no further resistance.

They entered a dark room at the end of the hall. Avi reached to his right and turned on the overhead light. When it came on, Zane realized they were standing in a small chapel. It had several rows of pews and a small podium on the far end.

Avi looked around. "Something's wrong."

Zane looked at him and frowned. "Are we in the wrong place?"

"We're in the right room, but there should be another door."

Zane swept his gaze across the four walls. Avi was right. There were two windows on the opposite side of the room but nothing that would indicate another exit.

"Let's check the walls," Esther suggested.

"For what?" Nathan asked.

"Creases or anything that looks out of place."

As the others set out in different directions, Zane walked toward the other end of the room, his eyes focused on the large decorative tapestry that covered the far wall. His heart beat a little faster. *The perfect place to conceal a secret door.*

He grabbed the edge of the tapestry and pulled it back. A small black door was set into the wall about ten feet away.

"It's over here," Zane called out.

As the others came over, Zane pulled the tapestry down completely. He then walked to the door and tried the knob, but it was locked.

"There is supposed to be a way to enter a code," Avi said.

"I guess we're not at that door yet," Zane said. "Maybe it's on the other side of this one."

"Assuming we're in the right place," Esther said.

Zane tapped the door lightly. It made a hollow sound, which indicated it was cheaply made.

"You going to pick the lock?" Nathan asked.

"Not this time." Zane lifted his foot and smashed it into the wood, which crunched inward. He kicked it again, this time knocking the door completely off its hinges.

"I guess that solves that problem," Esther said.

Zane directed his flashlight beam into the opening. A set of aged stone steps disappeared into the darkness below. Moving carefully, he led the others down. A half minute later, they entered a second room that was lined with stone walls. It felt like progress.

Avi pointed across the room. "There's another door."

"And that one has a panel," Esther said as they moved in that direction.

Zane noted that this door was made of solid steel. If the code didn't work, there would be no kicking it in.

Maya stood in front of the panel. She glanced at the numbers on her phone then entered them on the keypad. For a brief moment, everyone held their breath. Seconds later, there was a loud *click* as the locking mechanism disengaged.

Zane exhaled slowly. If the code hadn't worked, they would have hit a dead end.

Avi turned the long handle and swung the door open, revealing another set of steps that spiraled down into the darkness. The descent was going to get much more difficult, Zane thought. This stairwell was narrow and steep. Once they started down, it would be difficult to come back quickly if they encountered resistance.

"This should take us to the tunnels," Avi said.

"How far down are we going?" Esther asked.

Avi shrugged. "To be honest, I'm not sure."

Noting the narrow space, Zane suggested they go down single file. He would take the lead, and Esther would bring up the rear since she was armed.

As Zane led the group down the steps, his nostrils were hit with the heavy scent of must and stone. It was like they were entering a place that had been sealed off in time.

But he soon noticed something else that could pose a problem. The deeper they went, the harder it was to breathe. Was it possible they would eventually have to turn back as the oxygen levels continued to decrease? He didn't think so. After all, the Temple Guardians supposedly used this route on a somewhat regular basis. In fact, someone had recently taken photographs of the underground arch.

Just when it seemed like the steps would go on forever, the spiral staircase transitioned to a level passageway. Zane lifted his flashlight, illuminating a stone archway just ahead. "I think we're there."

He passed through the archway and kept going in order to make room for the others to come out.

"Are we near the chamber?" Nathan asked.

"No, we went straight down, so we're still west of the Temple Mount," Esther replied.

Zane noticed their voices echoed, which indicated they were standing in a cavernous space. He directed his light toward the ceiling. The others did likewise.

"Good heavens," Esther said.

As Zane swept his beam across the ceiling, the hairs on his neck slowly stood on end.

CHAPTER THIRTY-EIGHT

THE MORE SHE thought about her plan, the more Amanda believed it would work. But did she have enough time to carry it out? That would be the difference between success and failure. What she wanted to do would likely take more than the two minutes she had been given. That meant she had to either move extremely fast or convince her captor to give her more time.

Amanda whispered a quick prayer as she stepped over to the toilet paper holder that was attached to the wall. There were two prongs that needed to be pushed apart in order to insert the roll of toilet tissue. Since her wrists were bound together, she pressed her leg firmly against one prong while pushing the other one with her hands. The prongs slowly opened enough to release the roll, which fell to the floor.

"You need some help with those pants?" the man outside asked with a chuckle.

"Shut up, you pervert," Amanda whispered to herself.

Crouching, she examined the circular pieces that jutted out from each prong. Just as she had expected, the edges were sharp. While living in a dorm in college, she had once cut the side of her hand when putting on a new roll in the bathroom. That incident had given her the idea of how to free her hands.

Standing, she pushed the plastic tie up against the sharp metal edge. She then moved the tie up and down in a sawing motion. The metal cut into the plastic, but she could already tell it was going to take longer than she thought.

"Hurry up," the man barked from behind the door.

"You told me I had three minutes," Amanda said. "Now please, just let me—"

"I said two minutes, and we're already a minute in."

It hadn't been a minute, but Amanda didn't have time to argue. She sawed more quickly than before, pushing the tie harder against the metal with each successive motion.

She was about three-quarters of the way through when the man spoke again. "I'm gonna count to ten, then I'm coming in," the man said.

"That's ridiculous. I haven't even been in here for a minute yet." She thought about how to distract him. Unable to think of anything clever, she asked, "What's the big rush, anyway? It's just as easy to watch me here as it is the other place."

"Shut up," he growled. "You don't get to ask the questions."

Amanda looked down at the plastic tie and let out a groan. She was only about halfway through.

She needed to keep the man talking. "What are they going to do with me?"

"Ten."

Amanda's chest tightened. Apparently, he hadn't been joking about the countdown.

"Okay, okay. Just a few more seconds."

A soft snap sounded as the ties broke in half, freeing her hands.

"Nine."

Amanda felt a wave of relief wash over her. Her hands were free, and the man outside the door was letting quite a bit of time pass before he announced each number. Even so, she wasn't sure she had enough time to finish.

"Eight."

Amanda turned to the toilet and lowered the seat. Even though it was a commercial building, the toilet was the residential variety with a lid that attached to the rim with cheap plastic bolts. She popped off the plastic bolt covers, exposing the heads.

"Seven."

"I told you I'll be done in a few seconds."

"I don't care when you're done. When your time is up, I'm coming in."

Amanda snapped off her necklace, which her captors had failed to take off. She threw away the chain but kept the gold cross that had been attached to it. Reaching underneath the rim with her left hand, she held the nut in place. She used the cross like a screwdriver, sticking the bottom edge into the groove on the bolt head.

"Six."

She turned the cross as quickly as she could. The bolt was screwing free of the nut, but it was taking a long time. Finishing before the man came in seemed less and less likely.

"Five."

Once the bolt turned easily, Amanda started using her hand.

A few seconds later, the nut dropped to the floor, and she pulled the bolt out.

One down, one to go.

She moved to the other side of the bowl and went to work on the second bolt.

The man rapped on the door. "What are you doing in there?"

Amanda felt like punching him in the face. "I'm almost done. Just let me clean up."

"Four," he announced.

Amanda turned the cross as quickly as she could.

"Three."

She didn't have enough time to finish. The nut was still an inch or so from the bottom of the bolt.

Amanda reached over and flushed the toilet. "Okay, I'm done. Just let me get my pants on."

"I told you I can help with that."

A hand grabbed the doorknob and jiggled it. Amanda stiffened. Was it a bluff, or was he really coming in?

"Don't you dare come in until I get covered up."

The man chuckled. "Two."

Her adrenaline pumping, Amanda stepped over to the switch and turned the lights off. She felt around until she found the faucet then turned it on.

"One."

Amanda moved over to the toilet and reached around in the darkness until she finally found the lid. Gripping it firmly with both hands, she yanked it upward. Just as she had hoped, the cheap plastic bolt snapped off.

"What was that?" the man growled. "I'm coming in."

Amanda gripped the lid tightly and faced the door. Unlike the cheap plastic lids currently sold, the one she held was made of heavy wood.

The perfect weapon.

The man opened the door slowly, his silhouette framed in the dim light of the hall behind him. He took a step forward then stopped when he realized the interior light had been turned off.

Amanda moved toward him with speed.

At the last second, he seemed to see the lid coming out of the darkness. "What the hell are you—"

Amanda swung the lid like a batter connecting with a fastball hanging right over the plate. The hard wood smashed against the man's forehead with a loud crack. Unable to deflect the powerful blow, the man wobbled for a moment then dropped to the floor. Amanda whacked him a second time for good measure.

Crouching, she could see that he was unconscious but breathing. It was exactly what she had hoped to accomplish. She had no way of knowing how long he would be out, so she needed to make sure he wouldn't be a threat once he came out of the stupor.

After dragging the man's body completely inside the bathroom, she closed the door and turned on the light. She fished in his pockets and found several more plastic ties. She removed two and bound his wrists and feet. Just for good measure, she gathered a large wad of toilet paper and stuffed it in his mouth. She put so much in that it would be difficult if not impossible for him to spit it out.

Confident he wasn't going anywhere, Amanda collected the man's pistol and mobile phone. She didn't plan on using the phone, but at least it would prevent him from using it if he managed to get free.

She stepped out into the hall. No one was in sight, although she could hear voices in the distance. After a moment's reflection, she went back the way they had come, turning left down the corridor that ran along the back of the building. She went past the room she had originally been placed in then saw another connecting hall on the left. It was the one she was looking for, the one she had looked down when they brought her in.

As she crept up to the corner, the voices grew louder. Leaning out, she looked down the short hall and saw a cracked door on the other end. Seeing no one, she ran to the door and peered out. The interior of a large warehouse opened in front of her. People were talking loudly, but rows of stacked boxes hindered her view.

After waiting a few seconds, she stepped out into the room and ran to the left. As she went down the rows of boxes, she caught glimpses of a large crowd gathered in the center of the space. She wanted to see what was going on but knew if she went down any of the aisles, she might be seen if someone turned in that direction. As she neared the corner of the room, she noticed a forklift at the far end of one of the aisles.

Perfect.

Ducking down, she hurried forward and crouched behind the cab. She waited a few seconds then rose high enough to peer over the top of the seat. Dozens of people were gathered at the center of the space, their backs to Amanda. They wore dark robes and hoods. *The Drachen.*

She considered her next move. Several guards were positioned around the room. She thought about slipping out of the building and contacting Zane. But then she remembered the mayor. If he was here, she needed to get him out. And while she would love to have some help, she knew it would take too long to call Zane in. She didn't even know where she was. She assumed the building was in Jerusalem, but she had no idea what part of the city. For all she knew, Zane might be ten or twenty miles away.

She was on her own.

A hush came over the crowd, drawing Amanda out of her thoughts. Seconds later, a woman's voice came through a loudspeaker. Amanda couldn't see her, but something about her voice seemed familiar.

"Everyone, I need your attention. Please gather your things. If you need to use the restroom, please do so now. We go down in five minutes."

Go down? What was she talking about?

Most of the crowd began moving toward the other end of the warehouse. All except for one person. A woman broke away from the group and walked quickly toward the rows of boxes to Amanda's left.

The bathroom. She's going to the bathroom.

Hit with an idea, Amanda tucked the pistol in her pants and slipped off in the direction the woman had taken.

CHAPTER THIRTY-NINE

ZANE HAD NEVER seen, much less been in, a tunnel as large as the one they were standing in. The ceiling was approximately the same height as a three- or four-story building.

"I've heard stories from people who have been down here," Avi said. "But I had no idea it looked like this."

"So beautiful," Maya said.

Esther held her flashlight in one hand while she took photographs with the other. "To think all of this has been under our feet for centuries."

"We tend to forget that another world exists down here," Nathan said.

After taking a few more photographs, Esther looked at Avi. "Who built this tunnel? The Essenes?"

"No one knows for sure, but our oral traditions say the original Temple Guardians constructed it over a period of about fifty years."

"Did they also build the tunnel from the Dead Sea to Jerusalem?" she asked.

"Most of that tunnel is a natural fissure," he answered. "The

Essenes likely took what was already there and widened it."

Zane frowned. "What tunnel from the Dead Sea to Jerusalem?"

"While there's no archaeological proof, a few scholars believe there's a tunnel that runs from Qumran to the Temple Mount," Esther said. "It was said to have first been used during the Roman siege of Jerusalem in 70 AD."

"When they destroyed the Temple?" Zane asked.

She nodded. "During the siege, it's believed the Essenes relocated many of the Temple vessels in order to preserve them for future use. Some of them were hidden under the Temple Mount, perhaps in the very chamber we're going to now. But some were also transported to the Qumran community via the tunnel."

Zane found it all fascinating, but they needed to get moving. He pointed his flashlight down the tunnel, which ran straight out into the darkness. After referencing the compass on his watch, he noted they would be traveling northeast, a route that should take them in the general direction of the Temple Mount.

"I think we should go now," Avi said.

Zane set a brisk but manageable pace. Based on a rough estimate of the distance, he figured they should arrive at the chamber in about a half hour. That assumed they wouldn't encounter any obstacles, and it also assumed they would be able to continue at the same speed with such low levels of oxygen. Zane had strong lungs, but if he was already short of breath, he knew the others were as well.

Nathan came up beside him, a look of concern etched on his face. "You sure we're not just walking into some trap?"

"I'm not sure of anything," Zane said.

"That doesn't exactly fill me with confidence."

"I think it's pretty safe to assume the *Drachen* took the other route."

"I'm not as sure as you are. I think those two men were left behind to guard the entrance."

"I did too," Zane said. "That is, until I saw the tapestry."

"What does that have to do with anything?"

"Think about it. If they were bringing in a large group, I think it's pretty obvious they would have torn it down like I did. I think we arrived before the two gunmen had a chance to get back to the chapel."

"Maybe. I guess we'll find out soon enough."

As they continued on in silence, Zane glanced back. Esther had dropped far behind and appeared to be typing something on her phone. He found it odd that she wasn't taking in their surroundings. Was she texting someone? When he checked his phone on the stairs, he noticed there was still a weak signal.

While she might be looking through the photographs she had just taken, Zane still couldn't shake the feelings of suspicion. His intuition had served him well over the years, and it was screaming at him now. She had been hiding a gun she took off a dead man, and now it looked as if she might be communicating with someone. At a minimum, she was hiding something. At worst, she was a mole for the other side.

So what should he do? The calmer, more logical part of him believed his suspicions were probably misplaced. After all, he hadn't found any concrete evidence that she was working for the *Drachen*. They had a mole, and that mole was Rachel Hammond. And since Rachel had successfully completed her work, why would they need to leave someone else in place? It wouldn't make sense.

But that raised another question. What if Esther was aligned with a different group altogether? What if she was working for the Israeli government or some other group that wanted access to the chamber?

Zane decided to monitor her activities. If he saw proof that something nefarious was going on, he would take away her weapon and send her back to the surface. Until then, he would allow her to continue on to the chamber. With Amanda missing, it didn't hurt to have an archaeologist with them.

Looking up, Zane noticed that Avi had walked ahead. He also realized they were all walking at a slower pace. The lack of oxygen was taking its toll on their bodies, although he didn't get the sense that it was approaching dangerous levels.

A moment later, Maya came up beside him. While he had concerns about Esther, Zane had trusted the young Jewish girl almost immediately. Her kind and gentle demeanor seemed to have a calming effect on him.

After they walked in silence for a while, she said, "Avi tells me you spy."

"No, not exactly. I do investigate things, though."

She looked at him. "Tell me the truth. Are you going to try to take what is ours?"

He assumed she meant whatever they might find in the chamber. "Of course not. My purpose is to find the two people who are missing—my partner and the mayor." He looked at her and smiled. "But if we find something, I may take some pictures if you'll let me."

She returned his smile. "I told Avi we could trust you. I can see it in your eyes."

Zane was relieved to hear her say that. Their trust was mutual, and that was a good thing when going into battle together.

"How did you and Avi meet?" Zane asked.

"Through my father. He pay Avi to do things around our house."

"Did your father set you up?"

She frowned. "I not understand."

Zane realized it was a bad choice of words. "Does your father want the two of you to date romantically?"

Even though she was barely visible in the back glow of her flashlight, Zane could see Maya's face redden.

"My father claim he didn't know Avi well, but I knew there was more."

Zane let a few seconds pass then said, "And?"

She smiled at him. "So over time, Avi and I… we get close." She laughed. "I think that's my dad plan all along."

"I think you should listen to your father. I think—"

"Hey," a voice shouted from somewhere ahead of them.

Avi.

The tunnel had taken a slight turn to the left. As they came around, a cone of light appeared ahead.

Zane and Maya hurried in that direction. As they drew near, Zane realized that Avi was examining something on the tunnel wall.

"I found it," Avi called out.

Zane directed his beam toward the right side of the tunnel. A giant archway appeared in the light. His pulse quickened. It was the archway from Solomon Glaser's photograph. At least thirty feet high, the ancient structure was even more impressive in person.

"It's beautiful," Maya said.

Zane came up beside Avi. He could now see that the arch had been built with sand-colored blocks that were each the size of a refrigerator. It reminded him of the blocks that had been used to construct the pyramids at Giza.

"We have a problem," Avi said.

Zane was about to ask what that was when Avi directed his beam inside the arch. Instead of it being an open passageway, the space was blocked with what appeared to be a giant boulder or slab. Either it had somehow settled there, or it had been placed there on purpose in order to keep out unwanted visitors.

Nathan swore softly.

"All this way and now we can't get in," Esther said.

Zane looked at her. She seemed genuinely frustrated.

Avi turned and faced the others. "To be honest, I have something to confess."

Zane's heart beat a little faster. What information had *he* been holding back?

"I knew the entrance was going to be sealed, but I didn't know how," Avi said. "I expected to find a door of some kind. Not this."

"So what do you suggest we do?" Esther asked.

Avi shrugged. "I think we should—"

"Hey, look at this," Maya called out.

Zane looked in the direction of her voice. She was standing on the right side of the arch, studying one of the stones.

"Something is written on surface," she said after they joined her.

Zane followed her gaze. As she had indicated, a series of letters appeared to be etched in the surface of the rock. Zane was no archaeologist, but the writing looked like Hebrew.

"What does it say?" Zane asked.

Avi leaned closer. "I'm not sure. It's been worn down over time, and it's written in Ivrit Miqra'it."

Zane frowned. "What the hell is that?"

"Sorry, you would say Biblical Hebrew."

"Which is different than the Hebrew you speak?" Zane asked.

"Yes, in some respects. It's similar to the difference between modern English spoken by Americans and the Old English spoken hundreds of years before."

Esther laid a hand on Avi's shoulder. "May I? I can read Biblical Hebrew."

Avi moved out of the way. "By all means."

Esther stepped forward and placed her flashlight in a way that sent the light across the surface of the stone. It was obvious she had worked under these conditions before, because the angle sharpened the shadows in each letter, making them easier to read.

"Interesting," Esther said after studying the script.

"What does it say?" Nathan asked.

"Some of the letters are hard to read, so this is going to be a very loose translation." She moved her lips for a moment before finally reading the words out loud. "To him who would enter the sacred chamber, remember the place of Boaz."

Zane assumed the writer was referring to the Boaz from the book of Ruth. He was vaguely familiar with the story of how the two came together, but he had no idea what that had to do with finding the entrance to a hidden chamber.

"That's it?" Nathan asked.

She looked at him. "Yes, that's it."

"There isn't anything written underneath?"

She leaned closer. "I don't see anything, but I suppose it could've been worn off over time."

"Can you read again, please?" Maya requested.

Esther read the message a second time. As far as Zane could tell, her translation was precisely the same the second time around.

"Is that the Boaz from Ruth?" Nathan asked.

Esther nodded as she continued to study the ancient script.

"There must be more somewhere," Zane said. "That makes no sense."

"No, as far as I can tell, that's it," Esther said.

Nathan looked at Avi. "So what does it mean?"

He shrugged. "I don't have the slightest idea."

"So there was nothing in the information Maya got from her father?" Nathan asked.

Avi shook his head. "I can go through it again, but I don't remember any mention of writing on one of the stones."

"That's it," Esther said, her eyes still glued on the stone. "I think I know what it means."

CHAPTER FORTY

"WE'VE BEEN thinking about this all wrong," Esther said. "We've been focused on the wrong Boaz."

Zane frowned. "There's more than one Boaz in the Bible?"

"Yes, actually, there are at least two," Esther said. "You're already familiar with the man who used his right of kinship to marry Ruth." She paused as if waiting for someone to come up with the other Boaz.

While Zane enjoyed conversations that centered around history and religion, they needed to get to the answer. "So who is the other one?"

Esther held up a finger to make her point. "Not *who* but *what*."

A smile formed on Avi's face. He seemed to understand where she was going, but Zane was still in the dark.

"King Solomon appointed a man named Huram to build the Temple," Esther continued. "When Huram built the portico of the Temple, he placed two pillars, one on either side of the entrance. Let me read you the applicable verses." She looked down at her phone. "*Then he set up the pillars by the vestibule of* the temple; he set up the pillar on the right and called its name Jachin, and he set up the pillar on the left and called its name Boaz. The tops of the pillars were in the shape of lilies. So the work of the pillars was finished."

The group fell silent as each person digested what they had heard.

Zane was the first to speak. "So Boaz was the name of a pillar that was positioned at the front of the Temple?"

Esther nodded.

"So what makes you think it's the same Boaz referred to here?" Zane nodded at the stone.

"Think about it. What are we dealing with right now? We're standing before the entrance to an inner chamber."

Nathan's eyes widened. "Are you trying to say this is the Temple itself?"

She shook her head. "No, I'm just saying the pillars were placed at the entrance to the Temple, and now we're trying to get through an entrance of a different kind."

"I get the two-entrances thing, but how could this reference to Boaz help us get through the arch and into the chamber?" Zane asked. "There are no pillars here, and even if there were—"

"Think about the *position* of each pillar," she said. "Boaz was on the left."

Zane gave her a blank stare.

"I think I know what she's getting at," Avi said. "Whoever wrote that message was saying we need to look on the left side of the arch in order to find our way in."

"Precisely," Esther said. "That's where we'll find our answer."

Zane wasn't convinced of the connection. Then again, he wasn't a biblical scholar. For now, he would trust the curator and not his own intuition.

Esther led them to the other side of the archway. "Let's look for another message," she said.

The group used their flashlights to examine the surface of each stone. They all looked smooth to Zane, devoid of any script. If something was etched in the surface, it was too worn to see.

After several minutes of fruitless examination, everyone gave up.

Zane looked at Esther. "Well, it was a good idea—"

"Maybe this is it," Maya said.

They turned in unison. Maya stood several yards to the left of the arch, examining something on the tunnel wall. From his vantage point, Zane could see only a large, triangular rock. Was something written on it?

They gathered around her, but no one seemed to understand what she was looking at.

"What is it?" Avi asked. "I don't see any writing."

"No, not writing." She pointed her flashlight at the wall. "This rock… it look different than the other ones."

After studying it for a moment, Zane could see what she meant. The triangular rock was a much darker shade than the rest of the tunnel wall. But it wasn't just the color. Even the rock's geologic makeup looked different, like it had been brought there from another place.

"It looks different, but what does it mean?" Nathan asked.

"Maybe to cover something up," Maya suggested.

Esther crouched next to the rock and began sweeping pebbles and dirt away from the base. She looked at Zane. "Take a look at this."

He knelt next to her.

Holding her flashlight with one hand, Esther pointed with the other. "It's been placed on some sort of crude track."

Zane leaned closer. A notch was carved into the base of the rock, and it appeared to be positioned inside an iron track that was mostly obscured by a thin layer of dirt. It was like an ancient version of the track found at the bottom of a sliding glass door.

Zane stood up and stepped back for a better view. The stone blocks of the arch would prevent the triangular rock from being moved to the right.

"Should we try to move it?" Esther asked.

"Give me a hand," Zane said to Nathan. "We need to move it to the left."

After Nathan came over, Zane placed his shoulder against the right edge of the rock. Since he was shorter, Nathan crouched below him and positioned his shoulder against the lower portion.

"You ready?" Zane asked.

Nathan nodded.

"One, two, three."

Using their legs, both men pushed with as much force as they could muster. The track was filled with dirt and tiny pebbles, so it wasn't functioning as smoothly as it had when first built.

"Harder," Zane said through clenched teeth.

Both men groaned loudly as they strained against what seemed like an immovable object.

Zane reached deep to find an extra measure of strength. He knew there was another gear that could be obtained if the desire was strong enough. Athletes knew about it, and he had found it on occasion as well. Unfortunately, the low oxygen levels in the tunnel might make it unattainable.

Then, just as he was about to run out of energy, he felt something shift.

"It's moving," Maya said.

As both men strained with renewed vigor, Avi came over, placed his hands against the rock, and pushed along with them. He was a thin man, but what little strength he had seemed to turn the tide. The rock began moving down the track.

"Don't stop," Zane called out.

All three men continued moving their legs. Zane felt like his femur might snap if he applied any more pressure.

"That's enough," Esther shouted.

The men dropped to the tunnel floor, gulping in deep breaths as their muscles finally relaxed.

"You did it," Maya said.

Still breathing deeply, Zane turned toward the tunnel wall. The rock had been moved about three feet to the left, exposing a dark passageway beyond.

CHAPTER FORTY-ONE

THE PASSAGEWAY WAS more crevice than tunnel. Whoever created the alternate entrance had apparently taken advantage of a natural separation in the rock. Zane guessed the larger gate had been sealed at some point in order to prevent easy access to the chamber.

"It's narrow, but I think we can get through," Maya said.

"Since it was sealed up, I guess that means we were the first ones to arrive," Nathan said.

The Drachen. Zane had almost forgotten they could be close by. He turned to Avi. "Is this the only way into the chamber?"

"Yes."

"So where will the others be coming from?"

Avi pointed to the north. "They'll be coming from that direction."

The tunnel they were in continued north past the archway. As best Zane could tell, no lights or sound came from that direction. They had probably arrived ahead of the *Drachen*, and they needed to take advantage of the time they had been given. "Let's get moving." He pointed his light at the opening. "One at a time."

Maya had the smallest frame, so Zane told her to go first. She could traverse the route more quickly and let them know if she had any problems getting through. If it got too narrow for her, it would obviously be too narrow for them. She would be their canary in the crevice.

If the passageway proved to be a dead end, having that information quickly would allow them to retreat and hide before the *Drachen* arrived.

After Maya entered the crevice, Zane sent the others in behind her. Bringing up the rear would allow Zane to keep an eye on Esther while at the same time guarding their rear flank.

Before following the others in, Zane took one final glance north. A distant *thump* reached his ears. Was the sound some natural occurrence, or was someone coming toward him through the tunnel? He waited but heard only silence. He hoped the noise came from a natural source. If someone spent enough time in tunnels, they would probably hear all sorts of things.

Keeping his pistol out, Zane turned and slipped into the crevice. About ten yards in was a sharp turn to the left followed by another turn to the right. After taking the second turn, he could see the others had stopped just ahead. "What's the problem?" he asked as he came up.

"We've hit a tight spot," Esther said.

Zane looked ahead. Maya was turned sideways as she maneuvered through the tight space. His thoughts went back to the sound out in the tunnel. Once the *Drachen* arrived, they would surely see the opening to the crevice. That would be disastrous.

"We're waiting for her to give the all clear," Esther continued.

"The last thing we need is for all of us to get stuck in there together."

It was the logical approach, yet Zane still didn't like having to remain in place for so long.

A half minute later, Maya's voice echoed back. "I'm through. It look clear over here."

Zane breathed a sigh of relief.

Over the next several minutes, the others wiggled through. Once he received confirmation they had all made it safely to the other side, he turned sideways and entered the narrow space. Zane's large frame barely fit, but he still kept his pistol out. He still didn't trust Esther completely, and he also didn't want to be pinned down if the *Drachen* came up behind him.

A minute later, he stepped out on the other side. Much to his relief, the crevice was wider ahead.

"Let's pick up the pace," Zane said without explaining what he had heard out in the tunnel.

After traveling about fifty yards, Nathan said, "I think we made it."

A few seconds later, the crevice opened into a large space. Everyone stepped out and played their lights around. The darkness seemed to go on forever.

"Is this the chamber?" Esther asked.

Based on the echo of her voice, Zane believed they were standing in a large cavern.

Avi moved his beam back and forth. "It has to be."

"If it is, then there isn't much to it," Nathan said.

Zane made a motion with his flashlight. "Let's keep moving."

The five stepped forward while continuing to cast their beams around. To Zane, the darkness seemed infinite.

"I think I see something," Maya said.

Zane stared directly ahead. There was something at the periphery of his light, but he couldn't tell what it was.

"Come," Maya called out, picking up her pace.

As they followed her, Zane saw the outline of a large structure taking shape. It rose off the cavern floor like a giant stalagmite, but its angles were too straight to be anything natural.

Esther caught her breath. "Oh my…"

Zane felt the hairs on the back of his neck rise as buildings appeared in the light. Small ones that were made of mud and straw. Residential homes from ancient times.

As they continued on, Zane could see other multistory structures towering above the others. It was a city—Jerusalem from another time.

The group stopped about twenty yards out. They stood in silence, soaking in the breathtaking sight that spread out before them. Although the city was smaller and not as well preserved, the ruins reminded Zane of the underground world he and other Delphi operatives had explored underneath Mount Hermon.

Nathan was the first to break the silence. "It looks like some of the buildings are tilted."

Zane could see what he meant. Some of the structures were crushed together while others seemed to have fallen over.

"There have been many earthquakes in Israel over the last several thousand years," Esther noted. "That and the natural movement of tectonic plates must have pushed everything around."

Avi splashed his beam across the nearest homes. "It's so tight I don't see how we're going to get in."

"Let's have a look around," Zane said.

"What exactly are we going to do once we do?" Nathan asked.

"We need to find the Temple vessels before the others get here," Avi said.

"We also need to look for a place to take cover," Zane said. "If and when the *Drachen* arrive, we need to determine whether Amanda and Mayor Cohen are with them. If they are, then getting them back needs to be our first priority."

"I think I see a way in." Maya moved toward a gap between two large columns. *A gate.*

When they arrived, each person pointed their beam into the opening. What appeared to be a wide boulevard bisected the chamber's ruins. Assuming it continued straight, Zane believed the ancient street likely ran to the far end of the cavern. It would allow them to explore the city from one end to the other.

As they continued through the gate, other streets appeared to the right and left. Zane pointed his flashlight down each one. Some were blocked by buildings that had fallen over, while others seemed to continue on for some distance.

"That's a big one," Nathan said.

Zane followed his gaze. A three-story building rose up on the left side of the street. It was so high that it almost kissed the bottom of a stalactite. As best Zane could tell, the structure was in excellent condition.

"I think it's a palace or some official government building," Esther said. "First or second century."

"I think this is a good place to begin our search," Zane said. "Let's split up so that we can cover both sides of the street."

Nathan gestured in the direction they had been walking. "Why don't I see if there's something at the other end?"

Zane nodded.

Avi pointed at a flat building on the right side of the street. "Maya and I can start over there."

Zane looked at Esther. "You and I can take the three-story building." He turned to the others. "We'll keep working on either side of the street until we get to the far end. If we get some unexpected company, then we'll need a place to meet."

Nathan gestured toward the three-story building. "How about there?"

Zane nodded. "Copy that."

Then everyone went their separate ways.

Zane led Esther over to the three-story building. After searching for a couple of minutes, they finally found an entrance on the side.

Once they stepped through the door, Esther turned toward Zane. "So why don't you trust me?"

"What are you talking about?"

She gave a little laugh. "Do you think I'm that stupid? I can see how you look at me."

"We don't have time for this."

"What did I do to make you think that way?"

"All of you seem like nice people, but I've learned to never—"

"I'm not talking about some general caution that you professionals exercise in any given operation. I'm talking about a complete mistrust of someone... me." She pulled out her pistol and held it out. "You want to carry my gun? Will that make you feel safer?"

Zane had to admit it was a bold move, one that might suggest she was innocent. "Like I said, we don't have time to discuss this."

She shook her head. "Don't say I didn't offer."

Zane nodded at a set of steps to the left. "I'll start up top and work my way down. Let me know if you find anything."

Esther walked off but said nothing.

Zane went up the stairs slowly, testing each step before applying all of his weight. They were made of stone, but he couldn't tell if the underlying structure was stable.

Five minutes later, he arrived on the top floor and entered the first room he came to. Other than a few stray rocks and a few pottery shards, there was nothing of any importance. Before exiting, he stepped over to a window that faced the crevice they had come through just minutes before. He turned off his light and set his elbows on the sill.

As he stared out into the darkness, he heard a couple of hard *thumps* downstairs. *Esther.* He wondered if he had been wrong about her all along. Her offer to turn over the pistol seemed sincere, but he still couldn't shake the feeling she was hiding something.

Zane was about to leave the window when the beam of a flashlight flared about a hundred yards away. *The crevice.* Seconds later, two more beams appeared.

The *Drachen* were coming through.

Zane watched the lights. He expected them to remain in place as others came out, but instead, the beams began moving quickly toward the ruins. Whoever was holding the lights was running.

His heart pounding, Zane used the glow of his phone to exit the room and go down the stairs. Now that he knew the structure was sound, he was able to move with greater speed. He would grab Esther then cross the street to warn Avi and Maya.

"Esther," he called out when he reached the bottom floor.

There was only silence.

"Esther," he said, louder.

The stone walls were thick, which meant it was possible she hadn't heard him. Keeping his phone up, Zane began a search of the entire floor. Each time he entered a room, he expected to see Esther standing there, but as he continued on, a stark realization set in—she was gone.

As Zane returned to where he'd started, he remembered how quickly the men had come out of the crevice.

It was almost as though they knew exactly where to go.

It was almost as though someone had tipped them off.

CHAPTER FORTY-TWO

ZANE HAD BLOWN it. There was no other way to put it. Despite his misgivings about Esther, he was the one who had allowed her to accompany them to the chamber. Making matters worse, he had also refused to accept her offer of turning over the pistol. In retrospect, that was an obvious ploy to gain his confidence. She didn't need a pistol. She had armed backup on the way.

But while he was tempted to hunt her down, Zane knew there were more pressing issues at hand. He needed to find Avi and Maya, and he needed to find them fast.

As he exited the building, Zane realized how fortunate he had been. Had he not been looking out of the third-floor window, he wouldn't have seen the men enter the cavern. Esther had likely given away their location, so Zane had no doubt they would've found him.

Now in the alley, he hurried toward the main boulevard. Once there, he would cross over to the flat building and locate Avi and Maya. The three would then head to the other end to find Nathan.

THE CHAMBER

As Zane neared the boulevard, two flashlight beams sliced through the darkness just ahead. He was too late. The attackers had already arrived. Moving to the right side of the alley, he crept up to the corner then leaned forward and looked down the street. The two hostiles were only about forty yards out, and there were more behind them. Zane counted at least a dozen.

The sound of voices soon reached his ears. The two men were talking.

"There it is," one of the men said.

"There is what?" the second man asked.

"That's the building I saw the light in," the first man replied.

Zane swore softly. Apparently, they had seen his flashlight earlier. When he'd arrived on the third floor, he had kept it on for a few seconds before turning it off. And since he was elevated, the light would've been easy to see, even from far away.

Suddenly, the flashlights turned off. Had they seen him? Zane didn't think so but pulled back. He wondered if they were using night vision equipment. Typically, the devices didn't work in places with a complete absence of light, but the flashlights of the other men coming up behind them would likely provide enough illumination for the goggles to function.

"I saw you talking to the boss," one of the men said. "What does she want us to do after we take these people out?"

She? Zane guessed they were referring to Rachel Hammond.

"We're to rendezvous at the east end, the entrance to the chamber."

Entrance to the chamber? Zane considered what the man had just said. They were supposed to be in the chamber already. Did this cavern simply provide access to the actual chamber?

The *thump* of boots came toward the corner where Zane was hiding. He turned and sprinted down the alley. He continued on for two blocks then turned right on a street that ran parallel to the boulevard. Since the *Drachen* were going to gather on the east end of the cavern, he needed to get there and set up before they did.

Zane hated leaving Avi and Maya behind, but there was nothing he could do. Armed with only a pistol, he didn't stand a chance against a dozen mercenaries, particularly ones with automatic weapons and night vision equipment. Confronting them would be an act of suicide.

He could only hope that Avi and Maya had seen the flashlights or heard the men coming. If they had, there was a good chance they could slip away. There were literally hundreds of buildings and other structures to hide in, and Zane doubted the gunmen would take the time to search them all.

It took Zane a full forty-five minutes to reach the other end of the cavern. He had been forced to travel using only the glow of his phone, which slowed him down substantially. In addition, many of the streets had been blocked with boulders and large rocks. On two occasions, he had even been forced to climb over caved-in buildings.

As he neared his destination, Zane saw a glow of light to his right at about the place where he figured the main boulevard ended. It looked as though the *Drachen* had set up lamps at the entrance to the actual chamber.

Zane stood at the brink of an open space. On the far side was what appeared to be an abandoned mud-built house. Before setting out, he put his phone away. The *Drachen* had likely set up a guarded perimeter, which meant he would need to travel using the ambient light from the lamps.

Ten minutes later, he arrived at the house. He went to a door and paused at the threshold. He could hear the distant voices of the people at the *Drachen* camp, but no noise seemed to come from inside the home itself.

Zane was about to slip inside when he heard footsteps approaching. He turned and saw two dark figures rushing toward him out of the darkness. He drew his pistol and aimed it at the one on the right. The shots would give away his position, but he had no choice. He had to defend himself.

The men continued toward him, but strangely, neither seemed armed.

When they were about ten yards away, Zane saw that one of the men was bald and the other was slight of frame. *Nathan and Avi.*

Zane lowered his gun. "You two about got yourselves killed."

"Sorry," Nathan whispered. "We saw you move across the open space, but there was no good way to get your attention. There are armed men everywhere."

Zane suddenly realized one person was missing. "Where is Maya?"

"I don't know," Avi said. "We split up while searching the first building. I heard some men enter and was forced to escape through a window. I thought I heard her run off through the darkness, but I could never find her."

It was good that he had heard her run off.

"She's probably hiding somewhere," Zane said. "Once the *Drachen* leave, we'll find her."

Avi nodded but said nothing. Clearly, he was deeply troubled by his friend's disappearance.

"Let me check the house first," Zane said.

As the others waited outside, Zane entered the house with his pistol raised. Because the interior was dark, it took him several minutes to clear all of the rooms. Once he was done, he called Nathan and Avi inside then led them to a window that faced the activity at the east end of the cavern. The house was positioned atop a mound of rubble, affording a good view of the surrounding area.

Zane studied the scene below. Thirty or forty people were gathered around a crevice at the base of the wall. He assumed the entrance to the chamber was located at the back of the crevice. Zane also noticed that about three-quarters of the people were dressed in hooded robes.

"What are they doing?" Nathan whispered.

"They're probably setting up a camp. Once that's done, then they'll start searching the buildings."

"Why aren't they searching the buildings?"

Zane suddenly remembered that neither of the men knew what was going on. "This isn't the chamber," he said.

Avi frowned. "What do you mean?"

Zane told them what the two mercenaries had said earlier.

"So the Temple treasures aren't here?" Nathan asked.

Zane shook his head. "Not according to what I heard. That doesn't mean they're right, but it would make sense that the relics would be kept in a smaller place."

"So where is the chamber?" Avi asked.

Zane nodded toward the gathering of people at the base of

the wall. "Down there somewhere. Probably at the back of the crevice."

"I'm just surprised I never heard about there being two entrances," Avi said.

"It's probably something your elders kept to themselves," Zane said. "I would imagine some of the instructions were passed down orally. If you don't write something down, then it can't be stolen. The message Esther deciphered was another example. That wasn't in the instructions either."

"So how would they know about a second entrance?" Avi asked.

To Zane, the answer was obvious. "They must have found a way to force it out of the mayor."

Avi's expression darkened.

"Speaking of Cohen, isn't that him on the right?" Nathan asked.

Zane followed his gaze. Three people stood apart from the crowd—two men and one woman. The woman had dark hair and glasses. *Rachel Hammond.* Even from a distance, Zane could tell that it was her.

His gaze shifted to the two men. One of them held a rifle, and he seemed to be guarding the other man, who was wearing a dress shirt. Nathan was right—it had to be Cohen.

"Do you see Maya anywhere?" Avi asked.

"No, and that's a good sign," Zane said. "Like I said, there are a million places to hide in here, especially for someone so small. They'll never find her."

"I think something is happening," Nathan said.

Zane turned, and the robed disciples were moving quickly

away from the wall. Most of them entered a small building a short distance away, while others crouched behind large boulders.

"What are they doing?" Avi asked.

Zane noticed three men had stayed behind at the mouth of the crevice. A minute later, they, too, turned and jogged off. One of the men seemed to be holding an electronic device in one hand.

"Strange," Nathan whispered.

As the men entered the small house, Zane realized what was about to happen. "Get down!" he shouted.

All three ducked below the sill. Several seconds later, a thunderous boom shook the cavern. The house shook so violently that Zane thought it might come down on top of them.

Avi looked at Zane. "What's happening?"

"Apparently, the chamber entrance was blocked like the other one."

As the sound faded, Zane stuck his head above the sill and looked toward the crevice. A cloud of smoke filled the east end of the cavern, blotting out most of the light. As the smoke cleared, the three men came out of the house to inspect their handiwork.

Over the next several minutes, the others came out and moved toward the entrance. Zane wondered if the blast had been successful.

Nathan pointed. "Is that…?"

Avi caught his breath.

Zane caught more movement. An armed guard had just

marched into the lamplight, his rifle pressed into the back of a woman walking in front of him. Zane's heart moved into his throat. The woman had a slight frame and red hair.

Maya.

Even though they were at least a hundred yards away, he knew it was her. The slight frame. The red hair.

"Bastards," Avi said as he attempted to climb out.

Zane grabbed his arm. "Wait. All you'll do is get both of you killed."

"I can't just sit here."

"Yes, you can." Zane held his arm tightly. "I promise we'll get her back."

Rachel Hammond came out to meet the guard and his captive. The man shoved Maya forward. Not expecting the shove, she went sprawling on the ground.

Rachel said something to the guard, who stepped back.

"We have to do something," Avi said. "We can't just let—"

"Quiet," Zane hissed.

Rachel approached Maya, grabbed her hair, then yanked her onto her feet. The young Israeli girl cried out. Zane could feel Avi start to move, so he laid a hand on his shoulder.

Still holding her hair, Rachel pulled Maya out to the periphery of the light.

"I think Avi is right," Nathan said. "We need to do something."

Zane held up a hand. "I've been in these situations before. Give it some more time."

Facing the ruins, Rachel drew a pistol.

Zane tensed. Had he been wrong? Was she about to execute Maya right before their very eyes?

Rachel called out in a loud voice. "I know you're out there, and I know you're watching. You have ten seconds to come out, or the girl dies."

It wasn't what Zane had expected, but it beat the alternative of seeing Maya shot right away. He thought about possible responses and quickly realized there weren't any good ones.

"Ten," Rachel shouted.

Rachel lifted the muzzle of the pistol and placed it against the back of Maya's head.

"Nine."

Avi looked at Zane. "Do something. If you don't, I will."

"Eight."

He was right. There was only one real option, and he would be the one to take it.

Zane stood and placed his leg over the sill.

"What are you doing?" Nathan asked.

"Seven."

Zane dropped outside the house. "You two stay here. They may not know how many of us there are. They tried to kill me before, so it's possible that getting me will be enough."

"Seven," Rachel shouted.

Zane dropped his gun and began walking toward Rachel.

"Six."

As he went into the light, Zane held his hands in the air. "I'm here. Don't shoot."

CHAPTER FORTY-THREE

RACHEL SMILED BROADLY as Zane approached her. He had seen her smile once or twice before, but those expressions looked nothing like the one spread across her face now. This wasn't a smile that conveyed humor or happiness. It was a wicked smile of triumph.

The kind administrative assistant that Zane had known before was actually a cruel woman used to getting her way. Zane knew without a doubt she would have no trouble putting a bullet in his forehead. He needed to make sure she never had that opportunity.

This had to be a satisfying moment for her, he thought. Clearly, her order was responsible for the museum heist, which meant she had also probably given the order to have Zane assassinated. That operation had failed horribly, something that had to be a source of embarrassment for Rachel. But the tide had turned, and she would enjoy the sweet fragrance of revenge.

When Zane was about twenty feet away, Rachel gestured for him to stop. "It's nice to see you again."

"I can't say the feeling is mutual."

She laughed. "I'm sure it isn't."

He nodded at Maya, who was still on her knees. "I'm here, so let her go."

Rachel looked down at her prisoner. "Go where? This pathetic little thing would get lost trying to find her way out."

"Then it won't hurt to let her go."

Rachel was about to respond when her eyes seemed to fix on something over Zane's shoulder. Hearing footsteps approaching, he turned his head to the right and saw someone in his peripheral vision. Was it one of the guards?

"Avi Yosef," Rachel said. "What an unexpected surprise."

Avi. Zane felt like he had been punched in the gut. Why had he come out?

"What do you think you're doing?" Zane whispered as Avi joined him.

"I had to come," he said. "She would have killed Maya if I didn't."

"You should have given me a chance to work something out."

"There is no dealing with this woman."

Zane was about to reply but was cut off by a loud grumble that seemed to come up from the earth below. As the ominous sound continued, the cavern began to shake. The bomb had triggered a tremor. Zane had been through two earthquakes in his life, so he recognized the intense vibrations immediately.

As the shaking continued, Zane saw something in Rachel's eyes he hadn't seen before—fear. She knew her explosives had triggered the movement underneath them, and she also had to know they were in an unstable pocket beneath a city.

Despite the obvious danger the tremor posed, Zane wondered if it might just be their ticket to freedom. Once the cavern began to collapse, then it would be every man for himself. At that point, even Rachel would focus on making it out alive.

But just as Zane thought things might play out in their favor, the tremors slowly subsided. For now, it appeared as though the cavern would hold.

Her face showing signs of relief, Rachel said something to one of the armed mercenaries, who went to Zane and shoved him forward. This was it. There would be a quick series of executions. First Zane then the other two after him.

"I had planned on having a little fun," Rachel said. "But in light of what just happened, I think it's best we end this thing quickly."

Zane knew he needed to buy some time. "You know, I find this all very interesting."

Rachel's brow furrowed slightly. "You find what interesting?"

"The Rachel Hammond I met a few days ago had a moral compass and strong sense of decency." He allowed that to sink in for a moment. "I guess I just find it interesting that the real-life version is so paranoid. Afraid, even." He smiled.

"Afraid?" Rachel laughed. "I don't fear anything, certainly not you."

"If you didn't fear me, then you wouldn't have sent a team of assassins across the Atlantic to kill me," Zane said. "Did you tremble a little when you heard I had survived? Did you break out in a cold sweat when you heard we killed those incompetent goons in Bulgaria?"

Rachel's expression darkened. It was clear she wasn't going

to be humiliated in front of her people. She lifted her pistol and aimed it at his head. "Let's do this like the movies. Any last wishes before I turn out the lights?"

"Actually, I do have one," Zane said.

In truth, he had no idea what he was going to say. It was just another attempt to buy some time. He thought about rushing her. If he moved quickly enough, he might be able to take her by surprise. He would dive for her legs, which would make it difficult for her to hit him in the head or the upper torso. The guards would be hesitant to shoot in fear of hitting their leader.

As Zane prepared to act, he caught movement behind Rachel. About thirty yards away, one of the hooded disciples was hiking up their robe. What were they doing?

Zane tried to get a few more seconds. "If we're doing it like the movies, can I get a cigarette?"

"Sorry, I'm all out," she answered.

Behind her, the hooded figure pulled a pistol from under their robe, lifted it, and began to fire.

CHAPTER FORTY-FOUR

RACHEL DOVE TO the ground at the first crack of gunfire. It was an instinctive act that had come from years of living in a world of crime and violence. As her shoulder hit the hard surface, she heard two more *pops*, then the cavern went dark.

The lamps.

The shooter had taken out the two large lamps that had been set up to light the area.

But who was firing the gun? The shots had come from behind her. As far as she remembered, that was the same place where her disciples had gathered. Had one of them gone rogue? Had they been unable to stomach an execution? No, that wasn't it. Someone had infiltrated their ranks.

Another burst of gunfire rang out, and this time, it came from another direction. Pandemonium broke out among the crowd. People ran in every direction, screaming and yelling. If the shooter had wanted to create chaos, they had certainly succeeded.

Realizing she might get trampled, Rachel rose to her feet. As she stood, flashlights flicked on from several places, their beams crisscrossing the cavern like the dance floor of a nightclub.

Remembering the captives, she removed her flashlight and turned it on. She swept the beam in a wide arc, but there was no one around her. The red-haired girl was already gone, as was Zane Watson. They had probably fled the moment the lights went out. She cursed under her breath. Once again, the operative had escaped her grasp. But his escape wouldn't last long. She had left guards at the exit just in case something like this happened, and she had told them to shoot on sight if anyone tried to get out. One way or the other, the quarry would die.

Rachel considered her next move. All hell had broken out, but that didn't mean she had to abandon her plan. It just needed to be altered slightly. With her enemies on the run, she still had time to lead a small team into the chamber. They would grab as many of the treasures as they could and take them to the surface.

Three shots sounded close by. Rachel turned off her flashlight and ran toward the crevice where the entrance to the chamber was located. As she drew near, three of her guards appeared as a flashlight beam swept past them. They were kneeling in front of the tunnel mouth, guarding the entrance to the chamber.

Perfect.

"It's me," she yelled on approach.

Seeing her, the three men lowered their weapons.

"Follow me," Rachel barked.

Two of them stood, but the other remained in place.

Rachel looked at him. "*All three.* Let's go."

He stared at her as if debating whether to defy her order. "Our people are getting shot. I need to stay and—"

"No, you don't." Rachel lifted her pistol and shot him in the face.

The man slumped forward, dead before he hit the cavern floor.

Apparently, he forgot who was in charge.

As if eager not to suffer the same fate, the remaining two guards followed her into the dark tunnel without protest.

Once inside, Rachel realized it wasn't going to be as easy as she'd thought. Piles of debris, which included rocks with sharp edges, littered the tunnel floor. They were forced to move slowly, and it took them five minutes to reach the far end of the tunnel. Once there, Rachel took several steps into the open space.

The chamber.

She shivered with excitement.

As they continued into the room, Rachel began to cough, as did the two guards. The smoke from the bombs had mostly dissipated in the larger chamber, but it was thicker here in the confined space.

Her lungs burning, Rachel ran the beam of her flashlight clockwise around the room. At first, she saw nothing. The chamber seemed to be a much smaller version of the cavern they had just left. Then, as the beam reached the far side of the space, she saw a shiny metallic surface that flashed for a brief instant.

Gold.

"Did you see that?" one of the guards asked.

"Yes," Rachel said softly, her eyes riveted on the spot.

Intent on finding the source, they marched across the open expanse. The smoke cleared slightly as they went, allowing

Rachel to see that a large alcove had been carved into the far wall. It was approximately ten feet in height and thirty feet wide.

The gold. That's where it is.

As they reached the mouth of the alcove, Rachel swept her beam across the interior. She felt a rush of adrenaline as countless relics appeared in the light. Vases, decorative boxes, and other small items were piled in every direction. There were dozens if not hundreds of items, all of them undoubtedly tied to the Temple. But as Rachel studied the items carefully, she saw only muted colors. There was no sign of the gold they had seen before.

"I think I see something." The guard to Rachel's left had his beam trained on something at the back.

Rachel set her gaze in that direction. A stone altar was set against the alcove's rear wall.

If there's an altar, then there must be something on it.

Rachel moved her beam up until it illuminated what appeared to be a large square box. It was covered with centuries of dust and dirt, giving it an unremarkable appearance. But as she moved her light to the right, she saw a small patch of shiny gold.

Her curiosity aroused, she moved the beam to the right. A pole protruded from the side of the box, near the top. It was a pole someone might hold onto in order to lift the box.

The hairs on the back of her neck stood on end.

She illuminated the top of the box. A figure was affixed to the lid. As she splashed the beam across it, the distinctive shape of a wing appeared. The wing pointed toward the center of the box.

"My heavens," Rachel whispered.

One of the guards looked at her. "Is that...?"

"Yes... yes it is."

The Ark of the Covenant.

A jolt of excitement shook through Rachel's body as the magnitude of the moment hit her. This was the pinnacle of all finds, the greatest relic in the history of humankind. And it was hers. All hers.

Many wanted to find the ark because of the riches it would bring. Rachel knew there were people who would pay an unfathomable amount of money for it. But money wasn't what drove her. This was about power. Power over the Middle East. Power over Israel. It might even give her power over the entire planet. The Scriptures made it clear that whoever possessed the ark couldn't be defeated in battle.

Another volley of gunshots sounded in the distance, bringing Rachel back to the present. Finding the ark would do her no good unless they could get it back to the surface. Once it was hidden away under heavy guard, they could return and search for whatever else might be here. The giant menorah. The altar of incense.

Rachel turned to the two men. "Go get it and bring it out."

One of the men looked toward the ark then back at her. "Shouldn't we get one of the hand trucks—"

Rachel lifted her pistol and pointed it at his head. "There isn't time. Go!"

He didn't need to be told twice. The two stepped into the alcove, winding their way through the piles of relics and rubble.

"Hurry," Rachel barked.

As they neared the back of the alcove, the floor began to shake under her feet. Another tremor had started up, and it was as intense as the one before.

A *crack* sounded overhead. Rachel looked over her shoulder. At first, she thought it was a gunshot but then realized it was something more troubling: the sound of rocks splitting apart.

Turning back to the alcove, she saw the men standing in front of the ark. They were crouched down, trying to maintain their balance as the tremors continued.

The fools. Waiting would only make things worse.

"Bring it out now," she shouted.

Heeding her command, each man went to one end of the ark. After a brief exchange of words, each one slid his flashlight into his shirtsleeve. Rachel could see what they were doing. It would give them light without actually having to hold onto anything.

Both guards lifted their arms and stepped toward the ark. The guard on the right grabbed the poles on his end first, followed by the other one.

A moment later, a loud *pop* sounded in the alcove.

Rachel stiffened.

Brilliant bolts of light flared across the box. They sparkled and flashed like something from another world.

Rachel watched in horror as the bolts coalesced into balls that rolled down the poles. Frightened, the two men tried to pull free, but their hands seemed held in place by an unseen force.

Rachel's mouth opened in shock.

When balls of light reached the end of the pole, they jumped onto the defenseless men. Bloodcurdling screams came out of their mouths. The men writhed in pain as jolts of electricity surged through their bodies.

As Rachel watched the men twist in torment, the name Uzzah flashed in her mind.

Where had she heard it before?

She tried to focus her thoughts, but the answer seemed to dance just beyond her reach.

Then it hit her. The name came straight from the pages of the Bible. It was a story she had read many times while researching the ark and the mercy seat. King David and his men had placed the ark on a cart to take it to Jerusalem. Along the way, one of the oxen stumbled, threatening to tip the ark off the cart. Uzzah reached out to steady it, a violation of God's strict prohibition on touching the sacred chest. The Bible said the man was struck dead on the spot.

Rachel shuddered. The same thing was playing out right in front of her, and there was nothing she could do to stop it.

A moment later, the screaming ended, and both men sank to the ground.

Rachel waited for a few seconds then stepped gingerly into the alcove. She needed to make sure the ark was still intact. If it was, she would figure out a way to remove the relic without touching it.

As she made her way forward, the smell of charred flesh reached her nostrils. She felt a wave of nausea hit her but continued on. Nothing would stop her from finding out what had happened.

Once she was five feet away, Rachel trained her beam on the

face of the guard on the left. White eyes stared back at her from a soot-black head. A tendril of smoke rose from the crispy skin.

Rachel felt a column of vomit rise in her throat.

Covering her mouth, she turned and ran.

CHAPTER FORTY-FIVE

ZANE CAME TO a stop as they crossed the chapel.

"What's wrong?" Maya asked in a low voice.

Just a moment before, Zane was certain he had heard the faint sound of footsteps somewhere out in the synagogue. Had the *Drachen* posted more guards to prevent them from getting away? Had the police somehow learned there had been a break-in?

Zane turned toward Avi, Maya, and Nathan, who were standing behind him. "Stay here."

His first priority was to get the current group out safely. Only then would he go back to the cavern to search for Amanda and Ariel Cohen. He still held out hope that both had survived the mayhem. When Zane and the others had slipped out through the crevice, the tremors had reached a crescendo. Stalactites were falling, a sign that the entire structure might cave in. The quake seemed to subside as they left, but there was no guarantee that any left behind had survived.

Pistol in hand, he slipped out of the chapel and entered the first room on the left. He swept his flashlight around the space.

There was a desk, two bookshelves, and a small table in the corner. Scattered across the table were photographs of a man and his family. Zane guessed the man was the rabbi.

Seeing nothing out of the ordinary, he returned to the hall and entered the remaining rooms one at a time. All were empty. As he exited the last room, Zane wondered if he had been hearing things. He and the others had been deprived of adequate oxygen for several hours. That coupled with the clouds of smoke inside the main cavern could have impaired his senses.

Even so, he continued on. He needed to make sure they weren't walking into an ambush.

After entering the sanctuary, Zane saw that the body of the Hakham was still sprawled atop a massive pool of dried blood. The authorities hadn't arrived yet. After stepping around the body, he made his way down the portico on the left, clearing the pews one more time. Save for the bodies of the two mercenaries, they were empty.

Zane returned to the front of the sanctuary then went up the steps to the chancel. He checked behind the podium and the table containing the Torah scrolls. Finding nothing, he decided he had done all he could. It was time to go back and get the others. If he had heard steps, it was someone leaving ahead of them. He hoped it was Amanda and the mayor.

Upon returning to the chapel, Zane found the others huddled in the corner, whispering.

"All clear," Zane said. "I'm going to escort you out."

"Then what?" Avi asked.

"I'm going to come back. We still have two missing."

"Are you sure that's the smart thing to do?" Nathan asked.

"You look pale. We all need to recharge. Let the police go in."

"Amanda is my partner and my friend. I'll never leave her behind." Before they could protest, Zane took out his burner phone and handed it to Nathan. "Take this. There's no signal down there, so it won't do me any good. Amanda has my number memorized, so if she can get her hands on a phone, I'm sure she'll call."

Nathan nodded and took it from him.

"I also want you to call the authorities just in case someone else hasn't."

Zane led them to the sanctuary and across the transept. As they entered the hall on the other side, Zane realized he hadn't cleared the rooms there. He would do it as soon as the others were safely outside.

"Why don't I go with you?" Nathan suggested as they reached the rear exit. "Avi and Maya can call the police while you and I—"

"No, I need you to stay here with them. I appreciate the offer, but you'll only slow me down."

Nathan hesitated then nodded. "I suppose you're right."

Zane opened the door and led them outside. After making sure there were no hostiles waiting, he wished them well and reentered the building. After clearing the rooms he had missed earlier, Zane tucked his pistol in his waistband and sprinted back through the synagogue. Speed would be his primary focus. If Amanda and the mayor were trapped, they might not have long to survive.

When Zane entered the chapel, he came to an abrupt halt. A dark figure came toward him from the other end, having just emerged from the secret stairwell.

As the person drew near, their features came into view.

A woman.

Her height and general size seemed familiar. He frowned. "Amanda, is that you?"

The woman stopped about ten yards out. She had dark-brown hair that was pulled back in a ponytail.

Zane's body tensed as he realized who it was.

Esther.

Having focused on other things, he hadn't thought about the possibility that their paths might cross.

Her eyes were fixed with a steely gaze. She was going to kill him

Zane reached for his gun, but her pistol was already up. Even a child wouldn't miss from where she stood. If she pulled the trigger, he would die.

Having no other choice, he held up both hands in surrender.

Ignoring his act of submission, Esther fired twice.

CHAPTER FORTY-SIX

"MAYA, I THINK Nathan is getting hungry," Avi shouted in Hebrew.

Nathan shook his head. "Don't listen to him. I said no such thing."

"Believe me, I know who the impatient one is," Maya called out from the kitchen. "Avi gets grumpy when he's hungry. But don't worry. It's almost ready."

"Avi has just told me what a good cook you are, so I have no doubt it's worth waiting for," Nathan said.

"To be honest, I wouldn't even call it cooking," Maya said. "Let's just say I put a few things together."

The impromptu party had been arranged quickly. Maya lived in a small studio, so Avi had offered to host the gathering. His condominium was small, but it was nicely decorated, and its seventh-floor balcony offered stunning views of west Jerusalem.

Avi had come up with the idea. The group had formed a bond during the events of the last few days, and he feared they would all lose touch unless they got together. He wanted to celebrate all they had accomplished as well as the new friendships that had formed. He also hoped the dinner would help relieve the stress each person carried with them.

Nathan had another sip of wine as he took in the view through the floor-to-ceiling glass. Like a necklace of expensive jewels, the night-lights of Jerusalem sprayed in a circle around them. The city was getting back to normal, most of its inhabitants unaware of what had just taken place in the subterranean world beneath their feet.

"It still seems like a dream," Avi said, breaking the silence.

"Yes, it does," Nathan said.

"I still remember the moment I took Maya into my arms," Avi said, his eyes glistening with emotion. "I don't think I've ever been more relieved in my entire life."

"And I'm sure she feels the same way."

Like Avi, Nathan remembered that moment inside the cavern vividly. He could still picture Rachel lifting the gun and pointing it at Zane's head. Although he was too far away to hear what was being said, Nathan knew he was about to witness an execution. But then something completely unexpected happened. Shots rang out, but they hadn't come from Rachel's gun. Someone—Amanda, Nathan would later learn—was firing in order to take out the large lamps.

Before the cavern went dark, Nathan saw Avi running toward Maya. Not knowing what to do, he waited. He had almost given up when Avi showed up with Maya. The three then made their way out using back streets and alleys.

"The first course is ready." Maya came out of the kitchen with small, empty plates. She placed one in front of each man.

"It's not much, but I hope you like it."

"You always say it isn't much, and it's always perfect," Avi said.

Smiling, Maya returned to the kitchen then emerged a minute later holding a tray of hors d'oeuvres. "There is much more on the way, but this is a little something to get you started."

"Did you make your famous potato knish?" Avi asked.

"Not tonight," Maya said. "I guess you'll just have to suffer."

"It looks fabulous," Nathan said as she held the tray in front of him.

Maya nodded at the cold meats that were neatly stacked in rows. "You didn't mention being a vegetarian, so I put a little charcuterie together." She nodded at the snacks on the other side. "And these are feta and cucumber tapas."

As Nathan transferred several of the items to his plate, the doorbell rang.

Avi stood from his leather chair and headed down the hall. "The others are here."

"I'll get the wine," Maya said.

Nathan heard the front door open. Moments later, the sound of excited conversation carried down the hall. One of the guests was a man with a deep voice, and the other was a woman. Nathan smiled when he realized who it was.

A half minute later, Avi emerged with the two guests in tow. One was a tall man with long hair.

The man who escaped death.

***

Zane was finally starting to feel like a normal person again. After almost losing his life two nights before, the operative had endured two straight days of intense questioning by Israeli authorities, the FBI, and his own boss, Dr. Alexander Ross. He had just awakened from a three-hour nap, which was the first satisfying sleep he had experienced in days. He hoped it would allow him to enjoy this time with the others before flying out in the morning.

Nathan stood. "It's good to see you."

Maya came out of the kitchen. "Welcome. We're so happy you here."

"And it's an honor to be here," Amanda said.

After hugs and handshakes, Maya looked at her guests. "How about wine? It's wonderful cabernet sauvignon from Galilee."

Zane found her broken English endearing. "Why not?"

Amanda smiled. "Yes, please."

As Maya departed for the kitchen, Nathan looked at Zane. "I see you survived all the questioning today."

"It *was* a little intense." Zane nodded at Amanda. "It always helps smooth things over when your partner rescues the mayor of Jerusalem."

Amanda had shared her story with Zane over dinner the night before. She went into great detail, describing all that had taken place, from the moment they parted ways at the Western Wall Plaza until the moment they were reunited. The tale was so astonishing that it seemed like something right out of the pages of a major Hollywood film.

After escaping from captivity, Amanda had managed to

overpower one of the female disciples. Before tying the woman up, Amanda took her gun and her hooded robe. Attempting to infiltrate the *Drachen* in disguise had been a risky move. Amanda told Zane she would likely have been discovered had they not been operating in the dark tunnels beneath Jerusalem.

Perhaps due to the darkness, she didn't see the mayor until after the explosive device had been detonated. As the group reassembled under the large lamps, she noticed him standing a short distance away. His wrists were bound, but his legs were not. At that moment, a plan formed in her mind. She would shoot out the lights, which would give her the opportunity to grab the mayor and lead him to the surface.

As she waited for the right moment to launch her plan, one of the guards brought in a red-haired woman. Amanda watched as Rachel used the girl to draw Zane and Avi out of hiding. The timing couldn't have been more perfect. Shooting out the lights would give her the chance to whisk Ariel Cohen to safety, and it would also give Zane and Avi a chance to escape.

According to Amanda, the convergence of events hadn't been a coincidence. It had all been part of a providential plan. From the moment she had been captured, she had prayed that God would get them all out safely, and that was exactly what had happened.

Zane wasn't a spiritual person, but he had to admit the entire story was nothing short of miraculous.

"I know all of Jerusalem is thankful for both of you," Nathan said.

Zane bowed slightly. "We're just happy that everyone made it out alive."

Amanda moved toward the sliding glass door. "What a view."

"Thank you," Avi said with a smile. "I've found that if I sit here long enough, it will drain all the stress right out of me."

"Don't say that," Zane said. "We might not ever leave."

"You're more than welcome to stay as long as you'd like."

Maya returned with a bottle of wine. After pouring everyone a glass, she turned to Zane. "I'll be right back. Our special guest has been napping. She told me to wake her up when you arrived."

"I was just going to ask you if she was here," Zane said.

After Maya disappeared down the hall, Amanda looked at Zane and whispered, "You didn't tell me *she* was going to be here."

"It was never a sure thing. Avi told me there was a chance. She was pretty shaken up."

"I can imagine."

A minute later, Maya emerged from the hall. Behind her was a brown-haired woman who walked with a limp.

"You can see our patient is still not one hundred percent," Maya said. "But at least she got some rest."

The brown-haired woman broke away from Maya and limped toward Zane.

"So you are alive," Zane said.

Esther Navon smiled broadly. "I'll be fine. How are you?"

"I'm doing well." Zane put a hand on her shoulder. "And I have you to thank for that."

"To be honest, I didn't know I had it in me."

Zane stepped forward, and the two embraced. Squeezing her

hard, Zane enjoyed the moment. The two hadn't spent any time together since she'd saved his life in the synagogue.

As the two held each other, Zane's thoughts went back to that fateful night. He remembered Esther coming toward him in the chapel, a pistol clutched in both hands. Her grip was surprisingly steady, and he knew she wouldn't miss from such close range.

After Esther fired twice, Zane braced for the impact. He had never been shot in the chest or the head, but he hoped it would be quick and painless. A shot to the forehead would bring about instant death, and a shot directly to the heart would bring death in seconds.

Much to his surprise, he didn't feel anything at all. No burning sensation. No punch. No pain at all.

And then it hit him. He hadn't been shot.

In the seconds that followed, Zane heard a *thump* behind him. It was a sound he had heard many times—a body hitting the floor. Taking a quick look behind him, Zane saw a figure lying facedown. Even in the dim light, he knew who it was. *Rachel.*

Sensing Zane was shocked and confused, Esther then explained all that had happened, beginning at the moment the two of them had parted ways inside the three-story building. While searching one of the rooms, Esther had discovered a hidden stairwell behind a crumbling wall. Thinking a basement might be a good place to store relics, she decided to check it out. As she neared the bottom of the stairs, she lost her footing and fell the rest of the way, hitting her head and blacking out. When she finally came to, she discovered she had twisted her ankle.

The fall had also broken her flashlight.

After resting for a few minutes, she got up and felt her way back up the steps. By the time she reached the ground floor, she realized Zane was gone. She also saw the area was crawling with armed mercenaries.

Fearing for her life and realizing she couldn't help the others, Esther decided to return to the surface. After sneaking past two armed mercenaries the *Drachen* had left at the cavern entrance, she slipped out into the tunnel and began the journey back using the light from her phone. Just before reaching the stairs to the synagogue, she blacked out again. She wasn't sure how long she was unconscious, but after awakening, she was able to make her way up the stairwell.

When she entered the chapel, Zane was coming in on the other side. She also saw a woman sneaking up behind him. That woman was Rachel Hammond. Even though it was dark, Esther could see that Rachel was about to use a pistol to shoot Zane in the back.

Zane figured out the rest of the story himself. He *had* heard footsteps in the synagogue after all. Rachel had arrived at the synagogue first and had likely heard the others coming up behind her. She found a place to hide that allowed her to see Zane and the others exit the building. Realizing it would be foolish to attack four people, she had probably remained in place until she saw Zane come back in alone. That was when she formed the plan to sneak up behind and shoot him.

"Do you trust me now?" Esther asked as the two pulled apart.

He smiled. "With my life."

"Okay, I need a hug too," Amanda said.

After the two embraced, Maya gave Esther a glass of wine.

Avi gestured toward the couch and seats. "Please, everyone sit down."

Nathan looked at Zane and Esther after they were all seated. "So tell us what happened with Rachel in the chapel. We still haven't heard the whole story."

Zane wasn't surprised that they were still in the dark. The police had arrived at the synagogue not long after Zane and Esther emerged from the building. Once the scene was secured, the entire group was separated in order for the police to conduct preliminary interviews. Since that night, the group had exchanged a few calls and texts, but there had never been a full recounting of all that had taken place.

Esther looked at Zane. "I'm still groggy from my nap. Why don't you tell them?"

Zane spent the next five minutes describing what had happened after he left them at the rear of the building.

"So where did Rachel come from?" Maya asked. "You checked the whole place."

"I guess we'll never know," Zane said. "She's not a large person, so she could've easily squeezed behind something. There's also a second floor, although I can't remember where the stairs were."

"She may have been in the sanctuary," Avi said. "I noticed there was some upper-level seating above the portico."

Zane frowned. "How do you get up there?"

"The stairs are probably in the narthex."

"Wherever she was, I blew it," Zane said.

"Don't be silly," Amanda said. "It would have taken hours to search the whole building. You did what you could. The bottom line is you got everyone out safe."

Avi looked at Esther. "How did you know it was Rachel in the chapel? It was pretty dark in there."

"There was enough light coming in from the hall to see her face. But to be honest, I was never one hundred percent sure. All I know is that some woman was pointing a pistol at Zane, and I wasn't going to let him get killed."

Silence fell over the room. Avi plucked a tapas from his plate and popped it into his mouth. Zane took another sip of wine.

Esther turned to Zane. "Did you ever figure out what she said that night? I was hoping you might remember something after things settled down. Sometimes our mind works in funny ways."

"No, I didn't. What about you?"

She shook her head.

Nathan sat forward in his chair. "Rachel said something? I thought you told us she died immediately."

"I don't think I ever used the word *immediately*," Zane said. "She took two shots to her chest and one to her abdomen. She was alive for almost a minute."

"What did she say?" Avi asked.

Zane nodded at Esther, an indication he wanted her to answer. After all, she had heard Rachel's final words better than he had.

"When Zane and I went over to her, I thought she was dead. Then I saw her lips moving, like she was trying to tell me something. So I leaned in close and asked her to repeat herself.

That's when I heard her say, *'It's there. It's there."*

"What did she mean by that?" Nathan asked.

"I asked her, and to be honest, I don't remember her exact words. It was something like *'It was there... I saw it. It was in the...'* The last word was hard to hear, but I think she said 'chamber.'" Esther paused for a moment. "I assume she meant the actual chamber, the smaller one."

Nathan frowned. "She saw something there?"

"That's what it sounded like."

Avi's brow knit together. "I didn't know she went in."

"What do you think she saw?" Maya asked.

Esther shrugged. "We don't know, and I guess we never will."

"At some point, we'll find out," Nathan said. "They're probably searching the chamber as we speak."

"No, they aren't," Zane said. "The chamber won't be searched for a while, if ever. The entire area has been closed off."

"Why?" Nathan asked. "They need to send a team of archaeologists down there. There is no telling what they might find."

"I spoke to a friend of mine in law enforcement," Esther said. "A team of police officers and emergency personnel were sent to look for survivors. They were able to enter the large cavern, but they soon discovered that most of it had caved in. At least that's what he told me. Anyway, there are no plans to go back, because the entire area is unstable."

"Sad," Nathan said.

"Even if it was stable, I seriously doubt they would send in archaeologists," Amanda said. "The cavern and the chamber are located just north of the Temple Mount, which puts it in disputed territory. If word ever got out that Israeli archaeologists were underneath the Dome of the Rock digging around for relics, then there would be an uprising of epic proportions."

Maya looked at Esther. "So what do *you* think she saw?"

Esther shrugged then took a sip of wine before answering. "First of all, we don't know if she was even telling the truth. If she was, then I'd say she probably saw one of the vessels that was used in the Temple. After all, that's what the chamber was supposedly used for."

Maya pressed her. "Like what?"

Esther shrugged again. "There are so many. There's the copper psachter, which was used to remove excess ashes from the altar. Maybe one of the oil pitchers that was used to light the menorah." She hesitated then said, "Who knows, maybe she saw one of the menorah."

"Come on," Avi said. "You think she used her final dying moments to tell you she had seen an oil pitcher? I think we all know what she meant by *it*."

Maya looked down at him. "So you tell us, then."

Avi didn't answer, but he didn't have to. They all knew he was referring to the Ark of the Covenant.

Amanda looked at Esther. "Do you think she might have seen the ark or the mercy seat?"

Esther took a long moment before answering. "You want my honest answer? When I leaned close to her to listen, I noticed she smelled like smoke. I think she probably did reach the chamber, but I don't believe she saw anything of that magnitude. Her mind was clearly in a fog."

Zane thought back to the final moments of Rachel's life. He hadn't heard her words clearly, but he had seen the look of fear in her eyes. Something had frightened her, and women as tough as her weren't afraid of censers and oil pitchers. To him, the answer was clear.

"Zane?" Amanda asked. "That's an awfully strange look on your face. So tell us what you think."

He returned her gaze. "You really want to know what *I* think?"

She nodded. "Of course."

"I think I need another glass of wine."

A WORD FROM JOHN

Thank you for reading THE CHAMBER. I hope you enjoyed it. If you did, would you consider taking a brief moment to post a review?

Reviews are the lifeblood of independent authors. They also help recruit others who may enjoy my books as much as you did. It only takes a minute or two, and the review doesn't have to be long in order to be helpful. To post one, simply go to the Amazon sales page for THE CHAMBER and scroll down until you see the **Write a customer review** button.

Even if you don't post a review, please know that you are appreciated. There are a lot of ways to spend your entertainment dollars, and I'm thankful that you chose to spend yours on one of my novels.

WOULD YOU LIKE A FREE BOOK?

I enjoy building relationships with my readers. It's one of the primary reasons I write. As a way of saying thanks for being a part of the team, I'd like to offer you a free copy of my novella BETRAYAL.

You can get your free copy by signing up for my newsletter. The newsletter will give you periodic updates on new releases and special discounts, and you can unsubscribe at any time.

Visit www.johnsneeden.com/newsletter to sign up.

ARE YOU READY FOR THE NEXT THRILLER?

If you're new to the Delphi series, you may want to consider THE SIGNAL, which is the book where it all began.

If you like crime thrillers, you may want to consider DEATH LIST, the first book in my Silas Beck detective series.

Remember you can read all of my full length novels for FREE on Kindle Unlimited.

One last thing. I love hearing from my readers, so please drop me a line to let me know what you thought of the book. My email address is johnsneedenauthor@gmail.com.

ALSO BY JOHN SNEEDEN

Delphi Group Thriller Series

The Signal
The Portal
The Hades Conspiracy
Betrayal
The Island

Silas Beck Crime Thriller Series

Death List
Cold Blood

Made in the USA
Middletown, DE
04 January 2025